LITTLE WOMAN

Also by Ellen Akins

Home Movie

LITTLE WOMAN

A Novel

Ellen Akins

1817

HARPER & ROW, PUBLISHERS, New York
Grand Rapids, Philadelphia, St. Louis, San Francisco
London, Singapore, Sydney, Tokyo, Toronto

FIRST EDITION

Designed by Cassandra J. Pappas

Library of Congress Cataloging-in-Publication Data

Akins, Ellen.
  Little woman / Ellen Akins. — 1st ed.
    p. cm.
  ISBN 0-06-016362-3
  I. Title.
PS3551.K54L5   1990   89-46067
813'.54—dc20

90 91 92 93 94 CG/HC 10 9 8 7 6 5 4 3 2 1

For my parents.
This is what came out of the playhouse
and Cornucopia,
thanks to you.

I would like to thank the National Endowment for the Arts, the Ingram Merrill Foundation, the Mrs. Giles Whiting Foundation, and the Corporation of Yaddo for their generous support.

—*Ellen Akins*

S mall men have never been indifferent to me. The first was my father, whose position was complicated by paternal feelings, largely I would guess guilt and awe at his own part in making me—in the strict terms defined by the department of weights and measures—but let's not get mired in that swamp of mixed interests, paternity, since my father is only part of the story insofar as he gave me my start and my name, which is Beauty. When I was no tougher to consider and heft than a grocery bag (full) and, keeping my extremities to myself, as compact, my father was not ambivalent about me. He loved a baby and I was one and we went along having mostly good times until I grew progressively bigger, forcing him finally to say "Whoa" or words to that effect, I expect, since that was his philosophy vis-à-vis me from then on. Allegedly, I was an attractive infant, above and beyond the alleged loveliness of little ones as a class, and he called me Beauty, not to be redundant. As if to mock him, or me, the name stuck, and still does, though I have to explain it as often as I feel I must have something to say for myself.

Not understanding giantism, whose mental features became clear early on, my mother proceeded as if I'd got dumber with every inch I'd grown; the notion spared her the trouble of craning her neck. My father, however, viewed me with suspicion, as if

1

I'd become smarter and, in retrospect, sneaky for having started out tiny, and so he prepared me for one of the two common responses I could expect from little men: fear. The other is like lust but not quite, jocular or sly, obliquely intense, and then I'm the suspicious one, practicing a science devolved from phrenology, which once held that a mind could be known by the bumps in the head that housed it. Height, like the shape of a head or the curve of a back or the shade of a look, is telling; but what it tells is hardly ever heard, because the deduction mostly maps the mind doing the reading, and it takes more than a bump on the head to make someone admit that much. Little men look at me, and I look at them looking, and you might look at that but not for long since I must get to my mother:

With my growth she discovered that by saying I'd weighed seventeen pounds at birth she could start a conversation that would encircle her with curiosity and sympathy. Though she wouldn't tell this lie when I was within hearing distance, she needed my momentary appearance, which, upon my subsequent disappearance, would prompt a visitor to remark on my height. "What a big girl," for instance, a woman might say, and my mother would answer, "You think that's big," and spring her amazing figure. Learning of this tactic from a gymmate whose mother had been bamboozled by mine, I didn't know quite what to say, since I wanted to be interesting almost as much as I wanted to be normal, which I imagined I might be as long as no one mentioned my height, so I didn't say anything, and this was my childhood. It had started like that when the kindergarten teacher, consulting a card that mysteriously stood for *me*, read out my name and then, like an emcee adding that bit of color that makes a contestant familiar, said with a smile, "And her parents call her Beauty, isn't that nice?" and it certainly seemed so, the way she said it, so I dumbly smiled, too, and allowed the name into the system of public address.

Otherwise, my childhood was as normal as I liked to imagine it might've been. I grew up half-gifted—that is, I could get my foot into the door, where it got stuck. I was a wizard at math for a moment, could consult theorems and axioms and do speedy accurate work and then, in an instant, forget how. I could write what I had to, and well, but could make nothing up, see nothing

unassigned, if it took more than a paragraph. I could draw a fine likeness, which is something but didn't seem like something when I found that it wasn't fine art. The one area in which I truly excelled hardly seemed like a gift to me, since I couldn't hone it and make it my own, so I abdicated my natural place in athletics, embarrassed by the unfair advantage that put me a head ahead of other swimmers, head and shoulders above anyone I might meet on a basketball court. Until I received expert advice, I was not even tall well. I slumped. So I looked not just tall but also deformed. In this contorted posture, hunched and still hovering over my supposed peers, I longed so intensely to be one of them that my longing alone would have put them at an impossible remove if my height hadn't. At this distance, the social skills I developed were quite as keen in my imagination as they were blunt in fact; at the epitome of adolescence, I was silent, agawk, and inept, knowing enough to know that what I wanted wasn't what I knew and suspecting the rest. This was called potential. It's a myth perpetrated by elders and even well-adjusted coevals that there is a better world awaiting geeks. The maladjusted grade-schooler is promised more of her "type" in high school, when her "type" is just what she'd like to escape, and then, in high school, is promised a more congenial lot in college, and in college is encouraged to get out into the world, where she will be appreciated. A kind myth, this keeps the misfits moving.

I got out into the world, a hole in a cheap hotel, the Riverside, and, with the myth still clinging to me and my sketchy gifts sharpened almost to their vanishing points by a very liberal arts education, set out to make a career of potential: advertising. Among the samples I submitted with my application for a copywriting job, I included ads for a fictional perfume, Camaraderie, the fragrance that lets you live with yourself. I imagined it as something like water, Eau d'eau, or "Oh no" with a stuffy nose. This was a perfume that, I said, acknowledged that a woman has her own allure, and so, was so subtle it would be shared only with someone privileged enough to get so close. My sample book reached the man who handled the firm's lucrative perfume account, and (I got the job) I was assigned to this company's account. This company, acting on the advice of what was now my firm, which considered itself a marketing arm of the client, quickly developed a subtle fragrance that acknowledged a woman's own allure and told us to promote it.

For one reason, I was lucky to have found my place in perfume promotion: Advertisements that pretend to appeal to the nose are short-winded, as I was. Unfortunately, it turned out that I was shorter-winded than they are, but first:

Above a picture of a man who meant business, not just *the* business but also the business of holding controlling stock in IBM or some such Dow, I wrote, "This man has been wounded." Into his hand I put a bottle of our new perfume, which I was then calling Tout Doux, which might mean "softly, gently" or might become in vulgar translation "not so fast." At his hip I drew a box and printed COPY A in it. Copy A: "The notion that he can be led by the nose has injured his pride. Again and again his senses have been assaulted by aggressive perfumes. But he wants to know the woman before he knows her fragrance. He wants to be surprised, not stunned." "Tout Doux," the signature line read, "intimate apparel." I reproduce the whole thing here to prove that I once worked, and this is, in fact, all the work I did.

As I was contemplating this act of promotion, I discovered that I'd drawn another businessman, who was contemplating me from within fogging distance of my curved shoulder—my boss, one of the firm's multitude of vice presidents, the one the secretaries called The Nose. I married him. Before that, however, he gave me some advice on my campaign. He told me to drop the copy, of which no one would read that much, then tapped the tagline on my ad and told me to replace it with "Be gentle," a proper payoff for the headline. To do this, tap, he had to brush that shoulder of mine. The heat rose from there to ear and through the haze I vaguely heard him talk about my name, Beauty, how suitable for someone with a black mane like mine (he thought only highly of horses), but then again a little odd, like naming a city Truth. "Providence," I shyly offered and turned my head, coming eye to eye with him, and he said softly, "There you go."

I was on a stool that was shorter than my depending half, but even standing I was not much taller than the man, six or seven inches at most, though without the eventual embrace as measurement it would be hard to say exactly, since at that time it was my way to simulate medium height by keeping my eyes lowered.

Briefly, eye to eye, however, I'd seen a lovely sight. Almost immediately, I also saw how Mr. Silverman had got his nickname: as if trying to lift himself off the ground, he gripped the bridge of his nose from above, between thumb and forefinger, then lowered his face into his cupped hand, and thought. Doing as he instructed, I began to tell him about the name and kindergarten and everything since then, and when I paused for breath I found him staring at me over his fist with the baffled expression that I subsequently came to know as the sign of a big idea fermenting, which looked the way an idea fermenting felt to me, when "big idea" was not strictly an advertising term, that broad concept from which limitless little ads might come, like Marge's manicures and Mr. Whipple's admonitions.

My idea was broader still. In my lofted mind normality had achieved the status of a romantic ideal, and those things that might bring me closer to the ideal average state—office hours, dating, mating, family of four, lunch with the girls—had become a sort of dogma of longing, as far beyond question as they seemed to be beyond me, so I was not inclined to wonder about Max's courtship, which came next, any more than I was apt to ask "What girls?" or wonder why my mother, possessing almost everything I thought comprised happiness, sought to catapult herself out of her standard lot, using me, her most visible oddity, as a springboard. Instead, in a romance that occurred about waist-high, I dated and mated and slouched through the haze toward a mutual sort of bliss. I'm sure we had some happy times, and I'd like to pretend that I'm omitting most of them out of discretion and my wish to spare the short professor who'd preceded Max an unnecessary sense of discrepancy, but the truth is, I was too superstitious of my pleasure to come within describing distance of it.

Within two months we were honeymooning in Max's lake house in Michigan, and a week later I was back on my stool, which had become a dunce's. Extracting endless lines from a product whose merits were finite and, it now seemed to me, should be perfectly obvious, required more than potential. So, instead, I came up with excuses. The boss, my solicitous husband, was understanding. Standing at my shoulder and holding himself by the nose, he listened, looked at my doodles, and said: no matter, there might be something else I could do.

5

And indeed there was almost immediately a meeting for me to attend. Assembled were all those who droned over our fragrant account. Max, now and then making reference to a little Mary (the first, all those months ago, to touch my arm as my husband-to-be went by and say, "There blows the nose"), explained. Mary, this veritable goldfish in the secretarial pool, had, it seemed, come up with the idea, a perfume "we" were now preparing to promote, one developed simultaneously with Tout Doux. The new perfume, Feroc, was self-assured and strong, Max said, a bold scent for the fearless woman; at which, everyone turned to look at me. A woman who, Max went on, no one could doubt would have her way—after one glance at her, who could doubt it?

Yes, who? I echoed, both basking and shriveled in so much light, which illuminated me but also, in what looked like a back-wash of luminescence, the inspired expression of the early Max.

Little did he know just then that not all of my creative avenues had been blocked recently. Artlessly procreative, I was about to become a monument to all that perfume promises, and a model that no perfume manufacturer would touch. I didn't know it yet, either, so I blinkingly allowed the light to blind me a little.

For the next month I was relieved of the burden of myself. Wherever I went, charm school rose up around me. Palmed, my belly flatly retreated. Prodded, my spine uncurved. With lifted chin, I walked after dancers. Respectful hands measured and wrapped and tucked me, dressed me in clothes that, for once, I hadn't made. My hair went through so many transformations that, after a brief spell of daily reacquaintance with my reflection, I gave in to the mirror as well and watched there a parade of friendly strangers. Meanwhile, Tout Doux was evaporating, Max was doing his tardy part as an advocate of birth control, and I was finally happy to be of some use. Then, as if this had all been the celebratory embrace of the bride, I emerged with my news.

Max tugged on his nose. He made me dinner. "I love children," he said, watching me raise my fork. "I definitely want to have some."

Smiling, I said, "Soon."

"Yes, well," he said.

While my mouth was full, he said, "It would be good to plan a family." In the gentle grip of inertia, I kept eating, of course. "It might be a mistake to pass up the chance of a lifetime," he said.

I swallowed, slowly, said, "Which?"

There was a pause. "Which," he murmured and I lowered my fork and we looked at each other, eye to fist, in silent observance of the passing of one fearless woman before the arrival of another sort, the typical, fearless in the way animals are. "I love children," Max said. "I actually do."

Pregnant, the emphatic whisper went around, bringing to an abrupt halt all fiddling with and photographing of my passive person. Informal gatherings of informed copywriters parted before me. Little Mary interrupted herself repeatedly to give me descending looks. I'd become so accustomed to doing nothing at the office, to being a body, that it took me quite a while to realize that nothing didn't necessarily have to be done there, and then I became a body at home, wrapped in the gauzy contentment of being, of breathing and eating and sleeping, for the baby inside.

From this dream of Mother Nature's a woman must wake, usually only to be immersed in the all-encompassing care of a child. For me the awakening was different, beginning literally, in a hospital bed where I'd passed out shortly before the baby, which turned out to be twins trying to strangle each other, came out by way of an escape hatch opened by Dr. Cook. Drifting in and out I dreamed I saw at the foot of my bed the lovely man, my husband, sitting with his famous feature buried in an armful of crimson roses and his shoulders quaking. I tried to speak, but in this dream my lips seemed to be sculpted of lead. Waiting till I woke to find the room empty of nurses, I rose and robed my big body and crept down the halls, imagining I was sneaking, to the green room where the infants were arrayed. The window was the most comforting thing, like a huge monocle there to confirm, if not correct, my remote, distorted vision, and through it I found the two babies at once, elevated and separated, as if on display, in trapezoidal plastic oxygen tents. They didn't move. They were too small for that. I watched them until I couldn't see them for the fog on the glass, but I'd seen enough: the four tiny fists, no bigger than walnuts, curled at the babies' shoulders in twin shrinking gestures, the pea-sized sightless eyes, apparently lashless, looking up in horror as liquid dripped from an inverted bottle down a tube secured under a halved plastic medicine cup taped to each right foot. Then suddenly there was a woman, uniformed and matronly, on the other side of the glass, and she knew me. "Mrs. Silverman?" she mouthed, smiling confidently, and gestured an invitation to take a closer look. I smiled and gestured back agreement and, as if I hadn't understood, hurried down the hall as she headed for the door. In my room, on the window sill, there was a vase of crimson roses.

Anyone with half a mind might have guessed that the man didn't have to marry me to exploit me.

Waking to find that half missing, I knew I couldn't touch those two without losing the rest. Their miniature limbs were far too delicate to sustain my huge hands' interference. Even Max, so much smaller, was suspect, and when the nurse steered me wheelchairbound to the exit, I had to look ahead to avoid the sight of the little ones, by then each the three pounds ten ounces that the hospital deemed robust enough for worldly struggle, lost in his massive grip. At home he laid the sleeping twins in their twin bassinets, at which they promptly woke and began to cry. He reached for them, but I caught his arm, earning a look. I told him they needed to rest.

"Rest?" he said. "How can they? They're crying."

I told him, That's why they're crying.

But there was no stopping him. The man had to handle the children. Once he had them up again, rocked into stunned silence, he said, "Maybe they're hungry."

I told him that they'd just had bottles and that overeating could be fatal for anybody so small. This, Max said, was just the point: his boys needed something to grow on. He was bent on killing them, so I prepared a mournful formula, but when he thrust his arm out, as if he wanted me to go for a touchdown with Tim, I stood firm and maternal. They had to lie down, I told him, that was how they liked to eat. (It's true.)

Finally, as each of us tipped a bottle to the lips of a safely bedded baby, he said, "I wish we could breast-feed them," and smiled a wistful smile at Will. (I'd made up a story about cracked nipples, and Max had been good enough not to go to the doctor for corroboration.)

8

"We?" I said. That was my way of spreading the guilt.

Like most new mothers, I was preternaturally sensitive to the issue of my offspring's well-being. In me, however, maternal instinct was all eyes and no hands, and quickly, since the babies' survival depended on it, the instinct turned into paranoid cunning, with every contrary opinion about what was best seeming one more move in an obtuse conspiracy to befuddle me into manhandling the children. Every attempt by Max to foist Timothy or William into my arms registered somewhere deep and secret as an attack, as if I were the baby, too, but smart enough to recognize danger. When the man went to work, I circled the nursery in wild-eyed relief, at least it felt wild-eyed to me, but only until a wail went up to remind me that even tiny babies had to be changed, and there was no way to do it but manually. So I got on the phone and called for a nurse, a small one, and after going through two agencies that, probably thinking I had something kinky in mind, wouldn't make assignments on the basis of body size, got one.

This little nurse, then, came by day, watched soap operas between changing times, and was there for the news and gone when Max came home, free to imagine rough and tumble daytime adventures for the babies and me, which left the nightly balance of caresses to him if I couldn't convince him that now Timothy and William should rest. He liked to hold both the babies at once; I watched these orgies for as long as my stomach would allow, and then I left the room, knowing that my skittishness, which cunning told me might be perceived as a new mother's prerogative, would pretty soon, as the newness got old, come to be perceived as simply strange.

Sure enough, the rumor that I was "weak" soon made its way around the dinner table. "Weak" seemed as useful as "skittish," so I weakly agreed, then was damned if I had the strength to argue when Max suggested that his mother come to stay.

Minnie Silverman was one of those people who believe that a fear of water is best overcome by a dive into the ocean. That is, while I napped, trying to sleep through the sight of her brutal ministrations, she planted the babies on my person. I woke to find Tim gurgling against me, twisted in the sheets in an effort to evade my crashing elbows, and I leapt up, quick enough to know

9

that he hadn't got there on his own, so I shouldn't cry out—but when someone my size leaps, the floor shakes, and the woman came cheerily in, bouncing Will like a maniac and smiling like one, too.

I said, "Tim almost suffocated."

"Nonsense," she said, and when I pointed to the twisted infant as proof and added that I could have crushed him, she gave me her sinister assurance that babies know better than to be crushed without letting out a howl first. In support of this claim, she told me that Max had slept on her chest for the first six months of his life.

It was not a pretty picture, but I confined myself to saying: "Max was a big baby."

"And what, may I ask, is a big baby?"

She had me there. Minnie took advantage of my silence to comment on the distance I'd kept from my children since her arrival, and when I protested first that I was sick and then that the babies were still too small for roughhousing, she exclaimed, "Roughhousing!" and delivered herself of a nugget of what must have passed for wisdom in the Silverman household, where infants slept on chests. "Babies need fondling as much as food," she said, "more than adults even, and they need a little, too— everyone does. Why do you think hermits are shriveled and gray? No physical contact. Now you rest and think about it." Meanwhile, now in possession of both babies, she was smashing Tim and Will together and treating me to an armful of exemplary fondling, and I was thinking about it. I was much bigger than she, but who would get hurt in the fray?

"All hermits aren't shriveled and gray," I said, with great restraint.

Her pumping arm came to a rhetorical halt. "Which one isn't?"

"How do I know?" I screamed at her. "How do you know? They're hermits. You don't see them." She humphed me and retreated.

That night, while she dished out dinner portions and boiled the bottles and apprised Max of his immediate public's response to certain campaigns, the talk between those two, mother and son, was so small that I knew they'd been having big talk behind my back. The evening went by like a home movie shown too fast with lumbering me anchored in the middle of each scene, my limbs retarded, the tinny piano tune of a hysterical giggle tinkling in my ear. Suddenly Max stopped moving, stared at his bustling mother, flattened his hand on the table, stood, and, announcing, "A thought," lurched toward his study.

"I raised him to be a worker," Minnie said. "Be thankful for that."

"I am," I sincerely said and went into the nursery, which was running at my speed, both babies sleeping.

So far, their grandmother's supposedly salubrious molestations had only resulted in cradle cap. Otherwise the twins were intact, the asterisks in each belly where they'd been attached, the translucent eyelids, the tiny curls of toenails like claws, the minuscule fists still raised in a pathetic pretense of readiness for battle. Sometimes, as now, studying the two of them, I would have sworn that I could see them growing, but as soon as I lowered my hand into a bassinet, the proximity of my finger and a baby's wrist, first in space, then in size, showed me that my focus had only been shrinking to fit, almost caught in the conspiracy, and I retracted my hand.

Upon my retirement that night, a thumping and dragging commenced, a solid knock to a doorjamb maybe two rooms down (Minnie's), a grunt, a feminine snort, silence, a baby's whimper, hush hushing hushed. Max got into bed minutes later and, with his thumb shimmying the cloth of my nightgown up and down over the so-called small of my back, murmured, "Beauty?" I feigned sleep, preferring the thrumming of my vertebrae to the talk his tone and touch portended. When both died down, I turned to ask, "What was that noise?" but Max had fallen asleep.

That was the first night I dreamed about Wisconsin. My parents brought me here for vacations when I was little. It was a place where I could be at home without being home. Where we went, in the woods nearby, I had a dark hole to hide in, a tunnel into dewy undergrowth opening on a doorway framed by the trunks of firs. Sitting cross-legged with my back to a doorpost, I would conduct my version of business, that is, on stationery of white bark peeled off a birch I would write letters to an adult world of my imagination, where a secretary named Mary Lou or

Debbie or Susie was forever buzzing me to say that I couldn't keep someone waiting. It was an interesting business, with no product or service, just phone calls and meetings postponed and correspondence, and I dreamed of it so fondly that I awoke in a panic.

I went to the babies' room and found out what the noises the night before had been. There in the corner was Minnie's bed, sitting as if in judgment, made up. I sat on its edge with a long view of the empty bassinets. Almost at once, Minnie appeared, bouncing the babies, one on each hip. Talking in an unintelligible tongue to one, then the other, she crossed the room and, without any warning at all, dropped Will on my lap. I jumped. And Will— well, Will fell. He was helpless. I fell too, to my knees, a prayer to the carpet, its plushness, while Will cried and cried. Minnie swooped and reached, but I hunched in her way, reduced to a final parody of that last fearless woman, mother animal protecting her young.

"Did I tell you it was dangerous?" Minnie roared (referring, I suppose, to those hermits). "Did I mention you were risking their health?" She cribbed Tim so she could get at me with both hands, grabbing my shoulders and, when the strength of her righteousness proved useless against my brute size, hissing into my ear, "Give me that child." She was bent over me like an old goddess brewing us both. "Did I tell Max you were not a fit mother for my grandchildren?" that ominous voice said. "Did I say a dumb animal knows better? What kind of monster are you?"

Wasn't I a dumb animal? I was, and suddenly the silence was awful, no more wailing from Will, no more fierce whispering from Minnie, nothing. Into that thick air Tim ventured a burble. "You've killed him," the woman said, matter-of-factly. All the while, the baby—breathing, not killed at all—was staring up at me with an eerily adult expression that matched Minnie's tone for deathliness. He stared at me through the failure of his brother's whimper and into Minnie's second silence. Then, when he seemed sure that we'd understood each other, he opened his mouth in an abysmal O and screamed bloody murder.

I rolled back onto my heels. Minnie, moving with the regal certainty that there would be nothing to brawl about anymore, slipped her outspread hands under Will's head and bottom, and raised him. As if the experience had aged the baby, now she spoke English, or at least laced her speech with real words, and it wasn't till I reached the door that I realized that she'd been speaking her soothing gibberish to me.

Since she'd closed the door behind me, I could pack unobserved. Beauty and the beast ran away together.

▼▼

This was when, in response to widespread pressure, I became some kind of monster. At my old haunt, the Riverside, with under my pillow what little money was left in my checking account after nurse disbursement, I slept, rising only to forage when food appeared glaringly in my dreams, then returning again and again to Wisconsin. In the dreams now the kid I was would put pen to bark and transcribe letters that read like pages from a distorted, exaggerated diary of what I would call, for want of anything better, my adult existence so far. They included cryptic warnings to Beauty-at-ten to stay in the woods. No matter how bad the nightmare was—and it was a nightmare— I wanted to go back to it, and only got up looking for more than food when the dream finally disappeared. The sense of urgency that followed was, I realized, about money, which had dwindled, so I bought a newspaper and, on my way to the want ads, was seemingly sidetracked until the detour and the dream converged and my cunning revealed itself for the sensitive instrument it was.

Clara Bow—I met her in the paper, and it wasn't her money that drew me at first. Imagine an unnumbered crossword puzzle with no set solution and only one rule. Anyone who does the puzzle will create a unique diagram of words, its design dictated by the manner in which the puzzler answers the clues. The rule:

consistency—no leaps forward of intuition allowed, no outguessing a given solution, no punning unless punning has become the way. Without the rule, the product would be merely so many crossed words; consistency makes it a paradigm, a map of its author's perspective. That was how I was trying to read the newspaper, self-consciously, noticing the position of each news item, gleaning from ads what was most desirable, most available, or least expensive, checking these and the weather against the progress of sports and business, comparing readers' letters with editorials, and, yes, doing the crossword, looking for clues to my position in the times and the world. I'd just about given up the project when I reached the society page and was absorbed by a picture, a relief. This was a woman dressed in black, and so, reduced to an ink blot except for her bowed head, the tipped heart-shaped face and the pip of a nose and rising from her glossy parted hair a ridiculous periscopic curl. The woman was low in the picture, cut off at her rib cage, as if she were sitting, and bolstered on either side by a young man, each of whom rose pillarlike above her to where their crowns were cropped. The tips of her gloved fingers disappeared into the boys' sleeves, as if, if not sitting, she were hanging from them. It was the curl that got me.

The text identified her as Clara Bow Cole, thirty-seven, who had just inherited "the Cole fortune" on the demise of her husband, and the two young men as her stepsons. Cole was the woman's fifth husband lost and fortune acquired this way, it seemed, and it seemed somewhat odd that this implication and the announcement were made on the society page, as though an obituary were something else when money came with. Furthermore, the tone of the article, along with the fact that after the first mention of her full name she was referred to simply as Clara Bow, seemed to assume that everyone knew her and knew better, with the curl signaling over her head as proof. Far from everyone as I felt at the moment, here my place suddenly seemed clear.

Somehow, I mean, she got into the dream, where misfits went, and on my next foray into the world I proceeded to the library and looked her up. The woman was the subject of much newsprint, now microfilm, her marriages and bereavements well documented from the first but better documented later, when fortune was marrying fortune upon fortune and then the whole lot was periodically coming back into circulation. Her first husband, one Ray Hodges, a manufacturer of women's shoes, had apparently ushered her into the cycle and the society pages, where, as I was working my way back, an introduction was made at last: the only daughter of a movie actress I had never heard of (one who, the story implied, had made her way into silent movies a few minutes before their final silence) and the owner of a ship brokerage firm in Marina del Rey, California, she had briefly attended the University of Southern California, briefly done a stint as a staff writer in the news department at NBC, and then briefly gone unaccounted for. To earn her so much coverage, the marriage must have been a coup. Five months later, Mr. Hodges became a statistic, robbed and fatally stabbed near home, and Clara Bow was on her way, her appearances in print increasing in direct proportion to her real growth and bad luck; money seemed to want to wed her, despite the multiplying risks: one auto accident, one lung cancer, one heart attack, and, I've neglected to say, the last, another cancer—of the larynx. And then, the more money Clara Bow acquired, the more she seemed to give away; in fact, it was the amount she was shown handing out that gave me my first clear impression of how much the woman must have. There was a theme to her charity: to shelters for battered women, unwed mothers' funds, halfway houses for the fair sex just out of prison, ob-gyn clinics for the poor—and one of these, a free clinic on a mean street, was where I found her when I started looking in earnest, convinced by then that her idea of need and mine dovetailed somewhere.

She wasn't in the clinic (any more than she was in the phone book), but her name was on the wall, on a flier suggesting that anyone in need of help call: her number. Like all investigative procedures, mine took time, and meanwhile I'd come to think of Clara Bow as a temporarily misplaced dear friend who, because of her quintuple failure to find satisfaction in the schematic way of the world, would lend an immensely sympathetic ear and some cash to my wish to be elsewhere. In fact, we'd become so close in my mind that I didn't even have to ask; I would merely mention the Wisconsin woods as a place where there was no one to make me feel bigger than I had the character to be, and she would say: here. It took only the sound of a real voice on the phone to bring me up short. The voice was a man's and gruff and it said, "She's not here," making my need to say something next so suddenly clear, and thus difficult, that I hung up, feeling grossly betrayed. After a few more attempts to get past this grunt I was sure that he was our enemy, so I called one more time, pretending to have a computer-garbled address for a gift delivery from Saks, then went and stationed myself near the street number he gave me, not far from my own Riverside but worlds away.

She didn't come out. I patrolled the block for two weeks, trying out one approach, then another, the sincere surveillance of desperation, then the look of just happening to be there, finally rejecting both policies as flawed when the widow failed to appear and I had another possibility to consider, that the gruff telephonic entity had done something with her. I slunk half a block to my base, the Club Sandwich, to review the situation from a caffeinated perspective. It's amazing how the likelihood of failure can distract someone, and I mean me, from her task—if not amazing, then downright predictable to an amazing degree, and I shouldn't have been so surprised when, hearing the hasher at my lookout post hail a customer at my elbow, "Oh, Mrs. Cole!" I could only turn and stupidly stare, lips working like a goldfish's, no doubt. Then I looked down and saw her.

I don't know what dumbfounded me more, the sight of her or the look of her—not just her height, her hair too, barbered down to a burry skullcap, exposing her skinny nude neck, which stuck out of a fur—but all I could do was repeat "Mrs. Cole," and in my stupidity I must have been a sight, too, because she gaped back at me like a miniature mirror. As I mentioned, my prepared speech had been pruned by overfamiliarity, and now surprise pared it further so what I blurted out was: "I need help." Then, trying to recover, I elaborated. "Money," I said, underscoring the word as if I were searching for the one phrase a foreigner might know. Apparently, I'd found it. In a blink her dumb look became canny, and she opened her mouth to speak, but before she could say a word the man behind the counter, mistaking me for the petty panhandler I could well have been, reared up and said, "Miss, we can't have—" but stopped as if struck when Clara Bow Cole raised her hand and said, "Syd." When she did that, her fur gapped, giving me and anyone else who was looking a glimpse of herself underneath, completely bare. Slowly she lowered her hand, delved into her pocket, produced a bill, and put it, a twenty, into my palm, saying, "Here."

I said, a bit desperate, "That's not what I mean."

"It's not?" Wary around the eyes, as if watching her poise from behind, she said, "I thought you said you needed money."

"Miss," Syd said, "this is not the Salvation Army. This is the Club Sandwich. Where we don't allow impinging on our preferred customers."

"If you'd spent that twenty here," Clara Bow Cole said to me, "he'd prefer you, too."

The man made a pained sound. "You misunderstand me."

"I don't understand *anyone.* Do you like my haircut, Syd?"

"Of course," he said, he almost pleaded.

"What about you?"

It took me a second to see that she meant me. With the different scripts we were working from, mine a failure, hers a mystery, a new improvised one emerging at who knew whose will, I was just lost, trying to keep up and backtrack and figure at once, with Syd near to pleading frustration. "I didn't know you got it cut," was what I said.

She said, "Let's have a drink."

The passage from deli to bar was a difficult one, since I didn't know where we were going but felt obliged to walk in front of the little woman to keep the eyes of passersby out of her coat, which she made no effort to hold together. Once she ran into me, her face bumping flat into the scoop of my spine. "Oh great white woman," she said, "must we walk single file?"

I said, "Yes. Just tell me where to turn."

She said, "Here."

Here she was "Mrs. Cole!" too, and I began to worry about the recent fortunes of my Wisconsin funding. "Everyone knows you," I said.

She said, "They think they do," and I finally realized: The woman was soused. My experience of drunks so far had been limited to the obvious incoherent sort, so I was slow to recognize cagy inebriation, but once I did, still with the familiar kind of drunk in mind, I imagined an advantage just enough to think I must be thinking faster than she, which at last at least allowed me to think a little. I mean, of course, that by discrediting her script I had some time to work on mine; also, to study her. She was so short her height would bear repeating. The pictures, where she seemed to sit or sag, hadn't prepared me for it. And the heart shape of her face was much more striking with the hair sheared away, from the wide forehead, the perfect widow's peak—what else?—pointing like an arrow at her tiny chin. As I watched, she reached up absent-mindedly and clutched together the collar of her coat. Then, midway, she seemed to notice her own gesture, looked up to see that I'd noticed, too, and dropped her hand, the freed fur settling in a bulge on the tabletop, baring a triangle of her torso.

I said, "Your coat."

She said, "What?"

I said, "There's nothing under it."

"You disapprove of my appearance?" she said.

"I wouldn't approve or disapprove," I said. "But I'd worry about what might happen to a woman walking around in the altogether."

She pinched a fold of her fur. "This isn't altogether." I made a grudging gesture of *well* . . . and she said, "Nothing ever happens to me."

By "nothing" I assumed she meant anything that a naked body propelled by a woolly mind might provoke, but then again her mind was woolly. The woman was drinking Wild Turkey, which our zealous waiter kept pouring. With her elbow anchored on the table, she levered a fist between us and unfolded her forefinger upside-down, as if counting to one. "My fifth husband just died," she said. "What would you wear?"

"Black?"

"Black." She scoffed. "Black is for—" and she waved her hand, including everyone in the bar. "I wore black for my first husband. I wore black for my second husband. I wore black for my third husband. My fourth." She shrugged, opening her hand. "I was thinking red. You didn't say 'I'm sorry.' "

"For what?"

"My loss."

"I'm sorry," I said.

She said, "Shit."

I said, "Red?"

"If I'm going to dress for—" again she flickingly indicated everyone, "I might as well be flagrant." Here she was quite clear, and suddenly, "I'm not feeling sorry for myself," and then, "I'm feeling sorry for men, the marrying kind." She caught our waiter by the sleeve, pointed at her empty glass, and as he filled it, drew a finger across her throat and made a whispery croak. "I'm mourning the mere notion of number six," she said.

By now, it must be obvious, I'd decided to let her talk and get so drunk that at a later re-meeting she would have to take my word on what had been said, which I would dream up in the meanwhile. Of course, her next words were, "What was it you wanted?" It could wait, I told her, and she said, "Till when?" She waited, but I outwaited her. "I like to know what the future holds"—she stopped—"in her handbasket. What's funny?"

"Nothing," I said. "The future, a woman."

"So? The *man,* I know."

"If you're afraid of men," I said, "you could stay away from them."

"I'm not afraid *of* men. And where? They always turn up." Folding the finger she'd been pointing at my breastbone, she retracted her fist and hooked it knuckle-up under her cheekbone, like a child bemused. "And then," she said, "I like them. I like the way they put their hand on my back when I go through a door. And how every time I say a wish they think it's a hint. And the way they want to go out and do something without moving. How they want everything—everything in its place, life all settled and secure, but anything can happen, and then it does, and— I like—" She sighed—or did she snort?—and socketed her other fist into her other cheek. "I've been trying."

"Who answered the phone?" I asked her.

"What phone?"

"Your phone."

She said, "Oh, that." Briefly she seemed satisfied and sank into a reverie, then just as quickly rubbed her face, uncovering a shadow of the wary way she'd looked at me at the Club Sandwich. "You look like my sister," she said.

What sister? I said, "Your sister?"

"It doesn't matter," she said. "She died." She tried to stand, but her knees buckled, so she sat again, abruptly. "I've been drinking," she told me earnestly, then rubbed her face again. "What did you want?" She blinked. "Whatever's in my pockets you can have." And then, resting her cheek on the table, she slept.

When I tried to get into her pocket to pay for her drinks, the woman tossed her head and hand and clipped me in the jaw, the crack summoning the man who'd greeted her when we'd come in and who now told me not to worry, "it" was all right, did I need any help? I told him I could manage and he, a short man, said, "I'll say."

Clara Bow was no furry bundle. Her limbs, remarkably rigid for someone at her stage of liquefaction, stuck out every which way when I finally grappled her into my arms and carried her, also surprisingly weighty, out the door, down the curious street, to her building. When we reached her apartment, she opened her eyes long enough to say in a befuddled voice, "The front?" I kicked the door, but it was opened so fast that the thrust of my foot carried me stumbling into the compact body blocking the entrance, arms out for Clara Bow, who heaved into them, becoming flexible and folding in the transfer. The man identified himself as my telephone friend by grunting, "Did you do this?"

It took me a second to recognize this for the unnecessary nastiness it was, and when I did I hissed at him, "No, she did this."

"She's *forlorn*," the man told me. "Everybody wants to take advantage. Just because it's easy. Look." He tossed her limp form a few inches into the air, and then, when she settled, looked at me hard, as if this demonstration of Clara Bow's easiness implicated me. I could have broken his arms, but then what?—so I left, wrapped in the virtue of not having swindled, not much of a wrap against the cold thought of how much I might've got, which occurred to me quickly, as soon as the door shut, in fact, when I saw how the woman's drunkenness had benefited her more than me.

Disappointment promotes calculation, and I emerged from that building totting up my losses until they amounted to profit I'd never hoped to acquire from Clara Bow Cole, possibilities I hadn't counted on, but did now that they were certified as impossible by everything that had really passed. This, I mean, is where the plans began. That's not how they looked, though, like plans, as I reviewed what I might've said when I hadn't.

At least I had something to think about, along with how low I was, buying a paper again and bitterly observing that not one want ad asked for a major in English lit. With the thought that I probably couldn't even peddle my one small skill without word getting back to Max, I headed back to bed, stopping to gather food on the way but discovering that my wallet was gone, which increased my hunger tenfold. So I slept through what might have been one of the most distressful times of my life.

The slumbering distress would have ended sooner if I'd had a phone. As it was, at the Riverside we depended on the manager for messages, and it was almost a day before I got this one from him: "Clarabeau Co. Has your wallet. Please call." And there was the number I already knew.

This was such a wonder that it didn't occur to me until later that every piece of identification in my wallet had me living at Max's address and number. I called, and this time the woman herself answered the telephone. "It's me, with the wallet," I said, "or without."

She said, "Would you like to meet somewhere or come over here?"

"Meet somewhere?" I said, the compact man in mind.

"Why don't you come over," she said, not a question now. "I'm making breakfast. It's what? Six blocks?"

I said, "Five."

"I'll see you in ten minutes," she said.

There was no pugilistic welcoming party on my second arrival at the Cole apartment, only a bright voice calling me in and the beckoning smell of bacon. I plumbed the gray hall, plush, looking for the source of the voice, in vain, since the voice had stopped before I started looking. The bacon, however, continued to speak to me. "How did you find me?" I asked as I entered the chamber of sizzle and pop, having remembered by now what my wallet contained. I'd come into a bewildering white kitchen with mirrors making an infinity of the many cupboards and counter space enough for ice skating. "Do you have a large family?"

"I had your wallet," Clarabeau Co said. "I don't have a family."

"My wallet doesn't have my number in it, or my address."

"I got it from a Minnie Silverman answering at the number that *was* in your wallet. A very helpful woman."

As I was absorbing this startling bit of information, Clara Bow looked over her shoulder—she was at the stove—long enough to pronounce with a frown of what might have been concern or distaste, "The Riverside."

I was leaning on the counter, feeling foolish, not just because my incognito existence had been cognito after all but also because the counter was built for someone Mrs. Cole's size and I had to stoop to lean. "Why did you have my wallet?" I asked.

"Oh, yes," she said, very much like someone reminded of something, then scraped a skilletful of scrambled eggs into a bowl and, announcing, "Breakfast," carried this dish and one laden with bacon through a pantry into the next room, for dining. When she turned to find me trying not to stare at the enormous meal she'd made, she said, "You haven't eaten, have you? I forgot to ask."

Breakfast was the latest meal I hadn't eaten. I'd followed the food without thinking, and so knew where my mind would be as soon as I took a bite, so I resisted for a moment, still staring anywhere but there, at Clara Bow, as it turned out, and said, "About my wallet."

"I'll get it," she said and got up at once and left the room. There was no point in sticking to the subject while she was away, so I quickly gorged myself. When she came back and I was glutted and contemplating the empty dishes with all the restraint I'd shown them full, as if the food had simply disappeared, she laid the wallet next to my plate and, letting her fingertips rest on it, stood by my shoulder for a minute looking at me as a mother might after returning a misplaced valuable to her feckless child. "I took it out of your pocket," she said. "I'm sorry for whatever inconvenience it might've caused you."

After this little speech, she sat down, frowning to herself, then looking up again with eyebrows peaked. "That was petty," she said. "I'd like to blame it on the liquor, but I'd be lying. I knew exactly what I was doing—until later, when I didn't know what I was doing, which was the liquor, but I knew that, too.

The truth is, I thought you wanted to rob me—please don't take this personally—it's not you. Just an old incident." Dot dot dot.

"But you proposed the drink," I said.

"Clever, hunh? That's how I disarm danger—I run out to meet it wherever I think I see it. And then I came up with a scheme that I'm embarrassed to admit I can remember—that if I took your wallet and put it in my pocket, then told you you could have everything in my pockets, when you went for my money you'd find your wallet and experience chagrin and reform."

"You wouldn't let me in your pocket, anyway," I said, thinking, thinking, thinking. "You owe that man, at the bar. I would've paid, but I didn't have much money."

"I know," she said. "I had your wallet."

"In my wallet."

"I know," she said. "I had it."

I said, "How did you do it? I didn't even notice," and she dipped a flattened hand into an air pocket, a demonstration whose obviousness gave nothing away and so impressed me quite a bit. Then it occurred to me: Did she pick pockets on the basis of incipient suspicions? At the deli? The only other time we were within picking distance, she was dysfunctional. "When?"

"And *that* is the secret," she said.

I don't remember now if I believed her then, or if I even noticed, if I could've, since she didn't elaborate till later: in a few words she'd laid out her modus operandi—her way of not just coopting danger and difficulty, but creating them, forcing them out of fear, the little daredevil. I was preoccupied, not seeing myself in any scheme of hers at all, and this time when she said, "Now, what was it you wanted?" I was ready.

In view of the disparate elements it had to comprise, the plan was remarkably coherent and relatively simple: We would use Clara Bow Cole's money to found a charitable organization for women who wouldn't be likely to outlast its rigors and would eventually leave to me the paid-for-in-full, tax-free patch of Wisconsin where we made our home. This, however, was not quite how I put it. First, I created a category, "dependent women," which in turn called for a project that would free them up, and I knew just the place. You see the logic. I was defining dependence broadly, as reliance on a premade world of processed food, transported goods, water and power provided, found shelter; and the freedom our organization would promote was to be just what I'd need when the last of my projected dependents gave up and left me alone: the ability to do everything for oneself, from plumbing to farming to weaving and building and wiring and keeping house. Taking my cue from the widow's expressed fear for men, her at least ostensible wish to avoid them, and especially the gendered look of her good works, I was confining the project to women. But when Clara Bow asked, why only women? I could hardly tell her that this charity was custom-made to suit her, so I said that men would complicate things, that the women might be inclined to let them do the dirty work, which would defeat the purpose. She asked, "You think you'd get any worthwhile women to go where no men are?"

I said worth was our end, not starting, point.

"What's the level of interest?" she said, and I said, "Very high," then, when she asked, "How many?" realized that she'd meant interest besides mine. "None so far," I had to reply. It seemed unwise to recruit, I said, when funding wasn't certain. (Drum roll.)

Why Wisconsin? I told her land was cheap and good, there was wood and water, and it was wild enough without being too far off. Immediately, to my surprise and secret delight, the woman began to ask specific questions, which I deferred, about how much, how far, how soon. I was too pleased to wonder, as I might have, when she didn't ask: Why me? I mean, would you have adopted me, bought the project, and footed the bill on the basis of such a prospectus, presented more deviously but certainly not much better? For a while I liked to think that I was taken with her gullibility.

By the end of the meal, all mine, Clara Bow was making the plans, which included moving me out of the Riverside and into her apartment while we made the rest, as if by being robbed instead of robbing I'd proved my merit, among other things, as if, that is, for this woman disproved suspicion equaled trust, plus. We performed a polite farce in which I offered to pay for my upkeep with some of the money we both knew I didn't have and she acted the part of the offended hostess. This scene was replayed a few times before I had to laugh because the touch of her tiny hand on my elbow, her gesture of earnest persuasion, tickled. At once the brute appeared, as if alarmed by sounds of incipient merriment; he was dispatched to collect my things. To my objection that my suitcases weren't packed, the chastened creature grudgingly allowed that since I'd brung Mrs. Cole home he could at least put a few things in a bag for me.

And that was that. In I moved. For my room I was offered a choice of "dark or light" and, not to appear depraved, opted for the light, which turned out to be a sky blue bedroom furnished in petite white, including a rocking chair and an adjacent bathroom with a sink basined shallow and wide enough for bathing an infant. "Pretty," I said, since Clara Bow was watching me, and she sat in the rocking chair and smiled so happily that, oh God, I remember thinking, she wants company—a thought that, for some reason, at the moment, among those pristine furnishings, frightened me.

y ou've heard the good news about men from Clara Bow
Cole—they guided her through doors, etc., with touching finesse—so you might as well hear the rest. One
speech I remember well came when I asked her what else Minnie
had said and she, C.B., said, "Nothing," then, "Are you married?" and I said, "No. I was."

"Once?" she said. "Before my first marriage I was frightened sick. I put a lot of stock in marrying a man I could live with
forever—in the idea, I mean. But how do you know that about a
man until you've lived with him forever? And by then you've
either wasted a lot of time or you're in no condition to make a
choice anyway. But look: I've been married five times and I
could've gone on living with any of those men. Almost any man
can become compatible, given a chance and some time, I'm convinced."

I asked her if that was advice, and she said, "Oh, no. Maybe
it's me. You seem uncomfortable." It seemed wisest to admit I
was, so I did; I told her that I'd never been a guest in anyone's
home, except my own, and didn't know how to behave. To which
she said, "Be*have?* Don't be*have.* Just do what you normally do."

This was, if not impossible, then at least inadvisable, since
normally I would have been pursuing her through microfilm or

staking out her door. Instead I redirected my research, with my mind made up to get our claim laid in Wisconsin before the woman met her next doomed man and kept herself company in the usual way.

At the library I looked for volumes on soap making and windmill building and subsistence gardening and milking and ended up reading a book called *Wisconsin Death Trip,* which chronicled, in photographs and news clippings, a virtual groundswell of disease, necrophilia, infanticide, pornography, and arson in a small, turn-of-the-century community now defunct, no doubt, and at any rate far south of where I planned to go. This was edifying though not particularly fruitful, but I also managed to check out *Harnessing the Wind* and a Mobil Travel Guide to the Great Lakes states. When I returned, bearing these props, I was met at the door by Clara Bow, who led me to the den, a dim room of rosy cloth and satiny wood, and abandoned me to someone called Sal.

She was a big girl with a slouch rivaling the one I'd cultivated prior to my crash course for Feroc, the sight of which gave me my first clear sense of what the charm teacher had meant when, preparatory to wrenching my shoulders, he'd said, "You look like you're about to swoop." In the spirit of giant-bonding, I passed on a nugget of my learning.

Sal took this with a look. "First," she said, "I sit over books all day. If I held up this head," with a finger indicating which head, "I might just give myself a hernia of the neck. Second, I stand however I want when I'm the one handing out advice."

"Sorry," I said. This she allowed, but barely, lowering her weighty head at once to consult a clipboard.

"Clarabow" (slurred, first syllable stressed) "asked me to set you up for exemption. The steps are, first, create an organization. Second, the governing instrument, you have to submit it with your application. For you, a constitution outlining and limiting the organization's purpose and activities as tax exempt, say 'charitable'—it has a legal meaning. 'Philanthropic' and 'benevolent' don't. In the rules or bylaws put procedures for appointing or electing officials. Provide for distribution of assets in case of dissolution." Here I seemed to fall into a sort of trance, which one of Sal's points would penetrate now and then with all the force of death and taxes. Momentarily I was shaken from my numbness when the woman slapped a sheaf of pamphlets into my palm and told me to read up, adding in a burst of generosity, "There's an index." Then she talked me back into my torpor, where I stayed until a peremptory tapping on the literature in my limp hand summoned me forth again. "If you have any questions that aren't answered in these," Sal was saying, "ask me, but I wouldn't bother, because I'm going to be going over everything anyway. Clarabow doesn't pay me to give my private opinion, so I won't, as long as there's enough left to pay me."

She was an accountant.

As I was searching my gray memory for anything Sal had said, Clara Bow reappeared bearing a tray of iced tea paraphernalia, which she set on a coffee table between us. She winked, I think, as she bowed to pour and plopped ice cubes into a glass that she handed to Sal, who took it black, as her character dictated. By saying yes to lemon and sugar, I started Clara Bow on an elaborate ritual of squeezing juice onto a saucer, wetting her fingertip, then running it around the rim of a glass, which she upended in a sugar bowl, righted sugar-lipped, and filled with tea. Meanwhile I toyed with a knife (like a stiletto, though never having seen one firsthand, I couldn't say for certain) stuck in the glossy tabletop—and stuck it was, I quickly found. "Some knick-knack," I said, and she handed me my glass and smiled.

"Sentimental value," she said. "So, you have some studying to do. But first you have to point me at the land you want priced, so I can make my substantial contribution."

The words had that special sound, and I must have looked wary, because Sal said in her dry way, "More than five thousand dollars, if the amount is more than two percent of the total contributions received by the foundation from its creation through the end of the tax year in which the contribution is received by the foundation. That makes a substantial contributor. That is, Clarabow. That is, a disqualified person. It's in the book."

"I have to know all that?" I said, or moaned.

"No," Sal said. "You've got the book." She drained her drink and rose at least most of the way to go, led out by Clara Bow. I didn't bury my face in my hands and weep. I was too big a woman for that. In fact, if memory serves, I might even have snickered, the sound of nerves meeting relief, when the tea party broke up.

Here's what I learned: a "substantial contributor" or "disqualified person" can't be a member of a tax-exempt organization's governing body. (Oh, the tricky application asked with apparent innocence whether any such person was in that body, not saying anywhere that she shouldn't be; but I had Sal. Sort of.) This meant, simply, that Clara Bow couldn't be an official for our group-to-be. That left me.

When Clara came back in, she said only, "Sal," fondly, and I knew what she meant, since that woman's instructions had managed to show me mostly that I would be lost without her. Clara Bow climbed a ladder that ran on a rail along her bookshelves, and like a Halloween child dressed as a book, head and legs sticking out, she came down wearing a Rand McNally atlas of the United States, which she lowered heavily and opened to Wisconsin. I showed her where the land was. At once she got on the telephone and told someone named Brook to get her the names and numbers of real estate agents in the Bayfield area. This must have prompted a complaint, because she said next, in that sweet voice, "I know, humor me, I like to play employer."

Then she hung up and, with one last satisfied look at our page, closed the book and said to me, "We'll go on Friday." It was Wednesday. "I'll make the arrangements."

I wielded my reading material. "I'll do what I normally do."

"Beauty," she said, suddenly earnest and concerned, a pause. "I've taken you over, haven't I? If it's not what you want . . ."

"Oh, no," I said, just as concerned as suddenly, "you're much better at it than I am."

"But if you want to go out and, I don't know, do whatever, you will, won't you? Don't feel you have to put up with me all the time."

"You're the one who's putting up."

"But I'm enjoying this."

"So am I," I said quickly. "I guess I'm not very good at showing it."

"No, no, you don't have to show anything. See? I'm pushing you around again. Forget it. Have you had lunch?"

"No."

"I'll make some." She stopped at the door. "But you don't have to eat it."

"No, I like lunch," I said. "I really do."

I took this exchange to mean that my lack of a life was starting to seem strange to her, so instead of phoning in a classified ad for applicants as I'd planned to, I decided to go out and place it in person without telling Clara Bow anything, as a demonstration of my autonomy. I could then follow this up with mysterious outings on intimated personal business. It would be no more difficult than playing career woman in the woods had been, only slightly showier.

On the street, I consulted my pamphlets for some notion of the sort of women I was allowed to organize. After half an hour of this, I could've called Sal a genius. Bewildered, I wallowed for a while in Cultural or Educational Activities, Other Instruction and Training, Farming, Housing, Social, Community, Environmental and Beautification Projects. Scientific Research and Legislative Activities were out. At long last I ended up in a promisingly vague column headed "Other Activities Directed to Individuals," then ticked off its less and less promising possibilities. The IRS would recognize help to problem marriages, troubled families, students, ex-convicts, gamblers, alcoholics, drug abusers, the aged, the handicapped, the poor. The average needy had her handbook moment only under the unacceptable entries: Country Club, Hobby Club, Dinner Club, Variety Club, Dog Club, Garden Club, and that omnibus, Women's Club.

It was time I recognized the troubled, the infirm, the old, the poor. I wrote this ad: "Women: if you've been addicted, convicted, abused, broken or broke, wanton or wanted or stricken in any way and would like to retreat to the wilderness to behave well, live cleanly, and work long and hard for no pay but the gratification of having survived, come to the Rose Garden at 10 A.M. on Wednesday the 17th. Bring pen and paper." As a test of the ad's drawing power, I asked myself whether I, Beauty Silverman, nee Skinner, would have answered it two weeks ago. I said no. But then, I didn't know whether I was the kind of woman I'd want a lot of along. Then again, I didn't know whether I wanted a lot of any kind of woman along. So the ad seemed, so far, quite effective. Between this Wenesday and the next, I had to make up an organization that those who showed up, if anyone did, could join.

Meanwhile, Clara Bow took me to Wisconsin. Though I'd always had a sense of the power of cash, which came with my Coke-commercial vision of life and became even stronger when that expired, even when I was Feroc-ious I'd never been able to spend with authority or conviction, so it was strangely nerve-racking to see the woman so easily and carefreely disbursing great sums, as the sums seemed when I added up the tags on the plane tickets delivered to our door, the car rented and waiting for us on the tarmac in Duluth, the brokers reported to be ready and eager for our arrival. Her tips started to inspire a peculiar fear; I expected, perhaps, a thunderbolt. The idea that Clara Bow was actually going to finance my fantasy had finally penetrated. Destitution has a way of making money mythical, so that any commonsensical attempt to grasp its mechanics can seem profane, if not stupid. I could populate some of Wisconsin with windmills and cows and female strangers but I couldn't imagine a figure, a dollar and cents exchange for the goods. In the flat, bright light of day as it appears above the clouds I saw Clara Bow again with the atlas, peering down as my fingertip marked Bayfield. "Why are you doing this?" I asked.

She lowered her drink and said, "Because I don't trust the pilot." It was her third.

"I mean Wisconsin, my plan."

She said, "Funny you should ask."

I was learning this habit of hers, the reflexive comment made as a timing maneuver for regrouping or outright evasion. So I said, "Why?"

"I wouldn't think my motives would matter."

I didn't look her in the mouth. But, in keeping with my amateur understanding of money matters, according to which the two sides of a transaction somehow balanced, as if value had a standard, I started to wonder what Clara Bow Cole could possibly get from me; while she didn't trust the pilot.

Wan when we landed, she was silent and preoccupied from the airplane to the car, picking at her spiky hair as if pulling out burrs or encouraging growth. As we came to the car, she looked up, monkeylike, from under her busy hand, grinned in that way that made a heart of the lower half of her face, and said, "We got here. That's one thing."

She'd ordered a Continental, maybe with me in mind, because it fit me fine but required that she sit on both our coats—wadded—to see safely over the dashboard to drive. After a while, I asked, "Do we know where we're going?"

She said, "Eventually."

"Eventually?"

"It's irrational to be afraid of getting lost," she said. "There's always a way of finding out where you are—you're always somewhere—and sooner or later you'll get to where you're going." So we had no directions. I found a map in the glove compartment, had it half unfolded when she said shortly, "There'll be signs." A king-sized Marlboro Man cutout waved us out of Superior.

The trees had got shorter since my last visit. I didn't remember the road we were on, the pavement like rusted iron, and I didn't remember the birch woods as so delicate and airy, always shot through with light, as if there were a clearing beyond. On our left the trees toed the road, the feet of their slender etched white trunks fanned by pale ferns. On our right, they walked up and down hills, trailing trains of bending grass and tiny yellow flowers, filling hollows with their heaped treetops, parting suddenly for a stretch of rolling green dotted with immobile cows. Every now and then on either side there was a mailbox on a triangular frame, its opening flush with the edge of the road, and sometimes a house, tidy and plain and small, sometimes nothing but an overgrown path, a slash of pink earth. We went around a bend, and there was the Great Lake, Superior and smooth, bright as the sky.

Clara Bow said, "This must be the scenic route."

She read along with the small signs announcing Port Wing,

unincorporated, and Herbster, unincorporated, and Cornucopia, which for its brevity as a town, a glimpse of four buildings around a corner, had a surprising number of boats moored in its harbor under a sign that pictured a ship sailing out of a horn of plenty. After Cornucopia, our road strayed inland, over creeks, past narrow roads, some dirt, some paved, marked with letters. Spruces and pines, furry branches down to the ground, made the woods denser and darker and more like my memory's playground.

An hour later, passing through Red Cliff, where we got another glimpse of water, I asked whether we still knew where we were going. Clara Bow said, "We're still going to Bayfield."

Bayfield didn't have a sign. But luckily its First Bank of Apostle Islands, clearly marked "Bayfield Branch," could be seen down a road that turned off our own. "Bayfield," I announced.

She said, "Where?"

"That was it." In the rearview mirror, a sign: WELCOME TO BAYFIELD.

We returned to the town and perused its blocks until we located the two realtors we wanted, conveniently sitting side by side, sharing a wall. The smaller of the two buildings, hardly more than a lean-to, immediately drew Clara Bow. Inside we found a white-haired walrus of a man sitting at a desk papered with photographs of himself with, presumably, friends and, occasionally, a fish. "Mrs. Cole?" he said, looking at me. "You just missed a call from a charming someone named Sal."

"Sal," Clara said to me, by way of explanation.

"Charming?" I said.

"And you'll be Mrs. Silverman."

Still staring up, he rose and turned to reach for a ledgerlike book. "I assume Brook told you," Clara was saying as he turned its pages, "we need a square mile or so," and the man's hand stopped. It was my turn to stare.

"A square mile?" he and I said. He said, "All together?"

She said, "Yes."

Now the realtor laid a protective hand on his plat book. "You'd better go next door and talk to Nate or Donna," he said, "though I doubt they'll be able to come up with a parcel that big. I have almost that much, but it's scattered in acres all over the county."

Clara hesitated, her hands hooked behind her. She said, "But you're doing all right?"

"Ay," he said. "Donna, next door, she's your man." Smiling, he lumbered to the wall and knocked. "You did say 'need,' Mrs. Silverman?"

She stopped at the door. "Yes," she said. "But I'm Mrs. Cole."

"That's right," he said, and watched us go.

Clara murmured to me, "He thinks we're a cult."

As we walked into Bay Realty, the back door was swinging shut. On one of the desks inside, vacant, a half-smoked cigarette was burning. From the other, a plump blonde woman looked up at us and said with a wag of her head, "Those two," as if we all knew whom. When Clara Bow repeated her request, adding that we planned to build a home, Donna, for it was she, said wonderingly, "Six hundred forty acres for a home?"

Then I listened with amazement as Clara explained that, intending self-sufficiency, we needed land enough for sustenance, farming and grazing, and wood, and it would be nice to have a river or at least a creek. "Wouldn't it?" she said to me.

I said I'd always thought so.

Donna opened her plat book and turned it our way. "I don't know if you have your eye on any particular section," she said, "but I'll show you. See this? The squares are sections. All of these," where the page was white, "are the county's. The ones marked C.F.L. are managed for lumber—they won't sell those. The rest they'd sell like this," she snapped her fingers, "but you know why? Because there's nothing there, but nothing. See this, a road, it stops here, just stops. Where there's no road, there's no power. They'll run a line in off the road a hundred yards free, but if it's more than that, they charge, oh, we just had a man pay eighty-five, and I mean hundred, to get the line run in and he's looking at, say, eight hundred a month for electricity. Right here," a corner, "we have eighty acres. The previous owners started building a house and ran out of money, so there's the solid beginning of a house we were going to complete for sale and still could and a road runs by, not much of a road, but a road. Over here," the opposite corner, "we have another forty acres. Now the rest of this is land I can almost guarantee you the county

35

would love to have you bid on, all except for this ten-acre plat which is the property of one . . ." She ran her finger down the page to a lettered list of names: "Abbot. See this black dot? It means there's a house there, though how it got built without road or power or our help is a modern mystery. So if you don't mind this Abbot's few acres, this section might suit you. You can see, Racket Creek runs across the corner, looks like almost a quarter-mile of creek. This half-built house is a good sign, anyway, because it means they got a good perk test and dug a well, so you're not sitting on clay, at least not right here." She opened a drawer and produced a small glass jar. "What d'you say we oil up and go take a look?" She profferred the jar. "Muscal," she explained. "The bugs're bad, and I mean deer flies, or horse flies, or flies for something besides humans, but they aren't picky. Look at this." And she lifted her sleeve to display a lumpy arm.

Oiled and in a pickup truck, Clara Bow in the middle, surveying the cab and saying, "I think we need one of these," we went back the way we'd come, though riding higher, past Red Cliff, turned off onto a gravelly red dirt road, and passed two small houses that looked like expanded mobile homes and a farm where nothing moved except a threadbare brown dog who raced to the edge of the road, jerked to a rigid halt, and howled. The road's end was in sight when we stopped at a yellow Bay Realty sign framed by brush and climbed out. I reached to help Clara down. She flicked her hand and stung me.

Our guide barreled through underbrush, burrowed under low branches, talking as she went about how to approach the county, wait for appraisal and published prices, bid. "I don't know what kind of sustenance you mean," she said, "but these poplars are good for pulp, and Nekoosa Papers has the next section, so you might sell the timber, and there's that excellent grazing field and the creek, of course, for fishing—trout, maybe, we'll look at it." And, alongside, Clara Bow skipped over and ducked under, never faltering although she kept her head up and tilted politely in Donna's direction while her eyes went everywhere, now and then, at the sound of poplars, trout, the excellent field, briefly meeting mine with a smile of conspiratorial satisfaction.

We stopped, and I was sold. Now that, midair, the nitty-gritty of money had occurred to me and, along with it, intimations of nuts and bolts, I was relieved to see a house I didn't have to put together. It was a bare-bones structure, but with a roof, so I turned to beam approval at the benefactor, only to find her eyeing the building skeptically. "This isn't from scratch," she said.

"Scratch scratch," I said, then measured, remembering my prospectus, "This much a person could find." She smiled as she had for the flora and fish, but this time for me, as if I were the secret. I bent to scratch where the brush pricked my leg.

"You're not dressed for this," Donna said.

I said, "This is how I dress." Blue jeans don't come in my size.

Clara Bow said, "Donna, why don't you take us back to our car. We'd like to spend some time here on our own, wouldn't we, Beauty?"

In the pickup again, Donna said, "I could let you have the whole package for seventy thousand," bringing a hush to the buyer's side of the cab. In the city, seventy thousand would buy a skimpy house shadowing the sidewalk in a bad way, no yard. At our silence, Donna said, "The road access pushes the price up." This last line she delivered as she delivered us to the door of Bay Realty. We stood on the street for a minute, then said our goodbyes; then Clara and I stood a minute longer. We looked at each other. At once we said, "Well."

"Maybe there's something wrong with it," she said.

The "house" was a cement foundation with two wooden stories covered with what looked like tarpaper. Thick plastic, once transparent, I suppose, but by now beaten dull, hung inside the paneless windows. While bugs like tiny bombers circled our heads. Clara Bow picked up a handful of mud from the dirt yard and, with a listening look on her face, tossed it and caught it and then made a fist, as if testing its weight and resistance. When she lowered her hand, adopting a pleased expression, I said, "What do you get from that?"

"Nothing," she said. "But I've seen people do it in movies. I thought if I looked like they looked I might feel what they felt."

She told me about phrenology then, that direct correspondence between outer and inner. "Quackery." And she dropped our dirt.

"I think you have to taste it," I said.

"I didn't see that one."

"You know what mothers say: You have to eat a quart of dirt before you grow up."

"And I bet yours said that after you ate your share. Mothers say anything to—" She looked away quickly, spread her hand houseward and said, "But this seems all right?"

"Almost too right. There's no margin for error. Any mess-up has to be human."

"You don't know. This dirt might not be good enough to grow a dandelion."

"No, I think we're going to have good luck with weeds."

"But you like it."

I said yes.

She said, "It's your baby."

With so many acres to explore, we were stuck to the house as if our imaginations needed a familiar foundation to play on; where the wilderness of woods and field and creek overwhelmed, the house had built-in clues as to its disposition: wooden stairs, plateless outlets in strategic spots, suggestive plumbing protruding from floors and walls. Leaving an upstairs room whose size and pipes prefigured a bathroom, Clara wanted to know whether we planned to buy a toilet or dig an outhouse.

"Outhouse?" I said, adopting her forestalling tactic. An outhouse would surely discourage our women, the trip through the dark and sometimes rain and snow to a smelly hole where bugs bit and wild animals lurked, but when they deserted I'd like to be left with up-to-date flushing facilities. And then there was Clara Bow, who didn't know yet that we'd shifted from habilitating to rehabilitating and had not even fully approved of the house, just a shell. "I'll have to think about it" was my brilliant maneuver.

Turning to the bedroom window, my back to Clara Bow, I said, "How soon do you think we can get things settled and start up?"

"Whenever you're ready," she said. "It only takes a minute to write a check."

Which I would put into a bank account and draw upon to buy glass windows and a bathtub and a bed, a sink and a stove, wood and wire, seed and feed and a plow, cows and chickens. Once the check was deposited, Clara Bow would be a substantial contributor, with nothing to say about my—the board of governors'—methods. It would be mine. The house, the window, the plastic, the rip I looked through and the birch and pine bower beyond. It smells holy up here. I still think so.

"I think we should have a toilet," I said.

Being back in the city was like breathing air from an inner tube, a June oddly humid and hot, but not necessarily for us, because soon enough we were high up, hermetically sealed, and air-conditioned. In that atmosphere I drafted my constitution, while Clara Bow went out on undivulged business.

One evening as she returned, the telephone rang; and it occurred to me that this was the first time I'd heard this sound since I'd moved in. Clara stood still, her hand arrested in the act of pushing her sunglasses up on her head, and after a minute, said, "Bill?"

His voice came from the bowels of the apartment: "Wrong number."

Life came back to Clara Bow's limbs. She couched her shades in the brush her head had started to sprout and resumed her walk through the den doorway toward me. She was wearing what looked like a little boy's play clothes, a white T-shirt and red pull-on pants. When she sat down next to me I could see the cooling sweat on her forehead, a gumminess. "Why don't you ever get phone calls?" I said.

"It's a new number. No one knows it."

"It's on the wall of a free clinic on the south side and no one knows it?"

"Oh, that." She started to comb her fingers through her hair, forgetting that it wasn't there and running into her sunglasses, which she removed as smoothly as if that had been her point. "New since then," she said.

"Any reason?"

"Sure." As she turned to face me, her eyes fell on the paper I had in my lap and, nodding, she said, "Is that going to be ready by tomorrow? Sal's coming for it at two." I said yes, and she said, "We should have a copy." Then, rising, "I'm going to be in my bedroom. I have some calls to make."

"I might be going out."

"You don't have to tell me."

"I know. I meant: I could make a copy."

Ever since that flight to Duluth I'd been slightly paranoid, vaguely so, because I had nothing to lose except what I didn't have yet, which made the question of Clara Bow's character, where potential resided, my nervous focus. So this peculiar exchange prompted me to go back to the clinic where I'd got her number; I was going to call, as if this were a test whose results would enlighten me. But the flier was not on the wall anymore.

For fifty cents, the woman at the reception desk agreed to photocopy the constitution for me. While she xeroxed, I said, "Do you remember the sign that was up there a few weeks ago?"

"Sign?" she said.

"If you're in trouble?"

"Mrs. Cole's?" she said. "Yes." And then she became stern in the polite and kindly fashion of nurses. "We discourage the use of that offer. Mrs. Cole is already much too generous to us."

"Do you remember when it came down?"

"Exactly," she said. "The day of the monthly board meeting, which would have been the first."

"Any reason?" I said.

"I was instructed."

"Any reason?"

"Reasons weren't discussed. If they were, I couldn't discuss them anyway."

I said, "I see." What I saw was that the sign and I had been taken in on the same day, that first of May. This seemed significant. Next I went to the Riverside and cajoled the manager into looking up the number in his message book: Clarabeau Co. I called, got a busy signal, waited. When I called again, Bill answered (I hung up). This seemed significant, too.

The coincidence and the fib—about *when* she'd changed her number, it seemed, since she must have changed it, if there were no calls—were incomprehensible, couldn't possibly be as senseless as they seemed, since I'd gone to so much trouble to discover them. So I imagined a reason of the weight that would merit my trouble; just the weight, not the reason, I could imagine, and then my distrust was commensurate with my sense of how much I thought I was missing. This, I mean, was the significance. My imagination is generous to a fault.

▼▼

T he day Clara christened my organization Women Abreast, or W.A., an abbreviated wail, was Wednesday, a day of double-u: women, my wherewithal, my word. We were both up and dressed and ready for breakfast by eight in the morning, an amazing hour in view of our usual ante meridiem sloth. Clara's outfit was calculated ragamuffin—a man's T-shirt with the sleeves rolled up to its shoulders but not hers, white sneakers, blue jeans, all too bright. She said, "Are you going somewhere?" and I nodded and opened my mouth as if I were expecting speech to come out. She still didn't know what kind of enterprise we'd turned into, since I'd thought it wise to withhold this news until I'd gathered a moving group of women whose woes would work on her if my attempt to align rehabilitation with independence didn't. At my hesitation, she raised her hand boy scout fashion and said, "Don't tell me."

"You're going out, too?" I said.

She said, "I've been thinking about your wardrobe. Our Donna was right about your clothes being inappropriate—even though they look nice—you have a hard time finding jeans, don't you? I know, I have to get mine in boys' or girls'. But what I was thinking we might do is get some overalls. I'm sure we could find those to fit."

"As long as we're not going anywhere fancy," I said, and immediately she gave this sober thought. "I'm kidding," I said.

"Oh," she said. "Well, it's a consideration."

I didn't even think here: Wisconsin will make short work of her. I was too nervous, another good reason not to tell Clara Bow; on my own, I could loiter among the roses, waiting for the women to arrive and mistake me for one of them or for a woman unworthy of even the notice mistaking demanded, and, unobserved, I could contemplate losing my nerve. And this is just what I did when I reached the park early, waited and contemplated and imagined rising from the midst of the mistaken lot to reveal myself as the ad's perpetrator, thus gaining the added advantage of imagining the women's discomfort at discovering that they'd been secretly watched. If, on the other hand, only two or three showed up, and they looked truculent, I could just leave. If a mob assembled, I could leave. In fact, I was thinking of leaving at 9:40, since no one seemed to be coming, when two women appeared. They came from opposite directions, shiftily scanned the area, then began to meander among the flower beds. Toying with the tag on a lavender rose, Sterling Silver, and sniffing, I raised only my eyes to sneak a look at the curly-haired blonde of the pair and caught her, under cover of an American Beauty, peering at me. We sank into our respective roses and snorted like two people perfume-possessed. The other arrival, a girl-child floating the diaphanous stuff of a skirt on the breeze stirred up by her skinny legs, had circled around and was coming up on my left side, touching roses with a trailing finger as she went from bush to bush. As she came within breathing distance of me, I doubled over almost into the rosebush, afraid she might ask me a question, but instead the girl raised her whimsy-infected hand over my head and waved. By shifting my eyes I could see on my other side the approaching man, who returned the greeting and quickened his pace, looking ahead with a smile that relaxed then returned with every five or six steps he took. They were lovers. They locked, in plain sight of my desperate women, who were starting to arrive in earnest.

I had no idea that things were so widely accepted as bad, but they had to be if so many women, which is how many they were turning out to be, would turn out for nothing more than the slim hope of survival my ad had offered. Unless, of course, they suspected more, in which case we were all in big trouble. There were the girls between teenage and twenty-two or -three, the women of vague thirties, and the odd orphans, a plump pubescent dumpling, a few waifs, a fiftyish woman wearing a sleeveless housedress and towing a dachshund, Ma Kettle in a powder blue pantsuit, grandma on crutches and her friend in a wheelchair. Some of the younger girls came in pairs and talked, but the others staked out circles of grass or gravel from which they regarded each other with curiosity and suspicion. Whenever someone new approached, there was a general turning of heads but never past the most oblique angle that would allow observation.

The rose I'd been courting for about half an hour looked exhausted, baked, and bleached. I straightened and, as always, the sight of my full height, which amounted to an ascension, was enough to call an army of midgets to attention. The sitting and squatting stood while I waited for the rustle of turning and shifting to stop. The rose-sniffing blonde was standing right in front of me, looking up spylike from her downslanted face. Next to her was a scrawny girl, elbows and knees and neck, with long stringy hair parted low on the left and tucked behind her ears. She stared. The rest, except for a blinking eye or shaft of lit hair or slack lower lip, blurred beyond focus or feature.

"Hello," I pronounced, "I'm Beauty Skinner." For once I didn't feel the least bit inclined to explain my name. Authority went to my head. "I assume you're all here in response to the ad in last Friday's paper. Before I get started: we'll be demanding hard work without professional supervision or medical help, so we won't be able to consider anyone over fifty or under twenty. I'm sorry we didn't mention age limits in the ad, but those are the rules." The thrill of being able to make up rules was diluted somewhat by the women's indifference; the women over fifty and under twenty didn't move. I said, "What we have is some wild land in northern Wisconsin, on it an almost uninhabitable house, no water or electricity. Through the generosity of an anonymous benefactor, the U.S. government willing, we'll be able to turn this into a place where women can go and test their mettle. A pump has to be set up and a windmill built, crops planted and tended, cows fed and milked. It's going to be rudimentary and crude and hard. The thinking behind the project is this: by taking full responsibility for her own survival, a woman learns a deeper kind of responsibility, along with a sort of self-respect that can't be acquired any other way. That's the theory, in case anyone's looking for meaning."

Apparently they were not. Either that or—worse yet—they'd found it in my face, which they watched with the rapt impassivity of a cult.

"Anyway," I said, "no one's going to be around to teach anyone how to do what has to be done, so every woman coming along will have to learn a skill and help the others. I'm not talking about going to trade school and picking up a marketable craft. Fumbling along and failing a few times on the way is okay. We're starting from scratch. But fumbling too often and for too long could mean no food, no light, no heat. The rewards and punishments that are sometimes employed to encourage learning are going to be self-imposed in this case. And if you don't like it, you're free to leave.

"So"—I'm not sure I said "so," but I must have said something—"we'll be able to take ten women at first." I was thinking of the house's dimensions. "If we lose anyone, we'll take replacements. And in a while we'll probably have room for more."

And that's all I said, because just then, glancing over those heads all haloed by the sunlight in split ends and soft curls, I saw a double stroller with what looked like Minnie at the helm. So I ducked. It's hard to be inconspicuous at my altitude, especially when there's a riot-sized crowd looking one's way. Stooping and stalling, I stuck out my neck and pretended to search the ranks for someone or something, which prompted the grumbling women to look around too, except the blonde in front, who narrowed her forward eyes and put her hand on her hip. When my swiveling gaze got to that pointed elbow, there, closely framed by the blonde's bent arm, was Clara Bow's face, staring out at me as though she were trying hard to solve a charade.

We stayed like that for a minute, perplexed and perplexed; then her face disappeared, the blonde moved aside, and my little friend emerged smiling. "Thank you, Beauty," she said, too loudly, to convince the audience that this was all part of the act; and, as if under the weight of the tiny hand she put on my slumped shoulder, I sank to the ground. Down there I sat holding onto my knees and hoping to be forgotten. But I'd started a movement. I could feel the crowd lowering itself to my level. "Stand up," I hissed, "stand up." Around me many midsections froze midfold in uncertainty. "Stand up so you can see." Though this made no sense and was delivered croaking, it got the women up again. Through all of this Clara Bow kept smiling at me as if I were her own frightened child at a dance recital, faux pas de deux, only—the moment of magic—I was in the mother's seat.

While I watched her with that absolute and minute concentration peculiar to idiocy, she said, "You all have pencil and paper, don't you?" and held up one of each, visual aids. "Right now, I'd like you to write down your name, address, and phone number. Yes?" The smile, so happy to spot a question, took me back to kindergarten. "Use each other's backs. Okay? Then I'd like you to write anything you think might be pertinent—how you think the program will help you, why you want to be chosen, what you have to offer, whatever strikes your fancy. Don't worry. There are no wrong answers."

Now that I'd got over my first impulse on seeing the stroller-for-two, I rose a little to look again, but there was nothing as far as I could see. Clara Bow must have asked the women to pass their papers to the front of the class; she was rolling forward on the balls of her feet and reaching over my head and, when she rocked back onto her heels, had a messily gathered sheaf of loose-leaf in her hand. A paper airplane sailed over her head. "If you've given me one of these," she said, "that's all. We'll be getting back to you before long." She looked at me. "A month?"

"A month?"

"A month. Thank you very much."

For a moment, as if they were as reluctant to uncrowd as they'd been to stand close, no one moved. They shuffled, hardly speaking, then slowly, finally, began to disperse. During the leave-taking, I watched a bespectacled lady sneak up on the paper airplane and hunker down to smooth it out. A woman came up to me. Another followed and stood a few steps behind the first, who said, "What about kids?"

"Or guys?" the other said.

"No kids," Clara said. "No guys. Rank discrimination."

"What if you've got a kid?"

"How long does it last?"

"Indefinitely," Clara said, then turned to the woman with the kid, while the one with an answer looked around, fastened her incredulous eyes on me, and whined, "No guys. There's just rednecks up north." When she couldn't find a sympathetic audience, she wandered off.

"That doesn't matter," Clara Bow was saying. "You'll be sorry."

"I'm already sorry."

"Here, give me this." Clara took a piece of yellow paper out of the mother's hand and glanced at it. "I'll see what I can do."

"You will?"

"I said I'll see. That's not saying much."

The woman made a move to go, then seemed to stick, as if she thought Clara Bow might disappear, taking her slight hope with her, as soon as she turned away. "Thanks," she said, taking a step backwards. Laboriously—I realized I was leaning, giving her an imaginary push—she pulled herself around and started to walk.

"Wants to leave her baby with her sister," Clara Bow said.

I said, "Maybe her sister's a better mother."

From above me came a contralto voice, "Are you two in charge?"—the blonde from the front, still standing there. My yes sounded more like a query than her question had. She emitted a hard hiccuplike laugh and strolled away in snide time, dropping piecemeal from the fist that had been on her hip a red, red rose.

"Stage fright?" Clara said. She was talking to me.

I said, "I guess so."

"It took a while to take effect."

Seeing my fitness as a leader of women coming into question, I took the offensive. "How did you find out about the meeting?"

"Your ad."

"How'd you know it was mine?"

"I didn't."

"Then why did you come?"

Sitting down Indian style in the grass, with the papers

47

folded against her chest and her gaze skipping away along the path of red petals, she said, "It's dangerous here at night."

That was the gift horse speaking, but I said anyway, "If you didn't know it was mine?"

She smiled. "To be rehabilitated."

"From what?"

"Whatever ails me."

"What ails you?"

She lowered the papers onto her lap. "That's the problem." Frowning down at the pile, she said, "Don't you wish you knew which one of these is hers?"

"Whose?"

"That smart-aleck blonde."

If the ad hadn't been mine, she would've had to put whatever ailed her down on paper. But then again.

"Thanks anyway," I said. "For taking over. And everything. Maybe someday I'll be able to repay you. Not the money. Maybe I'll rehabilitate you unwittingly."

"You already are," she said, with a dismissive flick of her hand. "I like that—rehabilitation—that's a good angle."

Then I remembered that I still hadn't told her about our change of program. "Failure's the easiest thing to depend on," I said, "and the costliest." But she deserved better than a platform speech, and knew better, so I added, "And tax exempt."

She said, "Beauty?"

I said, "What?"

She said nothing.

We sat for a minute in silence, I clipping the grass with the nails of my thumb and forefinger, Clara thumbing idly through her cradled pages and shaking her shadow hair at a fly that was dive-bombing her head. When ambiguity ails you, go shopping, they say. This peculiarly feminine form of redemption was proposed brightly by Clara Bow on the tail end of a twitch, as if the fly had buzzed inspiration into her ear. Up we got, brushing off, and away we went, treading the hot air, in search of purchase.

The little woman believed we would find overalls at Lord & Taylor.

The city seemed different with her alongside. I was glancing down while I listened, looking where Clara Bow looked, occasionally blocking for her, and the street wasn't hairdos and bald spots and brims and peaks skimming by below, signs above and straight ahead, as it had always been. It dropped down and spread out and developed a midsection swarming with particulars. At the deep end, Penney's, I told Clara I was broke, again. Telling me it was bad form to broadcast this fact in a place of commercial exchange, she proceeded to the men's department where we found what we were looking for, overalls I had to try, turning this way and that, while she frowned and pulled back her head, like a rattler about to strike, and scrutinized the effect. "We'll get them altered," she said. We bought ten pairs. Then Clara marched me to the elevator, handing the parcel to me on the way so she could manually admire some doll-sized garments in the girls' department as we passed.

"Why haven't you had any children?" I asked her. My education in charm had been merely cosmetic.

"Why haven't I had any children?" She considered a baby dress. "I had a miscarriage once, when I was married to Ray. Then he died, and when I got married to Lou, I was afraid of losing the father, so I took precautions. Then he died, and I thought, 'Maybe if I had a kid'—I mean, maybe it was my fault, about Lou, maybe it was self-fulfilling paranoia—so when I married Edward, I tried. *We* tried, I should say, but he died, too, and I was still trying."

That tone, the tough and wistful mixture of someone reformed: Clara Bow's black widow complex hadn't been entirely liquor-inspired, perhaps not even liquor-enhanced. It occurred to me (Has it occurred to you that it should have struck me sooner?): What if she meant to make me honest for the sake of all marriageable and mortal men? What if she forced Woman Abreast to work for her self-policing purposes? What if she stayed? I had a vision of myself washing these overalls on rocks into perpetuity, the crack of dawn, the smoke of oil lamps, teats of cows. It was a Trojan nightmare. Clara Bow wanted to have a child, and now she was going to have one. Me. She was going to make me be good at camp.

Y ou can't get away with much," Sal said as she took my constitution.

"Sal, Sal," Clara Bow said, "you're such a doom-sayer. The money's in the bank, so you can stop with the dark warnings." The accountant looked from Clara to me, blinking between and after, as if taking snapshots to be developed later. "Now would you like something to drink?"

"No," Sal said, and ended with another shutter snap on me. "I'll go. I've got my work cut out for me." Fanning herself with the governing instrument, she slouched toward the door.

"Sal!" Clara rang out. "Why don't you come to Wisconsin? It'd be good for you."

My stomach turned over, but Sal didn't even slow down as she said, "And I'm sick of people who don't know what's good for them telling me what's good for me."

As soon as the door closed, Clara Bow said, "All bark."

While she showered, I pored over the applications. There were no wrong answers, but the closer to wrong an answer was, the better for the applicant, since, with some hedging where a woman looked like trouble, I picked the worst, the least likely to put up for long, as I saw it, from my aerie. Also, I was looking for a crew that would scare off Clara Bow, though I might've remembered the pickpocketing episode as an object lesson in how she took a scare.

I still have the papers. This is Molly, thirty-six:

If I had any idea of what kind of answer you wanted it'd be easier to answer. If you want someone to be ashamed and this is some kind of deal where everyone goes around being ashamed take my name out. I'm not ashamed. I provided abortions for girls who couldn't get them because of $ or they were too far gone and not like a quack. My mother taught me and a doctor taught her and I never hurt anyone only helped them. The law doesn't care about that. It's the law and somebody's brother found out and told and so I did some time. Also there are murderers who get off without doing time. Now even my patients forgot about when they were saying you saved my life, let alone everyone else that never heard that. I can't go anywhere because of $. I had a job on parole but as soon as parole was up and they could think of an excuse like the budget they layed me off and that's it. Everyone is trying to make me feel ashamed when I was doing a service. From the look of things, abortions, aboveboard or below, were not going to be a big problem up north, in the cloister.

Kathy wrote: *I was abused as a child so I know how they feel and I'd like to be rehabilitated of whatever makes me forget and lose my temper. Losing custody was the best thing that ever happened to me. I'm ready to try again, but I know I have to get my head together. This sounds like just the thing. I am also quite a hunter, anything from squirrel to deer. I've even done some hunting in Wisconsin. I could do that.* Already I thought I wouldn't mind losing her, though I wish I could say I was more sympathetic. And squirrel? That was the ticket.

The other Kathy, with a pencil-written past, had littered the country with abandoned husbands and children and proposed to do fission to another nuclear family. *By doing what I was brought up to do, but not having any faith in it I have got into an illegal situation.* This was cryptic, so I'll help: it seemed she hadn't bothered to divorce any of those husbands. *What I want is to learn how to do what I ought to do with feeling or learn how not to feel like I ought to. I have to get away and I'm going to, so this could be a way for me to do it without getting into the same thing all over again. Once I get my head together* (cheating!) *I might be able to go back for once or figure out how not to make the same mistake.* One for the loggers.

Gigi and Lynn were dependably undependable. Lynn used the form for first-class-of-the-semester essays. *What do I have to offer? That's a question I wonder about often and can never answer, which is part of my problem. Though I have an excellent education, I can't seem to find anything that I can do, partly due to a problem I have with falling asleep no matter what I'm doing. Perhaps this will hurt my chances, but it shouldn't, as I am very motivated to become a viable member of society, even a small one as described, possibly especially a small one which would allow me to become a complete person on a small scale first and prepare me for a greater contribution at a later date.*

Gigi applied for a position. *Why I want to be chosen: to become more responsible. What I have to offer: secretarial skills. Why I need it: to become more responsible (see above). To get over my sickness for taking little things which has rendered me on welfare. All employment has ended when pencil sharpeners or staplers or dictaphones disappeared from the office and the finger pointed at me, even though I didn't need any of these things except at the office, and I got caught every time which indicates a wish on my part to be cured.*

I felt sorry for the three battered wives (Elizabeth, Cora, and Mary Belinda) who did some drinking and always went back, but I admit that I didn't think much of the efforts they were all going to make this time, though for a while at least no one would be slapping them around.

Joan only got as far as *I been using for so many years* when her pen ran out of ink.

Barbie was different. She gave only her first name and phone number, and her hieroglyphic script was penned in blue onto the newspaper page with my ad in the middle, the ink staggering and fading, so I couldn't make sense of some of her marks. *I don't have anything to offer [   ] make me the best, but if you don't take me I'll [   ]. I'm not scared. I just know. I don't have [   ] I can go. Everywhere [   ] was to bad to live. I thought about [   ] but I always thought things [   ] better. I didn't want to [   ] just in case. Now I don't know. That's not to make you take me. Its just the way it is. I didn't think [   ] for me anyway. I just came in case.*

When I found myself responsible for filling in these gaps, my bogus authority became a burden, but one I had to assume. I dialed the number on Barbie's paper and got a voice that could have been a boy's or a girl's. It said that Barbie wasn't there, and didn't know where she was or when she'd be back but agreed to give her my name and number. After every two letters I recited, the voice said, "OK OK," and then, when I started to spell "urgent," "OK."

Then suddenly there was Clara, looking at me like a tamer gauging the margin of danger around an animal. "I didn't mean to startle you," she said. Withholding Barbie's composition, I tendered my two stacks, for her approval or veto, I said, but she insisted, "No, I'm not going to meddle. I don't want you to think my coming along means I'm going to interfere.

"In fact," she said, "you could drop me and take another one of these," the taller stack, "and there's nothing I could do. The money's banked, and you're the signatory."

I considered this. "You could put a stop on the check," I said.

She'd stopped walking earlier, but here she seemed to stop again, inside stillness. "You don't trust me."

"No, I was just being literal," I said, and she lowered herself into a chair, slowly, as if the weight of the papers were growing on her.

As she started to read, the telephone rang. The second ring was interrupted, and after a pause Bill appeared in the doorway, where he waited for our full attention before pronouncing, "It's for her." Clara Bow went back to her stack.

It was Barbie. I told her that we'd chosen her, and that we would call back with details. Meanwhile, I told her, sit tight. She was silent for so long that I finally said, "Hello?"

"That stuff I wrote?" she said. "It was just" another one of her gaps "I don't know. Can you throw it away?"

"It's confidential," I said and, over our good-byes, floated Barbie's page over to Clara Bow, who, despite her deep concentration, didn't blink when the paper lighted on the pile under her eyes. "I got it at the clinic," I said.

"What?"

"The number."

"That's funny," she said, turning over the page and reading

the side with nothing but newsprint on it. After a minute or two, she moved on to Molly's manifesto, then the next paper. Still reading, she asked, "What were your criteria?"

"I picked the worst. Off."

"How do you know they're not lying?"

This hadn't occurred to me, I'm embarrassed to admit, and I panicked, though I don't know why. "Molly, for instance," I said. "There's something sincere in her insincerity, the overprotesting. And 'I'm not ashamed'—that kind of assertion has to be a statement of the worst because it anticipates the hardest response. It makes a claim out of an admission. A claim of righteousness." This was absurd. As easily as someone—Molly, for instance—could become her own victim in this sort of reading, she could also use it, contrive the unconvincing pride to make a minor insincerity into an issue that would mask the bigger lie. There's no way of knowing the degree of someone else's self-consciousness.

Clara Bow was watching me, her head tilted, perplexed. "I was just wondering," she said, as if in defense. "Why the worst?"

The worst needed help the most, I said, so noble. Having suffered misfortune, I knew how to help those in need. That was a dubious reference. Clara's hair, shower-wet, was slicked against her head, except one tuft that lifted, drying as I spoke, then sprang straight up—I recognized the curl.

"I don't know how I'll fit in," she said.

"We'll make up a history for you. Something bad."

"I have a history."

"That's a good start."

"What about you?"

"What about me?"

"How do you fit in?"

"I'm the leader."

"So how do you gain their trust?"

"I pick them," I said. "It inspires confidence."

"That's something," she said, "but that's not what I mean. Once you've got them there, how do you keep them from resenting you? If they're dropouts or failures or whatever and you're, sort of, a representative of the system they dropped out of or failed at? 'Easy for you to say,' you see?"

54

I studied her. "I'll make up a history for me, too," I said.

"You make up one for me," she said, "I'll make up one for you."

"Okay. What?"

"It'll be a surprise."

▼▼

As a child I got to Wisconsin in a dream in the dark. It was where I woke up. But this time, driven through in daylight, Wisconsin became more than a destination separated from home by a long sleep in which gas stations and green signs blazed up now and then. Now it was the in-between too, a progressive state, the patched cement road cutting through leafy cornfields fringed with shocks of long, dust-colored grass gone to seed, the broad trees encircling shiny aluminum silos attached to farmhouses peeling white or brick red paint, then the businesslike farms with their untarnished buildings in brilliant rows and their dense green grass and their acres of corn and their hay for miles and miles, the seemingly flat land suddenly lifting the highway into the sky, a sprinkling of Queen Anne's lace. It was country with a lulling rise and fall like its own kind of sleep, a comforting swell, with, sharp against the vast spreading green, sign after black and white sign: NO TURNS, NO TURNS, NO TURNS; billboards announcing the Skelly's, the Stuckey's, the Wisconsin Dells, Storybook Land, Tommy Bartlett's Robot World, and Xanadu, the foam house of tomorrow; 55 MEANS 55.

For two weeks Clara had been on the telephone in her bedroom, emerging only briefly to eat and to confer with me, generally along this line: Clara Bow: "Why don't you sign one of those checks and give it to me?" Beauty: "Okay." I'd questioned her about the first, she'd said it would pay for the land, and after that I didn't ask because, left to my administrative tasks, which baffled me by not becoming quite apparent, I took more comfort from the mystery of Clara's doings than I might've from an accounting; and so here we were, a few days ahead of the women, who'd been given directions and carpool assignments, the only even slight hitch in the arrangements coming from Kathy number one, who, when I suggested that she should bring whatever might be handy or helpful, volunteered her gun. It was her hunting rifle, of course, and I asked that she at least pack it in her trunk. "What trunk?" she said, and I said, "The trunk of your car." "Car?" she said. "I have a van." "Car, van, what does it matter?" I said, and she said, "A van doesn't have a trunk. But it's a camper, fully equipped." Could she at least wrap the rifle and stow it under her seat then? I asked her, and she said, "What kind of people are they, the ones I'm driving?"

Indiana has road signs that say, ASK GOD. HE KNOWS. Wisconsin has signs that say, CHEESE.

We were in the cab of Women Abreast's brand-new cherry red pickup truck, Clara Bow sitting on a sofa cushion, driving, not that I hadn't offered, again and again, since she looked so uncomfortable, to say nothing of dangerous, her feet hanging short of the pedals while she adjusted our speed with the "coast" and the "resume" buttons on the cruise control, which entailed her moving abruptly, rabbitlike, one of the hands that were otherwise locked in the ten and two o'clock positions on the steering wheel. I suggested we stop at the cheese factory. Clara slid for the brake, ending up eye level with the dashboard. "Now will you let me drive?" I said.

She said, "No."

"Don't tell me you're afraid of driving, too."

"No, I'm not." She pulled herself up onto the seat. "I've never had an accident."

"Looks like the cheese factory's failed," I said, surveying the ghostly place, and she opened her door and leapt down. When I caught up with her at the gate, she was talking about buying the closed factory. "Branching out" was the term she used. I said, "Clara Bow, it's only a building."

57

"Don't be silly," she said. "It's the means of production." That was grand, and she swung open the gate, which was padlocked but not to anything, and swept in. The building wasn't locked either, and a glance inside revealed the reason. The factory looked long abandoned and more beaten by time than its obsolete billboards; of whatever had been, all that remained were three shoulder-high (Clara's shoulder) thick-lipped dull metal vats, over two of which hung huge kneading hooks (one broken), a long stone table, a rancid, musty smell, and the cold. Clara Bow rested a proprietary hand on the rim of one vat. "See?" she said.

"See what?"

"Everything waiting to be put to work."

To balance her theatrical gesture, I kept my hand clamped on the doorjamb. I said, "Can we work on roots before we start to think about branching?"

"You're humoring me again."

I said, "Let's get out of here."

We did. Her enthusiasm for cheese making disappeared as quickly as her interest in my last night's whereabouts had, as quickly as so many subjects and questions did that at times I thought her attention span wasn't a span at all, nothing more than the space of a synapse, in fact. But then I was back in the passenger seat, remembering the rusty road and the lake and the birch woods and skeletal house, and there Clara Bow was, crowding the windshield as if the visible half-mile ahead were her destination. She was moving her lips. In a minute, in response to my stare, she gave me a rabbit glance and murmured, "America's Dairyland."

This was, of course, on the Wisconsin license plates. "What?" I said. "Are you memorizing it?"

"Mother," she said. "I was naming our land."

"You were naming it Mother? Or, Mother, you were naming it?"

"For the milk."

I said, "Cheese."

In a minute, when I thought she'd dropped this, Clara said, "You really don't like it?"

I said, "I really don't mind one way or another. I don't really see us having the occasion to call it anything, since we'll be there."

As soon as I could, after we'd relaxed into our previous attitudes, intensity and reverie, I restructured the driving schedule so that her turn ended immediately. "Stay up there," I said as, thumb to the coast button, she veered into a rest stop; and I stretched out my leg and stepped on the brake.

She made herself small on the far side of the passenger seat. After a while, I thought she was asleep, but at my first approach of a slow car she said, "Watch out," fast and loud enough to cause an accident in anyone with quicker reflexes than mine. So, for the next three hours I was more aware of her balled up in the corner feigning sleep than I'd been when she was climbing the dashboard. Then she did fall asleep and, since she slept just as she pretended to, I didn't notice until, asking for directions, I woke her up. Where were we? she wanted to know, but instead of waiting for an answer sighed and sank back into sleep, finally freeing me, once I unfolded the map across the steering wheel and got my bearings, to exercise my peripheral vision, even turn my head and see some of what was going by.

We'd reached the hilly part, instead of a surprising sky after the too subtle lift, now a definite grinding upward followed by a gliding down, our truckload sliding away then barreling forward to batter the cab. The stretches of grass had become patches scattered with trees not as squat or stalwart as the ones that had hunched around farmhouses we'd passed, and whether these were farmhouses we were passing now it was hard to say, since the dirt with a fence around it or the cow or two or the horse or neat or mangy field might or might not belong to a house, which was usually two narrow stories and porchless, covered with what looked like pebbly roofing shingles, and dark and quiet as a ruin. But then there was the orderly garden in full bloom or the half-painted fence, its new white brilliant, or the window open, a curtain gusting in and out, to attest to life going on. Behind these houses, beyond them and ahead of them were woods, the birches delicate and full of light but dense too, growing so close together that the stricken dead trees leaned instead of fell.

There was nothing eerie or foreboding about the landscape. In fact, the weak word *pretty* might just be the best for the first glance, more sketch than painting, indication of a house, intimation of a tree, outline of a hill. But the look further on, where the woods filled in and the doorway got dark and the tire swing hanging from a bare limb hitched in the wind, seemed far too finished to be entered, anything but passed, and then what? Well, you know what, but at the moment, I woke up Clara Bow. At the moment, I needed the immediacy of her paranoia. Briefly I'd had the peculiar sense of being my own mother with Clara, heaped in the corner of the cab and emitting a whispery snore, as the child shadow of my dreamy long-ago self, sleeping and help-less, being driven. I had only itinerary, and it struck me that my parents, perhaps all parents, were impostors. The road narrowed, dug into the red earth, and ran below the roots of the trees.

Needless to say, my unnecessary phraselet, we had miscal-culated and didn't reach the place where we most needed light until it was quite dark. The northern Wisconsin night is unelec-trified. The sun drops behind the massed branches, leaving a sky of a uniform and seemingly sourceless brightness, and then it all goes black, and then you have to find your turn. The pitch air has started pulsing with the sound of crickets and another, strange insect. Eventually we dubbed this one, the stranger, which we never saw, the telegraph bug; but then, new to the clicking night, we hadn't yet discovered the small comfort of contriving a name for its sound. Driving at one speed above stopped and searching with a flashlight aimed out the window (Clara Bow's), we came to the dead end apparently without having passed our house or any indication of it, the yellow sign, for instance, a near monu-ment in an area so unmarked, which seemed to have disappeared since it had stopped applying.

Going slowly in reverse we arrived back at our "neigh-bor's" and were still homeless. Clara Bow equipped me with a flashlight, which froze my fingers since, for some reason, she'd had it in the cooler, and we walked, waving light. It should have been reassuring to know that we weren't lost, that everything we beamed upon was ours, but it wasn't. The night seemed propri-etary, its feet planted right behind the next tree, its eye looking through the ragged line where the branches met above us, its pres-ence elusive and oppressive as the crickets' humming. "Spooky," I said, just to hear my voice, which helped.

Suddenly Clara stopped sweeping the ground with her

flashlight, and there was the Bay Realty sign, fallen, cracked in half, covered with tread marks. The weeds around the sign were trampled. The mud was rutty with wide tire tracks. "Looks like the circus came," I said, but Clara Bow was unperturbed. She flashed her light into the woods and something in the distance sparkled.

"That's it," she said.

"What's that?" I said. She shrugged. A few steps forward revealed that, right where the tracks went through, a long portion of the swampy ditch along the road had been filled in. While Clara stayed behind as a signpost, I retrieved the truck.

Where there had been nothing but brush, dense and waist-high, we now had a veritable driveway, not smooth, but cleared and beaten. "This is very strange," I said. "Let's sleep in the truck and start over in the morning."

She said, "Don't be silly."

The crickets sang, "Be silly be silly be silly," but I drove on until the headlights spotlit the house, got out and walked into them, toward my own upright shadow on the front door, which was locked. I said, "Do we have a key?"

Clara said, "No."

As I stood there being irked about being locked out of a house I'd come to claim, Clara Bow opened a window and climbed in. Then it occurred to me: Our house didn't have windows. The door rattled and opened, letting the beam of one headlight and then me into the hall, where we were both stopped by a water heater. Clara Bow was staring at the water heater, too, not, like me, as if she were amazed by its presence, but as if she were merely perplexed by its position. She said, "Let's get the lanterns."

I said, *"What* is going on?"

"You don't like it." Her pathetic tone was a sure indication that the windows and water heater weren't all there was not to like. I swung the flashlight around and caught corners of furniture through the doorway on my left and the glimmer of a kitchen fixture down the hallway to my right. The flashlight cracked in my hand (I didn't know my own strength), and I reminded myself: I wanted windows, I wanted hot water, I wanted furniture and a driveway and a sink.

Clara had her light focused on my fist. Her voice came from the dark above the beam: "I wanted to surprise you."

I said, "You did."

"They're just the necessities."

"I thought we had those in the truck, the necessities."

I dropped my hand, and Clara Bow lowered her flashlight. "You're right," she said. "I'll have everything taken out tomorrow."

"That's ridiculous," I said. "Starting with next to nothing and working our way up to having what we need is one thing. But starting with what we need and getting rid of it so we can work our way back up to having it again?"

"We're the only ones who'd know."

"So," I said. "We'd know. I'm not performing a desultory exercise."

"Then I don't know what to do."

"Why didn't you ask?"

"I knew what you'd say." To that logical answer, I didn't say anything. "I didn't have the electricity hooked up," she offered. "I didn't have the phones installed."

"You showed some restraint," I said, and went outside. In a minute, when I was lighting the Coleman lantern, Clara Bow followed, that obliquely eager look on her face, as if she expected to say something any second now, her way of deflecting silence, mine. And so, saying nothing, we set about carrying in the diminished necessities. That expression, bearing the anticipation of speech, was exhausting, and it wasn't long before I couldn't wait to get to bed—I had a bed—and sleep, so I could wake up talking.

Circumventing what she must have thought of as *real* electricity, Clara Bow had had a generator installed (in what, for placement's sake, I'll call the pantry), and on the power it discharged, the water worked, but not, it seemed, the water heater. I found this out by running water in the "shower unit" until it was clear that it was not about to get hot, and then, feeling like a guest arrived before the host, I sponged off with a chilly washcloth, loomed through the upstairs, and fell into bed, sans sheet. What did I dream about? Wisconsin; another world.

★   ★   ★

62

In the morning the bed across from mine was empty, neatly made, camp style, and I could freely survey the effects of Clara Bow's long-distance handiwork. Calling in her orders, she'd obviously had to relegate quality control to some stranger, and the room (also, as it turned out, the house) looked like a rummage sale, with all the rummage new, my long bed with no head- or foot-boards to obstruct my longer body, Clara's with little picket fences at either end, a dresser of laminated pressboard supporting a mirror framed in frosted flowers, et cetera. The house and I coalesced in bemusement at our furnishings; rising, though I'd never risen in any room like this, I felt oddly at home.

In the living room downstairs, there was a fireplace, another "unit," the squat cylindrical metal type funneling up into a fat pipe that angled and tunneled through the wall. Sunlight squeaked in around the departing pipe. The women would have plenty to do. Caulk. Chop. Another necessity in the living room: a bookcase. Stacked on one shelf were my (library) books. I was noting this when I noticed the smell of butter melting.

Clara Bow was in the kitchen frying eggs—in a skillet on the Coleman stove, which was set up on the electric oven. She looked just like a picture of my first idea for raising funds: the primitive grafted onto the defunct advanced. "So here we are," I said.

She said, "So what do we do now?"

Eat. Then I went to meet the generator. One thing I knew about generators, no, two: My windmill would require one; generators, then, must run on something (if not wind, I mean). The specimen in the pantry, the size of two refrigerators, was attached to an engine which was attached to a hose and a pipe, both of which went through holes in the wall (our house was holy!). These sockets, like the other, leaked light. By putting my eye up to one of them, I could, besides burning my cheek, only see dazzling heat-hazy green above a horizon of pipe. I went through the kitchen. The pipe dead-ended in exhaust. The hose fed into a four-legged white tank with a conical cap. I found a switch and turned it off.

The clattering in the kitchen stopped and after a few seconds Clara called, "What happened to the water?"

"I'm conserving fuel," I said.

"Well, I'm doing the dishes. At least I was."

I hadn't thought about the water, worried as I was about conserving the little power we had, which seemed precious now that I knew we had it. I said, "You're rinsing in cold water?" Clara Bow was standing at the kitchen door, her hands dripping suds. "From now on," I said, "we'll boil one pot for wash water, then, while we're washing, boil another one to pour over the soapy dishes."

"Where will we get the water?"

"From the well," I said. "Remember the well?"

"As well as you do. That is, hearsay."

We circled the house, Clara Bow carrying her cupped hands ahead of her, stiffly, as if they'd just been painted. After three circuits, we came for the third time to a fat pipe stuck into the ground with a short red clay cylinder around it; and this time we stopped. Clara said, "That's *it?*"

"You could wipe your hands," I said, and she dropped them.

"Where's the water in the house come from?"

"The other well."

"The *other* well?"

"The one under the house," I said, as if I knew.

She said, "Let's use that one." Peering at the pipe as if something might crawl out of it, she said, "We couldn't even put a bucket down there."

"That's why we have to get a pump."

"We have to get a pump?"

"A pump."

She said, "Let me get my purse."

While I gassed up the truck, Clara Bow collected our key from Bay Realty, where I went to pick her up and found her huddled head to head with Donna. As soon as I appeared, the two of them shifted into a bright exchange over directions, which we followed, to a hardware and lumber concern in Bayfield. The man there, whiskery, wearing a baseball cap, squinted from Clara to me and said, "What do you want a pump for?"

Well, pumping, we said.

He considered this. Special order them from Duluth, he said, still squinting. "Hand pump," I said I meant, and he warmed up enough to tell us where to go, in Washburn. The man, also red-capped, in Washburn sent us to a junk dealer named Joe. She, as Joe turned out to be, had not one pump but two, both tiptop and shipshape. As she watched me measuring the base of one of these antiques (shipshape by Pilgrim standards, I suppose) with my hand, which was the instrument I'd used to take a reading of our well pipe, Joe asked if I was going to "join" it. "Yes," I said.

She said, "Just asking. Don't get testy up there. Wouldn't want to influence the weather." Then, fondling the pump, she mentioned that it was of course rebuilt, but worked like a charm.

"How do you know?" I said.

She said, "Why wouldn't I? Your well shallow?"

"Yes," I said. It had seemed shallow to me.

"Okey dokey. What you want to do is open this up," with her hand on the base, "and wet the valve."

"Prime it, I know," I said. "Make it airtight," I said aside to Clara Bow, to prove that I'd read a few books. "Otherwise it won't work."

When we got into the truck, Clara Bow said, "This is easy."

I said, "But just imagine building it."

She said, "But just imagine smelting the metal."

"Imagine mining it."

"Imagine finding it."

We spent the ride home imagining what it meant to be self-made, while our store-bought rebuilt pump bumped around in the back.

As soon as we turned into our road (W), I knew something was different. The morning air seemed so still that anything moving through it must repercuss, and that was just the sort of slight, ambient disturbance I thought I sensed, though it might have been the more pronounced intrusion of our own loud truck that bothered me, by blotting the rich silence: hindsight. Through the gaps between the trunks, as we turned into our drive, silver flashed, and I slowed. We skirted a tree that the movers had circumvented when they paved our way, and Clara Bow rushed the dashboard, yelling, "Beauty, stop! Get down!"

There was an armed woman on the doorstep. She had her knees braced against our electric stove, also on the step, and was aiming a rifle across it at a man. (A silver van was parked on one side of the door, a red truck on the other.) Just as Clara ducked, the woman clamped the rifle between her elbow and side, and waved. Under the dashboard, Clara Bow was hissing, "Beauty, stop."

I called around the windshield, "Kathy?"

She shouted a rousing, "Right!"

I yelled out, "Put down that gun." She didn't. I yelled, "What are you doing?"

"I caught this guy taking the stove!"

Then I remembered the huddle, Clara Bow and Donna. "Clara," I said, "any idea why someone might be taking the stove?"

"Because we don't want the stove?"

"So this isn't a theft?"

"No, it's assault with a deadly weapon."

I jumped out, saying, "He's supposed to be taking the stove. Put down the gun." Reluctantly, staring down her captive as if his innocence this time were merely a stroke of luck, which went against her, Kathy lowered the rifle. As soon as the muzzle passed the stovetop, the man turned his stupefied face to me. "Well?" I said. "Take the stove."

Clara had crept up behind me. "You *do* want him to take the stove?"

At first the man seemed not to have heard me; then he said, "Make her put it down."

"Kathy, put the gun down."

Her face was like a child's, beaten but bargaining. "I'll hold it just like this."

"Put it down."

She dropped it, and we all ducked. When no explosion occurred, I unsquinted my eyes to see Kathy leaning coolly against the door with her heel resting on the rifle. I pulled the man up from his crouch and, extenuating all the way, helped him ease the dolly with the stove on it down the step and across the dirt to his truck; he exhibited a fine professionalism—though he kept muttering, "I just want to get out of here," he wasn't about to get out without the stove. When I had him loaded up, I patted the door, only to feel it shudder and slide along my hand, so fast was the man on his way, spinning grit in a burst of speed as he left the tortuous drive.

Finally, when I couldn't reasonably look after the truck any longer, I turned around to find Clara's and Kathy's eyes on me. "So," I said. "You're early."

"I know," she said, bending to retrieve the rifle, slowly as if out of boredom with her other opportunities for action. "I got antsy. And everybody else got antsy, so we got together on it."

This was when I remembered everybody else. "Where are they?" I said. "The others?"

"I left them in the Dells. They wanted to stop there, they can stop there. It wasn't the first thing, I'm a slow burn, they were a total pain in the ass, total, from the minute they got into the van and had to make remarks about the carpet."

"The carpet?"

"The carpet. On the sides." (Duh.) "First it was stupid jokes with a sleaze basis, about why there was carpet on the walls. Then it was padded cell jokes. Then it was a debate about the color and the shag. That went on till something else came along, like how to drive—"

"Left them in the Dells." That was Clara, no inflection.

"Yeah," she said, and smiled in the rueful, ironic way of a woman who might cluck. If this were a movie without sound, Kathy could have been mistaken for a housewife called away from her mopping by the Fuller Brush man. She was round-cheeked and typically pretty in that none of her visible features were deformed or misplaced, wore blue jeans and a tailored shirt, and had her hair bandana-ed back. With the rifle not counted, she wasn't very big, five foot two or three, at whatever weight a home ec chart would say was right. She did, however, have a voice, harsh in contrast to this soft, soap-selling advertisement for the domestic mom. "Go get them," I said.

"Get them?"

"Yes. Drive your van down to the Dells and retrieve the others."

"I told you. They wanted to go there." She was squeezing her rifle against her.

"And leave the gun. We'll call it collateral."

"We'll call it my hunting rifle that I'm not leaving any-where."

We were talking over Clara Bow, who suddenly spoke up: "I'd like to call a meeting of the governing body."

She wasn't a member of that body, but this wasn't a time for quibbles, so we walked off a few paces and, when we could whisper without being overheard, she said, "I don't know if that's a good idea—her going back to get them."

"What else?" I said.

Always confident in her ability to buy, Clara suggested, "We could send them bus fare."

"Somewhere in the Dells?"

It was a bad start, I admitted, but we had to be firm, or who knew what this woman would think she could get away with next. Clara Bow was more concerned about the other women. "What could've prompted them?" she said, and frowned, and murmured, "The foam house of tomorrow?" (And I thought she'd slept through the Dells.)

While we conferred, Kathy must have consulted her inner counsel, since, this time, on being asked to go, she only smiled, almost placidly, shouldered her rifle, and marched straight to her van. Over the engine noise, Clara shouted, "Call if you have any trouble."

Kathy shouted, "Right!" and drove away.

I said, "Call how?"

Clara Bow looked up at me. "That's right," she said, and then, "And she didn't even ask the number."

For the rest of the afternoon, in air that seemed as still as it had been, I operated on the pump while Clara Bow stood ready to search out and deliver tools whose functions I was fitting willy-nilly to my needs as they arose, picturing the grip or blow a protuberance seemed to suggest, imagining the proper instrument, then naming it, something like recreating the Stone Age as a game of multiple choice. Clara, serious in Kathy's wake, never laughed at my charlatanism, not even when the pipe, after my ingenious but not quite accurate installation, required capping with a slit Crisco lid, which (the task) entailed taking the pump's handle off again and then putting it back on—but then, to test the damned handle, I pumped, and out came water.

Clara Bow took a step back to get a look at this phenomenon. Voice soft with awe, she said "They can't bill us for this, can they?"

I wasn't quite convinced by this evidence of success, so I kept pumping until the ground was flooded for yards around, and still the water hadn't stopped. Like a pair of idiots, Clara Bow and I stood there smiling down at our wet shoes. I said, "I guess we need a platform."

"Good," she said, with alarming eagerness. "I'll chop the wood."

"But you'd have to chop down a tree."

"That's what I'm going to do."

"Then we'd have to make boards out of it."

"Isn't that what people do? Make boards out of trees?"

" 'People' have saws."

She said, "We have a saw."

"Big saws."

Giving me a quick glance, lips pressed, she started picking up the soaked tools and distributing them among the official-looking loops and pockets of her overalls. Accessorized, she disappeared into the house. A minute later she emerged lugging an ax. "We have a saw," I said.

"Ax for the tree," she said, "saw for the boards."

"Don't be ridiculous," I said. "You'll kill yourself."

She stopped then, leaning on her ax. "And what would you use to cut down a tree?"

"Clara Bow, you're small," I said. She really wasn't that much bigger than the ax. "That's not a judgment. It's a fact. Common sense says act accordingly."

"I suppose that means you want to do it yourself." With an effort, she hefted the ax and held it blade up. "Due to an accident of birth."

"I just want you to use the saw," I said, but she was already striding, as much as her short legs allowed, away, and didn't hear me or pretended not to.

This was, somewhere in its inner workings, an argument, though about what it would be hard to say. In penance—or, more likely, political shrewdness—I assigned myself the weakling's task of making dinner; went into the darkening house, lit the lantern, considered our cache. As I fished through the bloated packages floating in one of our coolers, Clara Bow attacked a distant tree. The dull whack of her ax worked on me insidiously, killing my appetite as the icy water numbed my hands, and when I finally raised them, realizing they were dead, there was hamburger in them, so this was what I fixed, not listening to the strokes but forced to listen for them, since they were just faraway enough to give the silence in between a strain of expectation.

"Dinner!" I yelled out the door, although I hadn't located the buns or catsup or set the table. Ax met wood, right on time. Fine, I was thinking, starve; and then came silence.

I don't know whether it was pique or discretion that prompted Clara Bow to pick a tree such a trek from the house. It certainly wasn't discrimination; when I snuck up, following the path of sound the blows had made, even in the near-dark I could see that nothing but her assault distinguished the chosen birch from all the rest around. Clara Bow, her back to me, was standing in the wood chips strewn like a skirt around the foot of the tree. Though little more than an inch was left where the trunk was whittled, the tree stood upright, unshaken. Clara was breathing hard—not laboriously, like a winded worker, but deliberately, loud and deep, with long, hushed exhalations between her rich gasps. Suddenly she ran and hurled herself onto the tree. It quivered but stood. Monkeylike, Clara Bow clung to it. I backed up, behind a nearby fir. Just as I stepped aside, Clara dropped, scattering wood chips, and backed away from her birch.

She started the deep breathing again. It sounded a strange echo in my ear, not quite synchronous; but then I realized that this was someone else's breathing, close by, and turned my head and came face to face with a man. The shock I got felt like fear at first, and at first it might have been, but then I was left with the strangeness of seeing someone eye-to-eye. As soon as his height went from fright to observation, I noticed his expression, which was like Bill's when he'd said, "Did you do this?" but a little bit shrewder and not so easily spit upon. His position, behind the tree next to mine, and that appraising, reproachful look told me he'd been watching Clara, too, and felt as I did about her behavior—that she could hurt herself like this but also that, for some reason (maybe he knew it), a person shouldn't interfere. I'd like to describe that look, his face, but now I know it too well; then it was all expression, an afterimage of sternness. Also, white hair.

A scurry made us peer around our trees. Clara Bow again flew at her birch and wrapped herself around its trunk with a sickening thud. The tree shook in earnest this time, but still didn't fall; Clara did. That irked her. She got up and rammed her shoulder against the trunk and made the somewhat obscene noises of immense strain. With answering creak and groan, the birch gave up and toppled, taking Clara with it. As the tree made a crashing arc through a gauntlet of branches and hitched and settled, Clara Bow flat out, like an exhausted rider, arms and legs hanging limply from the level, her cheek against the bark, I saw a pale movement in the woods beyond, white hair receding.

Then a whimper came from Clara. I stepped out to help her, thinking she was hurt, but with a step the sound clarified, laughter, and I retreated, too, in silence.

In the dark I didn't find the house. I found the road. Then I tramped back to the strains of the cricket orchestra, telegraph bugs on percussion, down the drive toward the lantern twinkling in the kitchen. There are some theories as to why crickets beat their wings together, making music. One has it that they're showing off and calling mates, the night thick with crickets crying to couple. Another says they just can't help themselves; not even celebratory by nature, they chirp as we breathe. It seemed surprising that I hadn't sensed the man until I heard him, no disturbance of the subtle air; and then I remembered that our property boxed in someone else's, that Abbot, and the man might've had the air of someone who belonged. By then, it also might have entered my mind that I could secure my place by marrying Clara off, but this, if the man was that Abbot, a candidate, didn't seem like an especially propitious introduction.

Carrying the lantern now, I went back through the woods, thrashing noisily to announce my approach, into the deep night, and I got lost. I was telling myself that it didn't matter, everything around was mine, so I was really home, not lost, when Clara Bow found me. Suddenly she was swinging along at my side, her hands folded behind her, tapping her rear to the rhythm of her gait, the ax blade nestled against her bib, the handle bulging her pant leg like an extra femur. "Where are you going?" she said.

"To find you."

"Wrong way. I'm back there." She leaned into a cakewalk, pointing with her head.

We pivoted. "Well," I said, "do we have boards?"

"We have boards-to-be." She nodded; and there was the prone tree. "We have to mark the way—or I won't be able to find it tomorrow. Here, take the ax." Without unclasping her hands, she lifted her elbow so I could get ahold of the blade. "Chip trees as we go," she said. "I'll carry the light." She took the lantern and dropped it and, as I righted it, stood looking bemusedly at her hand, which was clasped midair as if still holding onto the wire handle. She said, "I tried to drag it. Before I had the path idea."

The tree was still attached to its stump by a hinge of bowed wood. I said, "It's not severed."

"I know." Then she turned over her fist and opened her fingers. Her palm was raw and bloody. "Who am I?" She clawed the air.

"A very stupid woman," I said and, armed with the lantern and ax, walked away.

"Sister of Usher," she called after me. Shortly I heard her tagging along. "Chip the trees, don't forget." Her voice kept a constant distance. "I'm starving."

One-handed, I swung the ax, smacking a tree on my left with the blade, "Good," one on the right with the butt, "we're having hamburger."

A ghost image of an animate house was dissolving around me when I woke in the middle of the night. I could see Clara's white pajamas standing up across the room, but I couldn't make out her face. "What," I said, "is going on?"

"You were having a nightmare. I tried to wake you up."

"I'm awake."

"You tried to hit me."

This statement, coming to me flatly from no face, seemed

72

a natural extension of an interrupted nightmare. "I'm sorry," I said, and was. "I don't know what I was dreaming."

For a few seconds she was silent, and I didn't have to see her to know that she was staring at me, that gaze uninflected, too. Then she said, "Was I in it?"

As soon as I said, "I don't know," I was stuck with the disturbing feeling that she was.

First aid was the first thing we discovered we'd forgotten. But that didn't stop Clara Bow, with her two wounded hands, from becoming a sawyer, especially after I'd voiced my reasonable opinion that her doing so would be not just unnecessary, since boards weren't an urgency: it would be idiotic. Hands picked clean of slivers (by wincing me—this much she allowed) and balled up with rags (good-bye, white pajamas), she went off into the woods, bearing the saw like an offering.

I can't say how much this irritated me, more than her apparent pursuit of martyrdom, something else. Thinking possibly as petty a thought as, "Improving the cosmetic value of a pump is child's play, but building a windmill is woman's work." I took *Harnessing the Wind* off the shelf and went to Bayfield to look for parts for my enormous anchored pinwheel. After I'd loaded the pickup with lumber and putty and nails and cable, my thoughts ran from electricity to refrigeration, and I bought bags of ice, meanwhile running on from perishable food in general to milk, which brought me to the thought of cows. Then I had to consider cow housing. Clara's efforts made it clear that hacking our own wood, even enough for the most modest shack for our projected cow, would either keep the women around forever or cripple them, and who knew what the lumber would look like? So my thoughts turned to money, what boards would cost, since I'd been writing checks all day, still with no idea of what my balance was.

When I got back to Mother, Clara Bow was puttering at the kitchen counter, a bucket of water at her feet. Turning around with a knife in her hand, she said, "Oh good, ice."

"I don't know which would cost less," I said. "Running the refrigerator or renewing the ice."

"Why are you always thinking about money?" she said petulantly.

"I was thinking about cows," I said. "But how much money do we have?"

Pausing to show me her disapproval, prim and superior, she walked to the window and touched the pane with the point of her knife.

What I saw was, next to the pump, a tidy stack of boards. The stack was tidy, not the boards, which even from that distance looked a little rough and not exactly uniform; but relatively straight and square, there they were. The woman, no doubt trying not to look smug, was waiting, face smooth and expressionless, but eyes distinctly on mine. When I only responded by staring, she smiled slightly and tapped the window with her knife. That was when I noticed her hand: it was bandaged with gauze, neatly, whitely taped. The other, holding a peeled onion, was just as sterilely wrapped. Clara was still watching me. "I met our neighbor," she said.

"He did this?" I'd nodded at the boards, but she was admiring her hands and didn't see.

"He's a doctor." She said this with simple pleasure, apparently unsurprised by her good luck. "That solves one of our problems."

I managed to say, "It does?"

"Weren't you worried about medical attention?" Now I was.

"He doesn't practice?" I said. "Up here in the middle of nowhere?"

"Look at this." Again she showed me her hands.

"So? I could've done that if I had the stuff."

"He has a bag."

"Pretty impressive."

"He practices. What I mean is, we don't have to worry about getting Pap smears."

"Pap smears?" I said. "From some quack in the woods?"

"Quack?" she said. "He's perfectly reputable."

"Judging from his way with a bandage."

"When I found out he was a doctor, I researched his credentials, what do you expect? Anyway, he helped with the boards, so we had time to talk."

All I said was, "Oh."

She squinted up at me. "Oh?" she said. "What's that supposed to mean? I was half done when he showed up. There'd be boards if Frank Abbot never existed."

"Oh," I said. "Frank."

" 'Oh, Frank,' what's *that* supposed to mean? What's got into you, anyway? I found us a doctor. Which we need. You, too."

"Me? Do I have an appointment?"

"Actually, an appointment with this doctor might interest you."

I said, "Why?"

The quality of Clara's pause told me that she'd gotten ahead of herself. "He's a nice doctor," she said finally, "very smart. Not bad looking," she added, tentatively, but not a word about height.

"I'm not looking for a doctor."

"Why not?" she said. "You haven't had any fatalities, have you?"

"If he's so nice, you go ahead."

Her face went hard. "I told you—" she said, but didn't finish, since for emphasis she'd slapped the windowsill with her hands, and that hurt.

"Okay," I said. "Let's drop it."

"Okay," she said, but then, when she went back to the onion, began to talk about the doctor anyway, how odd he was, insisting on wrapping her hands and then, when she let him, acting irritated, not a word, as if the injury were something she had done to spite him, a stranger—funny, hunh?

I said, "If you still had the rags on, that wouldn't have hurt."

We settled into a working routine, Clara hunkering with hammer and nails near the pump and occasionally crossing to where I sat constructing sails to borrow my cellulose filler, since her boards turned out to be not quite as square as they'd seemed from the window; where she couldn't match dips and bumps, she filled gaps. In the house, the generator hummed. We'd decided to run it until the women arrived, when I hoped to be ready for their help in hauling up the tower. For the most part we were silent and when we weren't we were mundane, deploring powdered milk and Tang, our current beverages, and planning to wean ourselves to water, which was sulfur-rich and stank, counting on cows, agreeing to buy lumber for their shed, wondering how long the Coleman fuel would last, it went so fast. We needed a range. My saying so prompted a look of disbelief from Clara Bow. So, I wasn't thinking straight, I said, the woman had a gun. Then we tried to remember the legend on the man's red truck, but couldn't, but Donna would. Why not take a hike to the doctor's and use his phone? Clara suggested, meaning me. Why not? I agreed, sitting fast. Giving me a martyred look, she rose from her carpentry, rinsed her fingers under the pump, ran them wet through her bushy hair, and, with a puff of purpose, headed off.

Just as she disappeared into the thicket of thin birches, a gunshot sounded in the woods. I leapt up. She came running. We met in a skid at the edge of the yard and stood shoulder to elbow, peering into the trees. This stupidity passed fast and, feeling like an ample target, bigger than ever, I retreated to the house. When I noticed no accompanying patter, I turned around to see Clara Bow going back into the woods. I shouted: "What are you doing?"

"Going to borrow the phone."

"Don't be ridiculous. Someone's shooting out there."

"Trespassing," she said.

"*So?* Would you prefer manslaughter?"

"I'm not going to let someone who's got *no* right to be on *our* property scare me out of walking through it. That's final."

"It could be."

Her laugh came back faintly, as she went. I was not about to go after her. I was too big, a coward, and, especially, the one who'd said, "Go get them," provoking the wrath of Kathy, if I were guessing right, although a little late. I held off hammering for a long time. There were no more gunshots, but the silence made me nervous, too, and then it started to get dark.

Keeping quiet, I'd moved to the pump and occupied myself with planing the edges of Clara Bow's boards. I did some sand-

ing, then planed the edges even smoother, or, I should say, further. I was polishing away and the crickets were sawing at full
volume when Clara, right behind me, said, "What are you doing?"

I noticed I needed a lantern. "Well?" I said.

"I couldn't get Donna, so I kept trying."

"So?"

"So, I never got her. Have you eaten?"

"Have you?"

"Fish," she said, "from our river. What a wise investment."

"Trespassing," I said.

"I don't mind a trespasser who feeds me fish. Only one
who shoots me."

"She could be hunting," I said.

"Kathy?"

"Just guessing," I said. "Don't forget the squirrels."

Clara made a nauseated sound. I felt her toeing the board
that lay under my hand. "I could've done this. If I had that." The
plane twitched, nudged. We were silent for a minute. "We're going to have to go look for them. Those women."

"I know," I said. "When?"

"When?"

"Soon?"

Clara Bow murmured agreement, then a soft, "Pretty
soon."

It's not that we *forgot,* or that it finally mattered, but we
had work to do. Sometimes the diagrams I consulted seemed
hopelessly naive and, wondering how they could be right and my
renderings wrong, I prided myself on my inadvertent complica-
tions. When I had my four warped sails, the pine spars angling
along the sail-stock as directed, the plywood slats in place, and
knew what these things meant but not whether the wind would;
when I was ready to mortise the sails into the poll-head and Clara
Bow had reached an impasse at the pump, was staring more than
putting wood together, we decided to take a vacation, a visit to
the lake, maybe, a moment, one of the last of "pretty soon."

O ur legs were wasted from six days of squatting and sitting, so we thought we ought to walk. By the time we reached the main road, 13, and noon, we thought we ought to drive instead, but we were halfway to water and would've wasted half a day of walking if we went back for the truck, so we walked on, as if there were more purpose in the lake, the end of walking, than in the woods, the way. When we finally reached the lake, we really did need a rest, and had only a few hours of daylight left in which to get it and get back to the road.

From 13, we'd taken a northbound dirt road with rutty red tributaries branching off into the woods where we caught glimpses of sometimes a cabin, sometimes a cement foundation, sometimes a clearing, hole of light, each red drive with a shingle posted or hung from a tree: Anderson's Acre, O'Leary, Potter's Place, Shangri-la. It was at Shangri-la that we noticed our road was veering south. Up this drive, someone had cleared and leveled a square of earth, leaving the felled trees lying like stricken sentries, and had planted four little red flags for corners. There was no one around, and we could see blue ahead, a hazy line through the trees, so we proceeded, surprising flies, who regrouped and followed for a while, then fell back.

We'd come to what looked like the shore's northernmost

78

outjutting, a ledge above a steep, rocky drop to the lake, the land on either side of us receding. With our towels draped around our necks, we started down, grabbing stony knobs or roots sticking out of crevices, swinging our feet and tapping with the toes of our sneakers till we found rocks flat and dry enough to hold us. Halfway down, where the occasional slapping wave had turned the moss to slime, the going became difficult. I tied one end of my towel around my arm and told Clara Bow, the lead explorer, to take the other end. She reached for it, and landed in the lake.

I scrambled down, lighted on a flat rock, a little island. "Let's not go in after all," I said. That was a joke.

Clara Bow was standing waist-deep in the water, making broad blinks that involved her entire face. "I can't speak," she said. "I'm frozen." Just then a wave lapped at my feet, turning them to ice. "Help me up." I reached, she hung her whole weight on my hands, and I slid in. That, she thought was funny. As I stood there spluttering, lungs shrunk, she said, "I'm getting warmer. Once you're used to it—"

"You're dead," I said. "Our clothes are never going to get dry before we go."

"Go? We just got here."

"From here, home looks like a vacation."

Her skin was turning the fishy white of frozen chicken, her lips were purple, her face was grim. "I'm having some fun," she said, then, slotting her fingers in the cleft face of my deserted islet, she tried to scale the slimy rock. Her attempt was comical, climbing in place, one foot sliding as soon as the other held, and all the while she was expounding her approach to fun. Whenever she was happy, she said, having fun, feeling safe, things going fine, something happened—always awful and always a surprise, so she tried to imagine every awful thing that could occur. It was her way of guarding against disaster, since nothing she could contemplate would happen. (I made a stirrup of my hand and boosted her.) But she always knew she was forgetting something. She couldn't think of everything. And the one thing she forgot—that would be what got her.

Grabbing the rock where it jutted, I hoisted myself up next to her. She was trying to wring out her towel, beach-sized, that is, twice her armspan long, and soddenly unwieldy. I took the twitching end where all the wrung water had pooled, and twisting, said, "That's very superstitious of you."

With a level, sensible tone, she said, "If you knew, you wouldn't think so."

There were a few minutes of silent wringing then, Clara Bow paying profound attention to the task. Finally she tugged the towel out of my hands and, laying it out flat on the rock, still intensely preoccupied, said, "That's not all." She patted and smoothed where no ripples were. "There's always been a man. But now." With one forefinger, she was making adjustments to the terry's nap. "You're the only one around who . . . person, I mean." Rocking back on her heels, she frowned to herself as if she'd got sidetracked and missed her point. Then she looked up at me and said matter-of-factly, "Something terrible is going to happen to you."

In spite of myself, I shivered, not because I put much stock in superstition, but because, in view of my plans, this seemed quite a close call from someone who did. "Not if you think hard enough about it," I said, and a quick hurt look crossed her face, as if doom had been a gift, then disappeared.

"Cancer of the larynx," she said to herself. "I never thought of that."

I believe she was sincere. I believe she actually was feeling guilty, that her husband had died through a failure of her imagination. "But you thought something would happen to him," I said, "and that didn't stop it from happening."

She said, "It has to be specific."

My second attempt at arguing along her line went, "If you think you could've prevented disasters by anticipating them, couldn't you just as easily think you precipitated them?"

"I *didn't* anticipate the things that happened. And anyway, I didn't think of anything the first time, except good times, and look."

I did. Standing at the edge of the rock, facing the horizon, Clara Bow looked like a figurehead at the prow of our small, anchored ship. The sun was beginning to set, lighting lake and sky alike, and never was the world so still and blue and brilliant. Abruptly Clara stripped down to her bathing suit and started spreading her clothes on the sunny rock. I did the same, and shivered. We were both wearing Speedos bought in town, Clara Bow's idea, since I couldn't swim. She was outlining her dialectic of temperature adjustment: the water, if we got into it, would seem warm, since the air was brisk; then once we got out, the air would seem warm, since the water had been so cold. And by then our clothes might be dry.

Stiff at least, I said.

Without waiting to see if I'd been convinced, she sprang off the rock into the lake, with such force that I was surprised to see her rise no shorter than before. Flapping her arms, spreading wings of water with each sweep, she shouted up, as if I were seventy instead of seven or so feet away, "Watch out for the pebbles! I think I just acquired cleats!"

The water was still as cold as water can get. Being big, I was half in, half out next to Clara, who was under almost to the neck; and in the slight blue breeze my suit clammed to me. "This is too much fun," I said. "I'm going to get out."

"Go under," she said, "you'll get used to it," and ducked.

I've always thought the cold could kill me, that in my deceptive frame I housed a delicate, consumptive being, and already I was standing on stalactites where I'd once had legs, but with a show of bravado to preserve my cover, I dunked my head. When I unbent, not mindless but numb, Clara Bow still hadn't surfaced. Suddenly, yards away from where she'd submerged, she shot up like a slightly retarded missile, then settled chin-deep. I treaded out toward her while she looked at me oddly, as if she didn't quite recognize me. "Are you all right?" I said.

"All right?" She sounded mildly baffled. "I told you it gets better."

My teeth were starting to chatter uncontrollably. Clara ducked again, did whatever slithering she did on the bottom, and sprang up a few feet away from her point of departure, then came down a few inches deeper. Leaving her to her game of jumping waves where there weren't any and being carried without current, I headed back, convinced that in a few more minutes my blood would gel and in a few hundred years I would turn up as a perfectly preserved but misleading specimen for anthropologists. Behind me, Clara Bow erupted sporadically. When I reached the rock, I looked back to see that she'd pogoed in over her head and was still bouncing. I couldn't tell how deep she'd gone, only that she disappeared between jumps and was much farther out than she'd been.

I started to climb out but found that this softened the numbness, so I slid back into the water and watched Clara while I waited for the strength to face recovery. Her showings—allowing for the distance—weren't as boisterous as before; it took me a minute to realize that if she were in as deep as I guessed, she couldn't be springing off the bottom anymore and must be propelling herself upward on aquatic angel wings.

She bobbed and said something. When she came up again, I bellowed back, "What?"

There was mild suspense, the feeling of waiting for sound to travel. She yelled, it seemed, "It only goes out," a garbling in the transmission, I thought. Her next message was clear. "I can't swim." So I understood the first: She couldn't bounce back.

You're thinking of the boating accident? It never even crossed my mind, though I believe it was supposed to. In fact, my first response was irritation at her stupidity in going so far out when she had no way of getting back. And then it struck me that *I* was the way that she'd been counting on. If this was a test, she'd overlooked one important variable. She yelled again, "I can't swim," and disappeared for what seemed like a very long time.

When her head came up again, I shouted, "I can't either." Two more times she popped up, at increased intervals and not saying anything. I shouted louder, "I can't either!" Then, as far away as I was, I thought I could see her expression: stricken. But I wasn't as far away as I'd been; as if in an attempt to shorten the delays between communications, I'd been pressing toward her. Like those suicidal romantics in movies and literature, except in one crucial respect, I walked deeper and deeper, while Clara's struggles to the surface became weaker, silent.

Walking in water when it's over your head is not an easy thing to do. Your airy marrow buoys you up off the bottom. To keep Clara in sight (and to breathe) I was forced to use her method, sinking to the floor on bent legs, then shooting to the surface at an angle. The going was slow, and when I'd been in water deeper than me for at least five minutes and still hadn't reached Clara Bow, worry made me lightheaded; the lack of a retrieval plan, occurring to me just then, had almost the force of an idea.

The next time I went down I could see her legs pumping the water at eye level four or five yards ahead of me. Our ups and downs had got out of sync. I jumped up in slow motion for my last gasp of air, then dove under her, tried to anchor myself, grabbed her pedaling feet, and fastened them to my shoulders. Exhaling was the only way to gain weight and stay grounded; it also deprived me of air. So, bursting to breathe, I trod shoreward (I hoped) with my hands clamped onto Clara's feet. She responded to my ever-so-slight momentum by falling backwards, lying nearly flat in the water behind me like a lame little submarine in tow. Letting go and treading up for air, I met her at the surface and, between pants, uttered: "Paddle." Thrashing, she nodded, with a somewhat hysterical smile.

After that, we were an efficient machine. The undercurrent was negligible and, except for the inconvenience of my topside propellor, walking toward shallow water was no harder than bounding into the deep had been. If my mind had been more than a lump of matter frozen into the shape of survival, I might have thought about that fact and dropped my passenger right there. However, hours passed and I'd thawed to mellow before I realized how suspicious her distress had been. But by then I'd also thought about the boating accident, and reconsidered Clara's stricken look. At the moment, though (lump), I had no trouble believing that the quiver in my spine signaled a change in my form from flesh and bone to jellyfish. Then I tilted my trembling neck and looked up through the brightening blue and saw that Clara Bow was halfway out of the water. Taken as I was with the protean explanation, it took an effort to understand that the strange sensation in my back was caused by Clara juggling her weight to stay upright.

I released her wriggling feet and met her in the air. Too winded to speak, I gripped her hand and dragged her into water that reached my upper lip. From there, she held onto my shoulders and floated behind me until we could both walk with our heads above water. When I got used to being able to breathe whenever I wanted and heard Clara Bow splash-splashing after me and saying lightly, "Some vacation," relief, if it had its mo-

83

ment, gave way to fury, and turning on her, I started to scream. Specifically, I remember screaming, "What possessed you?" but the rest is lost in a haze of screeching reproach, like a stereo distorting at peak volume; and then it all seemed too ridiculous for words, so I splashed a fan of water in her face. "Stupid stupid stupid," I remember muttering as I climbed the rock, crawled onto a damp towel, and collapsed on my face—and breathed, breathed, breathed, breathed.

I had to wake up to find out that I'd fallen asleep. A full moon made the lake look milky. Clara Bow was sitting behind me telling me the story of her life. I don't know whether she had skipped her childhood and teens or whether I had slept through them, but we were well past adolescence when I woke. I don't know whether she thought I was awake or was telling me because she thought I was asleep; waking, I shook myself and grunted, settled, and sighed, and she went on anyway.

At first, accustoming myself to the chill and the stiffness in my limbs, I could only understand her cadence, as storytelling. From the measure of her words, I gathered that the story was a long one, this the middle. She was saying something about a contact of her mother's, and I was thinking of the few feet of water between our rock and Wisconsin, the stony ascent to Shangri-la, the dark walk home. I was wondering if some vision of death in the deep had prompted Clara to review the events of her life, or if she were merely what my own little mother would call "touched," since my concern over our return seemed saner than the characterization of the anchorman who'd just entered her account. Somehow, "the network" connected her mother's contact and the anchorman. Then I remembered my research into Clara Bow's background and knew what she was talking about: her stint as a writer for TV.

Her status reflected the tenuousness of her mother's friendship, she said; she was assigned to cover a newscaster deemed worthy of a TV obituary only because of his standing at the network. He was old, too, had grown up with the medium, and was not expected to last much longer. Other people, she said, researched Elvis and Nixon and Tennessee Williams.

It had seemed like dues-paying until she got to like the

man. First there was pity, though, and chagrin over her position. She could even date the pity, which had arrived with the actuary's report. Bill, she said (Bill? I said. She said: Not that Bill.), was already living outside of his life expectancy as figured by the statistician. She'd remarked on this to one of her co-workers, who said Bill did it because he knew he'd have less time on the air the day he died than he did now, and, after that, none. Then there was the attached medical report, the fact sheet, according to which the anchorman had an operable lung condition, but had refused the operation. The same co-worker said that the last operation had kept Bill off camera for a month. At his age, that kind of lapse in exposure was almost as good as death. Clara Bow felt sorry for the man, not so much because of the facts on the sheet as because of the way they were bandied about by gofers in a busy room with short partitions for walls, so that Bill had to know that he was living in an unforecast future. Every day, she thought, must feel like a sanction that could be revoked as easily and mysteriously as it had been granted. She felt bad about *knowing*. When she watched the news, she couldn't understand why Bill wasn't paralyzed by the information. She pitied him for his *exposure*.

"Pity seems so condescending," she said, signaling a digression. "Whenever I pity someone, I get to thinking about how far off I have to stand to feel superior enough, and pity starts to look like a pathetic excuse for feeling—compared to what provoked it. The truth is, I almost always end up admiring—actually envying—anyone I pity. Well—" There followed a critical pause, then Clara Bow, as if she had a dialogue going on inside, said, "Not anymore."

I didn't know any newsman Bill. Back then, at the time she meant, I must have been a child (she was thirteen years older than I). The man's consistency, out of bravery or stoicism, was, she said, what moved her most. Anyone else, she thought, would be doing every extravagant thing he could to prove he was still alive. And his refusal to have an operation that would allow him to live longer simply baffled her, proving that he was also profound. Her work was supposed to be deskbound, the compilation of data with which a scriptwriter could highlight a life as soon as it ended. But once her pity played out, she started to follow Bill around.

"I was only a kid," she said. "It was a kind of crush." To convince herself that she was merely working, only more actively, she carried a pad and pen while she shadowed Bill and, like a cub reporter on the human interest detail, took notes: Is harrassed by vendor into buying hot dog which he discards a block later; notices his makeup in store window and takes it off with handkerchief, looking in glass; second time this week; asked to sign autograph, borrows my pen, seems to know me, not sure why.

After a few weeks of following him from studio to apartment, apartment to studio, sitting behind him in bars and restaurants, she stopped taking notes. They seemed to reveal nothing but her own tenacity. By then she'd become so familiar with his habits that she began to think of the man as someone she knew quite well; and it began to irritate her that he could be so oblivious to her, right there as she always was. It began to seem possible that he didn't know what the gofers were saying after all.

For one more week she trailed Bill, now hoping to discover his secret resources so she could stop doubting that he had any. In her preoccupation, she nearly bumped into him a few times, assuming that whatever he might do she'd seen him do before. This was the state she was in, wrapped up in wishful skepticism, when one night he slipped on ice on the steps leading up to his apartment building. She looked up and saw him coming down backwards, headfirst. She caught his hat. Next thing she knew, she was dizzily trying to sit up under a huge and immovable weight, which suddenly shuddered and rolled to one side.

"I'm little and skinny," Clara said, "but I'm better than a sidewalk." I do believe she was taking credit for saving Bill. At first she was dazed from the knock of her head on cement; then she was dazed by the implications; then Bill was huffing over her, asking if she was all right, but shaking her so vigorously that she couldn't answer. Finally he let go of her shoulders and, saying how sorry he was, helped her onto her shaky legs. I'm sorry, too, she was saying, so amazed by the fact that she'd cheated the actuary that she wasn't clear about much else, except her trembling. Bill invited her up for a glass of brandy—to wipe the chill and spill from immediate memory, he said—and she obligingly followed. "Puppy of fate," she said. "I walked behind. I remembered the ice."

As soon as she got warm and undumbfounded and slightly tight, she told him everything—about her job, following him, her bafflement at his behavior in the face of a long-since-predicted death. He said, "Ah, yes." Bill was utterly unimpressed with the actuary's statistics, which he'd discredited by living. They'd worried him once and for a while, he told her, but he'd counted on the fallibility of statisticians. And when time proved him right, he started to think his life was just beginning, differently, no longer circumscribed by logic and mathematics and probabilities. As he saw it, this was just confirmed once more by Clara's chance presence behind him when he happened to fall down a flight of stairs.

Clara said that if not for those statistics, she wouldn't have been there. Her interpretation of the event, which she didn't voice, was that his time had come just then, and gone. The man was moved by her concern. He accused her of being a "sensitive little creature." And then he fell upon her.

"You know how I am about men," she said.

I said, "You *didn't*."

"Of course not, that old man?" she said. "The thing is, I was so innocent, it took me a minute to catch on—just like one of those dates where you're going along with things, taking it for granted nothing else'll happen, it's understood—and then the guy undoes his pants. I mean, I had to see evidence before I could accept him as a lecher. Then I kicked him in the leg and left. But that's when it started—about men."

Instead of elaborating, she went right on to the next morning, an airplane ride. She'd quit her "stupid, useless" job and taken off to get a new one from someone she'd met at a party, a man who claimed to be the director of the network's Chicago affiliate. The previous evening had left her confused. The fact of its significance seemed obvious, but not the sense. Buckled down and frustrated, she imagined that figuring out whether providence or coincidence was implicated in the scene would teach her something about how to conduct her own life—with premeditation or abandon. It seemed a great misfortune that she hadn't been paying attention when Bill slipped, the key moment. Then the plane hit an air pocket and, to Clara's significance-saturated mind, this looked like a clue.

In all her flying, she'd never experienced a sudden drop, and so had no way of seeing it as a minor, not uncommon occurrence. So this, her first plunge, sped her heart and made her hyperventilate. Coffee and soda hit the ceiling and rained down around her while she waited to die and tried to think of a decent parting thought. When the airplane righted and word came whispering back that stampeding meal carts had hurt a stewardess's leg and another stewardess, intact, was passing out promissory notes for dry cleaning, Clara Bow could think again. (At least she said so; that hyperventilation might have left her giddy.) Having her meditation on probabilities and proper action brought to a shocking stop by weather—the unpredictable, arbitrary, absolute—robbed Clara of her will. Her helplessness, her brief mindlessness, was a message interpretable only at the moment of impact, when all a person could do was wonder. It was as if all along she'd been sitting in the palm of a big hand ("I'm not talking about God," she said. "I wouldn't presume.") and seeing what she thought might be all the world through the crack between the fingers. Then just when she'd started to see through the fingers—the way you see through your own when you hold them close to your eyes—and to doubt they'd ever been there, the hand tossed her into the air to let her know what it would be like if she really were sitting on nothing at all. "I got this feeling, it was physical, in my stomach and lungs, this feeling that it didn't matter what I did. If the plane had crashed, I couldn't have done anything but go down with it, and that didn't really have anything to do with my decision to fly, or the pilot or the plane, for that matter." She stopped a second. "That's the state I was in," she said.

"You walk into a studio and the first thing you see is a TV tuned to the station—suspended up in the corner across from the security guard, where most businesses hang their surveillance monitors." While she waited for the guard to telephone her cocktail party acquaintance, Clara watched a few minutes of soap opera, a commercial for shampoo, and then a "news brief." There was Bill, still photo, the newscaster telling of a heart attack. At the supposed time of death mentioned by the man, Clara Bow had been in Bill's apartment. Then there it was, her research, clipped through in one minute and summarized at the end with "the passing of a newsman who was like a family member to a million viewers."

"I'm sorry, Miss," the guard was saying, "he didn't know about it." Then, when she turned, "Mr. Merton. He isn't expecting you."

Clara said, to me, "This is the thing: I thought I should've stayed. I told you that was how it started."

"By 'it,'" I said, "do you mean the fatal effect you think you have on men? Or how you think you have to have them?"

"Both," she said. "They're related, you know. If I hadn't been there earlier, he would've broken his neck. But if I'd been there later—he was fine, perfectly fine when I left, except for the obvious. The point is, all the time I thought I was acting on whims, and I was fulfilling a contract. That's how it seemed. Almost crashing in the plane made sense, then.

"So I armed myself."

She was not about to get onto a plane, so she stayed in Chicago. There followed a time of no job, no money—and, for me, another digression, this one about her money being "second generation," which meant that her parents had worked so hard at looking like people with infinite funds that she grew up completely stupid about every aspect of finance except spending, so that even what she'd recently earned, like play stuff compared with the constant flow of cash from her folks, hadn't seemed to have any practical purpose. She literally had to run out of money to get a grasp on it. With her traveling cash, she'd rented a room about a half a block from my alma mater, the Riverside (which was how she'd known of its unsavory reputation before I did). She knew where danger was.

On impulse, she bought a stiletto—a clever thing, made like a lipstick—from a man who was selling jewelry and pretty knives out of a suitcase in a parking lot. Then she took her stiletto for walks—into what she called "the sleaziest, bummiest, darkest places." She might have been carrying around an arc light for all the trouble she attracted: none. "Chance or whatever's behind it," she said, "isn't interested in the insane, which is what I must've looked like, being who I was, where I was. They're too close." Everything systematic was now suspect. The apparently logical structuring of family precluded any further contact with home.

She wasn't going to be fooled by the sense of security that membership in a social unit could inspire. Instead, she was looking for the kind of reason that expressed itself mysteriously, in accidents and coincidence and unlikely encounters. We're still primitive, she said. What good does being able to lock a door or fasten a seat belt or visit a doctor do? As she saw it, the skills developed by civilization were merely actuarial.

For two months she frequented places where a person could expect to be surprised, where time and opportunity and deviance might combine to make a victim of someone; but Clara couldn't be surprised. She meant to tempt fate and, when it tried to close in, be ready for it. "You know the beach along the Drive? By North? It's dangerous at night. So I went there."

For a minute she said nothing, and the lapping of the water was loud. It seemed to be the sound of night, in Wisconsin, in Chicago, around the island of Manhattan Clara had abandoned. "You try to take advantage of chance," she said, "and it takes advantage of you by turning human. Making itself into the commonest instinct—self-preservation. I'm sick. I think I'm going to be sick." But she didn't move, and she didn't get sick. After another long minute, she returned to the beach in Chicago.

It was the perfect place for misadventure, and the perfect night. The sky was black. The water, black. Between the bright spots from the streetlights the world disappeared. Clara walked along the shore, doing her best to look vulnerable. Resisting the temptation to be too prepared, she didn't hold on to her stiletto, but kept her hand in the pocket where the knife was and would bump against her knuckles as she walked. She'd been out so long that her mind was wandering—the point at which she generally went home—when she heard someone behind her. The wind and the muting sand and the sound of cars on the Drive had kept her from hearing the footsteps until they were close. Till then, she hadn't thought about guns; but suddenly a gun was all she could think of, and how unfair it was. In another second or so she could almost feel the person at her back. She whirled around, right into a jacket with a hand reaching into it. Then the figure rocked on unsteady feet and fell, and the jacket fell away, revealing the hand with a pistol in it and a woman's chest with a knife sticking out of it.

"She was a big woman," Clara said, "about your size, on the ground, twitching, with the blood making a spot on her shirt. Her eyes were closed, and she was making a whimpering sound. That sound—I didn't know what to do. I didn't want to leave her there to die or get mugged or killed the rest of the way while I was trying to get help. So I used the magic strength that comes in a panic and dragged her up to the Drive. Think about it: me, carrying you. That's how it was. Either way, leaving her or pulling, I thought I was doing her in, but I felt better taking her with me than running up alone."

When she got to the sidewalk, Clara straightened the woman out and ran the few more yards to Lake Shore to flag down a car. Nobody would stop until she flung herself into the street, waving her arms. The driver who stopped didn't stop fast enough and knocked Clara into the air. She was fine, she assured me, merely unconscious for a brief time. When she came to, she was lying by the curb, with a semicircle of flares next to her on the Drive, containing a circus of sirens and flashers and voices and bobbing and bending uniformed men. Despite her declaration of how all right she was, she was hustled into an ambulance with the stabbed woman and taken, siren screaming, to a hospital. During the ride, an attendant squatted between the two women, obscuring Clara's view. She asked him if the other was alive, and he said, "Just."

When they reached the hospital, Clara's and Sarah's ("Her name was Sarah," she said) stretchers went their separate ways: Sarah's to surgery, Clara's to a ward full of people mending, where she told anybody who would listen that there was nothing wrong with her, she was all right, they couldn't make her stay there. A doctor appeared (not the one who had examined her and palpated her head) and told her that she had a mild concussion and, no, they couldn't *insist* that she stay; but he said this in such a dire way that she got back into bed.

That night she was visited by Sarah's brother, another giant, a soft-speaking, slow-moving man. He'd talked to the police, he said, so he knew his sister was alive right now thanks to Clara, except that he thought her name was Claire, so he said, "Thanks to you, Claire," just as mother and father and a few intimate friends at school had always abbreviated her name. Other than that, he'd only said, "What was she doing? There? Alone?" and then, "I know you can't answer that," speaking very softly, as if he thought she was asleep and didn't want to wake her. Then the nurse drove him out; and Clara lay all night in her bed with walls, looking up at a ceiling she had to imagine was the pastel blue or green of a public restroom. By morning she was truly sick.

Maybe it was the milieu she'd taken me into, the drowsy nighttime ward, the hallucinatory morning, the wide, pale room; or maybe it was the rhythmic slapping of the waves, the cool breeze, the hum of Clara's voice; something was lulling me to sleep. Maybe it was exhaustion. I caught my head sinking and snapped it up in time to hear Clara Bow say that she was sitting up in bed, banging on the bars, until they had to move her to a room of her own. I had missed something.

She'd finished with her hysterics by the time Sarah's brother visited her again. The first thing he said was that he'd come to see her while she wasn't herself. He'd upset her the night before, he said, he knew it. He knew what she'd done and he wished there were some way he could repay her, but. The "but" was a mournful one, and she was afraid to ask. Instead, she asked him his name. Ray Hodges.

The next thing I knew, Clara Bow was living in his apartment. Sarah had dropped out of the story. Again I was aware of having missed something, that earlier item, which I might've nodded through but kept trying to recover. Then Clara was shaking me, telling me I was freezing. "No, I'm not," I said, "I'm sleeping."

She said, "That's how it starts," and kept roughhousing me. I must have flailed, because there was a splash that sounded very much like someone Clara's size falling into a lake. That got me up. Figure of authority that I was, I rose to my full height and told her to get out of there, we were going home. There she was, treading through the water in the blue light, only darker than before, as if I'd only missed more of the same and might have dreamed the rest.

suspicious-looking, mud-spackled Buick sat in the drive (suspicious-looking because it was there). The kitchen window had a hole in it big as a fist. Without a notion or Clara Bow to get behind me, an act of faith like force, I would never have walked in there, but I had both, so I did. Chairs had been moved around in the living room, but no one was there. The kitchen was empty, too. Before going upstairs, I switched off the generator. Clara whispered, "Ambush?"

"I'm guessing they're some of ours," I said, and the change in her expression was something to see—a sudden thrilled smile, whether of relief or plain hospitable delight I couldn't tell, and she sprang to the stairs, taking the lead.

There was a woman in each of our beds. Clara Bow sang out, "Hello!" and they were instantly up, the one in my bed black and bony with hair pulled back so tight it seemed to be stretching her face, which looked extremely annoyed, the other pale, puffy, and snub-nosed, blinking in baffled alarm. "You have us at a disadvantage," Clara said.

The black woman, narrowing her eyes, said, "What?"

I said, "She means: Who are you?"

That was Gigi. She was wearing only bra and underpants, with a kind of flagrant ease that had the unsettling effect of making me feel like a matron in a jail, while the other, fully dressed, springing up and announcing herself ("Kathy"—though now, to distinguish her from our renegade huntress, I will call her "Cathy"), immediately started fussing with her clothes, straightening, smoothing, fingering one wrinkle in the general rumple, touching the curls of her crisp, permed hair as if each had a place. Minus two, here was the lost Dells contingent: our kleptomaniac and our family-abandoning bigamist.

I said, "You broke the window." Clara Bow touched my back.

Gigi said testily, "What'd you want us to do? Sleep in the car?"

There was a shuffling at the door, and Clara was saying, "Hello, I'm Clara Bow Cole."

"Lynn Kozinski." Our narcoleptic. She was a dark blonde, tall by normal standards and solid-looking, wearing a quilted bathrobe and slippers with furry balls at the toes. She squeezed past me and took her place between Gigi and Cathy, giving the assembly a them-and-us appearance.

"Where'd you get the car?" I said.

The three of them looked back at me with bland curiosity, as if I were still speaking. Finally Cathy said, "A Denny's parking lot," then sat down on Clara's bed, folding her hands and looking up at me with the bleary, expectant eyes of a girl waiting for the last question in a tough exam.

"Shit, stole it," Gigi said. "What do you think?"

Behind me, Clara Bow was saying, "They stole it, what did you think?"

"Shit yes," Gigi said. "That bitch left us flat. All we had was our clothes and we only had that because I told everybody that custom van was a perfect mark."

Cathy explained, "We were afraid somebody'd break into it. We did bring canned goods and blankets, but we left them in the van. Sorry."

"Sorry? How did you steal the car?"

Gigi said, "Hot-wired."

Cathy said, "Gigi did it," and I opened my mouth to say I didn't care *who,* but she went on, "but we all agreed."

Clara Bow said, "They all agreed."

I said, "You'll have to take it back."

Gigi said reassuringly, "We switched the plates three ways. No one's gonna find it. They're sure not gonna find it here. 'Specially if we ditch it." She glanced at the window.

"They're not going to find it here," I said, "because it's not going to be here. You're going to have to take it back and leave it in a conspicuous spot where someone can find it and assume it was borrowed."

Gigi made a whinnying sound. "That's what we say if we get stopped? We borrowed it? That'll be a good one. Least they be in a good mood when they take us in."

Cathy roused herself from an apparent trance to say, "Then we'll be stuck at Denny's again."

"Someone can drive along in the truck. You can come right back."

Finally Lynn spoke up. She said, "I'll drive the truck."

I delivered a little pep talk then, about how everything would be all right and how if it wasn't, if they got caught, I'd do my best (no elaboration of this point) to make it all right anyway. As I said it I believed it, touched as I suddenly was by the peculiar logic the women had exhibited in stealing a car to drive to a place of supposed rehabilitation.

Cathy said, "What about Barbie?"

The fourth; I'd forgotten. "What about her?"

Gigi said, "She doesn't have to come."

"Where is she?"

All three shrugged. Lynn said, "Around."

We found her in the living room, curled up in an armchair that had been pulled up to the fireless fireplace so that its back faced the door, a big-eyed, wistful sketch of a girl, like a Kewpie doll never quite finished. Other than returning our first curious glances, she didn't react to our appearance. When I said, "Barbie?" she said, "You found out about the car."

"You could hear?"

"The way your voice sounded," she said. "I could tell. I couldn't believe we got away with that."

"They're going to return it."

"They?"

"They said you don't have to go along."

"I can go," she said, sounding slightly offended.

"I'm sure you *can,*" I said. "The point is, it's not necessary." Frowning, she looked sidelong at nothing, first one way, then the other, as if following voices behind her. "Anyway, I forbid it."

She slumped further into her chair with a resistant "OK," just to show how reluctantly she stayed.

As soon as we left the living room on the pretext of making breakfast, Clara jumped in front of me, hissing, "How *old* is she? She's thirteen. She's twelve! We're not qualified guardians." Malnutrition and the childish way she'd been tucked up into the chair might have made Barbie look young, but she was at least sixteen; I could see it in her face, and I said as much to Clara Bow, who wasn't convinced or comforted. She seemed to think that enraged parents were going to swoop down on us.

To which I said, "Why would she be here?"

"That's what I want to know."

I said, "You read her sheet."

"I don't trust anyone who achieves despair by the age of twelve."

"Sixteen," I said. "Didn't you?"

"What? Des*pair?* At six*teen?* I got my ears pierced. My driver's license. My first date. That was the year all my stupid misconceptions got started."

"And how come she missed all that and caught up with you anyway? Is that what you're saying? Is that what's bothering you? You know what I think? That stinks."

"You didn't believe me," she said. "You didn't believe a word I said."

"Believe what?" I said. "I just want to know why you want to get rid of that kid—when you don't know the first thing about her."

"She's trouble, I can tell."

By now I knew how to short-circuit Clara's instincts. I said, "Send her home."

Predictably, she said, "How?" as if she were resigned to the hopelessness of such a proposition.

"Yes, how?" I mournfully agreed. Then I walked around

her into the kitchen where, while I scrambled eggs and, because there were only six left, heated up a can of chili, I caught myself wondering more than once: what kind of trouble?

While Clara Bow said good-bye to Gigi, Cathy, and Lynn, I, like a baby-sitter distracting the child from Mom and Dad's departure, led Barbie to our store of blankets and told her she could make up four new beds if she wanted work to do. Something about her demeanor said she wanted to be occupied; or maybe the restlessness was mine, a vague uneasiness prompted by her passive, unfocused presence at my side, which gave me an insight into Gigi's willingness to spare her the trip.

Holding the blankets I'd piled into her arms, she wandered from the room. When I came out, she was standing in the hall. I pointed out the rooms with beds in them, but still she stood there. Finally she said, "But which ones?" so I assigned beds with great specificity, and Barbie wandered onward, as if she'd merely been pausing on her way to work.

She had a lazily mechanical walk. Contrary to what her compactness in the armchair indicated, she was tall—taller, at least, than the thirteen-year-old she looked like, five-foot-three or -four. Her hair, an antique gold, fell frayed and uneven past her shoulders, and her eyes had a dullness in them that seemed deceptive, assumed; almost from the first, I had the impression whenever I looked at her that she'd just dropped her gaze, or lowered a film over it. Again, it might've been my own uneasiness. I never caught her staring.

With Barbie busy, I went to my room and changed, and was listing toward the bed when Clara Bow came in to change, too. From the eye of a storm of flying garments, she announced that she was going to Dr. Abbot's to make appointments for everyone. I looked at her skeptically, but of course there were those garments getting in the way. So, "Don't bother that man," I said. "Nobody wants a doctor."

Moving obstacles stopped for her own skeptical look. There followed a gruesome account of a bout of dysplasia she'd suffered some time back, then the ensuing education she'd received, on modern medicine's near-eradication of cervical cancer through early attention to malforming cells like hers, a common prelude. "Common" was the key word here, with an ounce of prevention for freight.

She was already halfway out the door by the time I could say, "Don't bother to make an appointment for me." Gigi would be with me, I thought, a sensible woman. Then I remembered Lynn's offer to drive the truck, and her condition. Luckily, since there was nothing I could do at this point, Barbie distracted me by coming to the door and, by nothing more than the way she stood limp-limbed, declared that she was done.

Any remaining hope of sleep I'd had evaporated at the thought of this listless girl roaming the house. We faced each other for a while, and when the situation seemed about to reach a crisis of immobility, for lack of a better—or another—idea, I suggested that she cut firewood. So my days as director of activities had begun. Barbie stood looking dreamily at me, not the least bit uncompliant except that she didn't move. After a few minutes of this, she said, "With what?"

I ferreted out the chain saw. Accepting it pleasantly, with a little dip of her spine, Barbie drifted off and soon enough was whirring away at the outskirts of the yard. Contented, I went to my corner, laid out my lumber in the last uncluttered space, and began in my primitive fashion to construct the tower that would support the sails. I'd been hammering for less than an hour, at least it seemed like an hour, when a whistling whoosh and crash sounded behind me, a severed fir falling with a bounce of its branchy head on my poor sails. Barbie came running with a stuttering sound like an attempted cry. I was screaming, it seemed. Then we were face to face, both suddenly silent again.

While I wrestled the treetop off my week's work, Barbie softly explained that she would have felt stupid saying "timber." I and my sails, excellent craftsmanship, were fine, I assured her, to which she responded in her disappearing voice, "Is it a good one?" I looked up to find her eyeing the felled tree. As if either of us could tell—it was for burning, how good could it be? But she seemed so troubled by the question that I told her it was probably the best.

This was the first time I saw Barbie smile—at the fir—and it was a strange expression, maniacal or melancholy, I couldn't place it, with the odd feature of wide-open eyes above a grin so deep it should've made her squint; nothing disturbed the girl's gaze.

There was still no sign of Clara Bow when the sun retired, Barbie and I with it. Barbie carried in several armloads of wood, a load being two logs, and went back out to gather kindling. Shortly, from the kitchen I could hear the scratch of matches being struck, then the sizzle and purr of paper and twigs catching. I was surveying the prospects for dinner with mild distaste when I smelled smoke, heard Barbie cough, and looked up to see the ceiling hazing over.

Barbie was standing over the fireplace as if she meant to stare down the smoke. Choking and teary—duct damage, not despair, I guessed—she kicked the pile of logs at her feet and called it: "Stupid wood."

"The fire should dry it out," I said. Till then, however, we had to breathe, so I ran to the kitchen to open the door, calling to Barbie to open the front. As the house was exhaling its tainted air and I was inhaling fresh, Clara Bow came running out of the woods, flying a line of strung fish behind her like the tail of a kite. "Fire!" she screamed at me.

"Only smoke," I said.

"What is it?"

"Fire," I said. "We're seasoning the firewood."

"Where's Barbie?"

"Out front."

Right behind me, Barbie's soft voice pronounced, "Fish." When I glanced back at her, she said, "The smoke's almost gone." The draft from the front door had swept the smoke through the kitchen, and it churned around us as we clustered at the door. With a pale cough, Barbie listed toward me. I'd caught her and was lowering her to a sitting position on the steps when the pickup, its engine sounding sickly, pulled up in the drive and, with an enormous belch, braked. Clara Bow was stooping over Barbie, saying, "Don't worry, I made a doctor's appointment for you."

"She's not sick," I said. "It's smoke."

Doors slammed, feet slapped, and Gigi, Cathy, and Lynn

burst around the corner, shouting, "Fire!" Our apparent uncon-
cern slowed them to a halt.

"Hey," I said to Barbie, "look what you started," and the
car thieves, compact, swiveled to look down at her. Quickly, I
started to explain, but was interrupted by Gigi saying, as if hailing
a friend on the street, "Hey, fish." Then they all looked at the
fish.

"A doctor?" Barbie said, and the collective stare shifted
again. (She had no sense; thinking of her application, it occurred
to me that this girl could have contemplated suicide without suspecting it could kill her.)

"Yes," I said, "the famous fishing doctor. Other doctors
give away lollipops."

Getting into the spirit of the company, Clara gave me a
nasty look and said, "It's dinner."

"Good," Gigi said. "I'm sick of canned."

"You only had it once."

"That you saw."

"You're early," I said. "Where did you take that car?"

"To the Dells," she said. The others echoed. "To the Dells,
the Dells." Cathy added, "Denny's." And together they con-
fronted me with that blank expression that tries to pass for innocence.

Their guilt established, they scaled and gutted Clara's catch
with barely a grimace, heated and swallowed the supplementary
canned hash that the fewness of the fish made necessary, and
washed afterwards in cold water. Tired, they went to bed, Barbie
to her armchair by the fireplace, and Clara Bow and I went outside to talk about tomorrow, which we agreed needed planning.

"We're exhausted," Clara said. She'd been preoccupied
through dinner, looking up with a small, tardy smile whenever
the rest of us fell silent, and she seemed thoughtful now. We'd
been sitting against our respective birches, the lantern drawing
bugs between us, for five minutes or more, when a window
upstairs opened and Cathy called down, "Can we use the
john?"

I said no.

"Somebody already did." She closed the window, then
promptly reopened it. "What're we supposed to do?"

"Go outside. Take the toilet paper." This time the window slammed.

As if the woods were full of spies, Clara Bow whispered to me, "Maybe we should turn it back on." No, I said. She agreed, "You're right," so quietly that I couldn't catch her tone. Gigi, Cathy, and Lynn came down the steps, placing their feet with meaningful emphasis and, mumbling, rounded the corner.

"Hey," I said, "take the shovel. By the door." Lynn swung back for it and, shouldering it like a standard, rejoined the others, who'd waited frozen, facing the woods, their stiff backs eloquent: We are not sorry anymore about leaving that hot car short.

If the women were this short-tempered the first time out, I had to get the windmill going if I were to have working plumbing by the time they lost their patience for good and left. This made the planning easier. Though Clara Bow was most concerned about grocery shopping and laundry (quite a sizable pile of which we'd already accumulated), I convinced her that our structural problems were urgent, and by morning we had divided into two teams: Clara Bow, Gigi, and Lynn to construct a cow shelter; Cathy, Barbie, and I to raise the tower. Then Lynn, extrapolating from her firsthand knowledge of winters as far south as Chicago, where there weren't stockyards anymore, she said, because the cows couldn't stand the cold and it cost too much to heat them, suggested that if we wanted to keep our cows alive up here we should bring them inside; so I shifted her to the windmill detail and sent Barbie with Clara.

The next day, Lynn was begging to be put back on the other crew. I masked my incompetence with taskmastering, but Clara made no effort to conceal her lack of expertise. She and Gigi and Barbie spent half of our first workday buying lumber, going on no other criteria than "what looked good," as Gigi put it, and the other half considering it—circling the stacks they'd unloaded, apparently discussing them, occasionally stopping to shift a board from one pile to another. At about 4:30, they started banging something together. Barbie held the pieces in place while Clara and Gigi took turns hammering. By 5:30 they'd outlined a square and called it a day.

In the middle of dinner, Clara said, "Damn. We forgot the door."

I said, "You forgot the walls."

Gigi tipped her fork at me and explained, "You got to start with a concept. No problem," she said to Clara Bow, who returned to whatever reflection this observation had interrupted. She raised her fork and, without noticing that every Spaghetti-O had fallen off, put it in her mouth—and swallowed. Then, though no one was talking, she clicked her knife against her plastic glass and, when we'd stopped eating, too, announced that she'd scheduled appointments for everyone with the "neighborhood physician." This was greeted with silence, broken at last by Gigi, who said, "Who's gonna pay for that?"

Clara said, "He'll do it as a service."

I said, "He will?"

Cathy said, "That's nice."

Gigi said, "No way."

Lynn said, "You'd pass up the chance for a free checkup?"

Gigi said, "Yeah."

Cathy said, "I wouldn't."

Barbie was looking dimly from mouth to mouth, as if she were lipreading. Tilting back her head, Gigi slanted a glance down at Cathy. "You wouldn't," she said.

"What's that supposed to mean?" Cathy turned on Barbie. "What are you looking at? *I'm* not a criminal. I—"

"Stole a car," Gigi said.

"You mean *you* did."

Gigi smiled narrowly and pronounced an extended, "Yeah. Don't give me any more 'we agreed' bullshit," she said. "Next time I hear that shit—"

"LADIES!" Clara Bow was rapping madly on her glass. To clear the air of hostility, she told her dysplasia story in graphic detail, which was enough to keep any woman away from doctors for years.

The tension at the table turned dumb, but it didn't disappear, and Clara Bow must have absorbed it. In her sleep that night she babbled some unintelligible urgency, like a foreigner trying to describe an emergency, until her own voice disturbed her. She woke up exclaiming, "What?"

"Nothing," I said. She fell back on her pillow. Then, when

she'd been silent, her breathing regular, for so long that I thought she was asleep: "Beauty?"

"I'm awake."

"What I told you? The other night?" I didn't say anything, waiting. "I made it up." This was when I started to believe it. She whispered, "Beauty?"

I said, "I'm awake. I heard you."

The rest of the women arrived the next day, in two install-
ments: Mary Belinda, Elizabeth, and Cora in a white
Cadillac that Mary Belinda called Alimony; Joan and
Molly—the maverick abortionist, who turned out to be the cool
blonde who'd put the whammy on me in the park—in a rusted
Honda hardly bigger than a refrigerator box. Informing us that
Joan was in "a bad way," Molly pumped some water on the
bewildered woman's head, then told her to lie down and rest, and
Joan did, right there.

Luckily this sudden crowd, too much, robbed me of most
of my mind and, on automatic, I proceeded with mechanical pre-
cision: Joan to bed; Lynn, known by now as the chronic com-
plainer, and Elizabeth, a doughy woman with gray hair in curlers
and a sour whiff of liquor about her, to the laundry problem, as
Clara Bow liked to think of it; Cora to Clara's gang; Molly and
Mary Belinda to mine. Mary Belinda would have been a fine
addition to my crew, if she'd been inclined to move. She was a
massive woman, not soft like Cora or Elizabeth, but solid as a
fullback, with a helmet of nappy black hair to round out the strong
impression. However, she was mostly inert. Molly, on the other
hand, merely tried to *look* inert, but the somewhat dated suburban
languor she affected, a heaviness of limbs and eyelids, could hardly

mask the power of spite and longing underneath, since she had to keep her wilting eyes at least half open. After her sarcasm in the rose garden, I took some pleasure in telling her what to do, and I was only sorry that when she left she would think it was her idea, not mine.

Shortly we discovered that we didn't have tools enough to go around. At about the same time, a shout came from above, "She's in my bed and she's muddy!" (Lynn, re Joan), so we effected a quick reshuffling. Cora went upstairs to make up new beds and get Joan into one, and I sent Molly to bring firewood out where it could get some sun, then to make dinner. In no time, Molly and Lynn were brandishing spatulate weapons at each other, contending for possession of the stove. Laundry versus dinner, we voted, and dinner predictably won. In response to this verdict, Lynn added bleach to her bathtub of cold water, so that everything spotted and streaked. That was petty.

Dinner was a dismal something featuring tough strings of unidentifiable meat and kernels of corn. During the meal, Elizabeth kept slipping out of the kitchen until finally I followed and found her swilling gin from a canning jar, which I appropriated and took to the table to say: "There'll be no more of this." As I moved to the sink, a chorus of voices suggested that waste was a sin. Outnumbered, I gave up the jar and the women passed it around, except Elizabeth, who stayed in the living room prostrate in the armchair until Barbie demanded her bed—Barbie's way of demanding was to stand and stare until the woman became so uncomfortable that she relinquished the chair.

Back at the mess, Mary Belinda drank off half a juice glass of gin and loudly pronounced it "Rotgut."

From the living room, Elizabeth's rasping voice testily answered, "It was good enough all the way up here."

Talking to me, but loud enough for Elizabeth, Mary Belinda said, "She has four more." Then, no doubt kicked under the table, she jumped.

From the living room: "Three."

Mary Belinda: "Four."

"Three."

"Four."

I had to act or sacrifice credibility, a position I didn't much care for, but I went in to Elizabeth and asked for the rest. She whined, "You said bring food."

"That's not exactly what I had in mind," I said.

"That shit in there? That what you had in mind?"

"You don't like it, don't eat it."

"I won't," she said, and she didn't, unless on the sly. Sustaining herself on the gin she didn't declare when she directed me to her bag—or so I assumed, since she continued to smell—she sagged within a few days and became loutily, petulantly lazy and was the first to leave. She just disappeared; and she'd been so unhelpful, so little around anyway, that it took us a day or so to notice her absence. By then, I suppose, she was sleeping among the cattails somewhere up the road, curlers caught in the rushes, lips clamped on a reed. She may still be there. We spread out and searched, but when Cora and Lynn each returned with a fish in her hands, I suspected that the search hadn't been thorough. With my tax-exempt status in mind, and some question as to whether Sal still had a say and what that would be, I carefully documented Elizabeth's disappearance.

But I'm anticipating. Before Elizabeth left, she did put in a few days of grudging and gradually stuporlike labor, along with the crude living everyone enjoyed. Starvation and shortage of gin were only a few of her problems but made her weaker than the others about facing the standard allotment of trials. Trudging into the woods whenever nature called didn't endear the ticklish, bug-ridden wilderness to anyone; and it certainly didn't improve the outlook for the next call. In fact, for a while the yard was downright rank, and the prospect of venturing out of it, even guessing where it stopped and the venture began, was enough to cause painful procrastination. But the situation, upon getting worse, got better, because the women, revolted at the smell and the thought of stepping into it, became more apt to carry a shovel and use it.

Knowing that the food we faced three times a day would end in such ignominy didn't make the meals any easier to bear. The menu, comprising every imaginable tasteless potato- or pasta- or rice-based dish, was bad enough in the first place. Everyone griped; but since the women who'd brought the food in question were its loudest critics, I learned to disregard their complaints, especially when spoken through half-masticated mouthfuls. The women didn't like to talk to one another. During dinner, they cast out their remarks without looking up, as if there were a kitty in the middle of the table where conversation collected. From this and the fact that they ate heartily what they damned I deduced that pooled complaining was their safe way of turning their strangeness to one another into a sense of community. They could be together against the food without hazarding an alliance to anyone in particular—that would come later. At first, aware of the range of misfortune and deviltry that qualified a candidate for Women Abreast, each was arrogant of her own and, at the same time, suspected every other woman of having similar qualifications, and so, distrusted her with the intensity of the knowing. The complaint was for a while their favorite mode of discourse; it worked as greeting, observation, opinion. For instance, a woman coming out to join Clara's or my construction crew could expect a volley of statements denigrating the work she was about to do. She'd answer with an insult of her own—to her health or the weather or the job she'd just come from—and everyone would turn pleasantly to the business at hand.

I walked into the kitchen one day to find Cora, a plumpish, dumpling-skinned black woman, drinking off the juice from a short can of what a blue-and-white label identified as Vienna Sausages. Holding back the little wieners with her hand and draining the packing juice through her fingers into her mouth, she looked at me over the tilted can, kept her head cocked, and kept drinking until the sausages plopped audibly into her palm. She gave the can a shake and emitted a shallow burp. " 'Scuse me," she said. "While I kill myself."

This was before I learned the language of amiable detraction, so her remark perplexed me, until Mary Belinda, Cora's kitchen helper, responded, "Yeah, but taste those little turds and you'd think it was gin." The lethal juice, she meant; they were making friends. Not one of those little turds made it to the table that night.

Because Cora and Mary Belinda were contagiously weary, I kept them in the house, domestically busy, as much as I could. While Women Abreast was at full strength, there were too many hands for the available tools and my powers of productive management, so I had to keep at least four women at a time occupied with tasks other than construction. Joan was a housebody, too. She stayed in bed. The others took turns doing laundry, which got pretty dingy as the detergent diminished to minuscule rations per wash.

Out in the yard, we weren't quite merry, but made a racket that had the raucous overtones of merriment to come—elves before Christmas, decoration committee pre-prom. Around the house it looked like the party had already been. Anything anyone couldn't make fit or saw straight or carry alone, she dropped in the spot where the material's shortcoming or hers became apparent, which, from the looks of the lumber-strewn yard, was just about everywhere, twice or thrice. In the midst of the clutter we sawed and nailed and puttied and drilled to the occasional report of a distant rifle.

I liked having Molly and Gigi on my crew, since they were both tough and inventive and, despite the type of ennui that each cultivated, tireless—though Molly accelerated her superior glances at me after I refused to let her wire us up to the county power lines, which she could do, she said, without a second thought. She indicated with an extreme roll of her eyes that my protest of the proposition's illegality was only an inferior form of cowardice unworthy of the least form of vertebrate. "Electricity is a gift of the air to mankind," she said. "It's in the public domain." Nothing comes from nothing, I told her, and electricity comes from fuel. She said, "What about lightning?" What about it? I said. A hard source to tap. Hunh-uh, she said, and opened her hands like a magician who's just made a hat disappear, "Where's the fuel?" Then she pulled her head back and smugly locked her jaw. Lightning, I said, comes from the friction of thunder clouds—a brainstorm—and though it was there for all to enjoy, who could rub clouds together or take advantage of their unpredictable meetings? We were trying to take what was ours, but from the wind, so there was no need to get righteous over the power lines passing us by.

"What is it we stand for again?" she said.

I said, "Survival."

She was also unhappy about Clara's plans to shuffle everyone off to Dr. Abbot for an examination. After her long practice

108

at unburdening women, Molly considered herself a common-law physician. Clara Bow had of course treated the new arrivals to a discourse on dysplasia. Her eloquence on the subject was odd, especially since, with the coming of the new women, she'd turned almost as taciturn as they were. Also odd, in this medical business, was the staggering of appointments, as if the woodland doctor had a waiting list that necessitated long stretches between visits. When I asked Clara Bow about this, she said that the doctor, reclusive, could only stand seeing patients at widely spaced intervals—and that seemed odder still.

Clara's appointment, the first, came up a day after her second call to make arrangements. What with scheduling, checkup, and test results, she left her crew on the cow shelter unsupervised for three days of our first full working week. And yet, the structure rose. Clara and Gigi, who acted as foreman in Clara's absence, had solved the door problem by hinging a whole wall to the upper framework—a flap. Their initial solution had been to hinge at the bottom, drawbridge-fashion, but then I pointed out that the snow would impede opening, at which Cathy said, "Snow?" and Lynn blanched. Then, when they turned their plan upside down, I pointed out that raising a whole wall to open the shelter would defeat the purpose of housing the beasts. "Shit," Gigi said, "It's just cows. You act like it's family." Then, no doubt inspired by her interjection, she said, "What about us? I'm not goin' bareass in snow." The windmill would obviate that, I said. Among other things.

The support structure for my four blades, sturdier than the intuitive cow shelter and planned to the last mote of sawdust, was slowly, painstakingly, but surely becoming something that would stand and stay put. It was beautiful, no words to match its wood for grain, its lines for elegance, its tapering construction, its silvering red cedar, honed struts, terrible height, but why try, when its success was a matter of time, not space:

That rare day, for instance, that Cora worked in the yard instead of the kitchen. For a few days she'd been slumping around looking abject and snapping whenever her abjection was interrupted, so I prescribed fresh air and exercise. While Gigi and I worked on the tiller which, attached to a shaft at the center of the tower,

109

would turn the sails into the wind, Cathy and Lynn were outfitting the prone four-legged tower with braces. I told Cora that Cathy and Lynn would tell her what to do. But they didn't (and, to be fair to them, Cora didn't ask). She watched them for a while and tried to mimic their work. She was inept. Every time I looked across the yard, she was sawing a board or trying to install it—each successive board cut longer, but none cut long enough to neatly wedge. After she'd made firewood of three twelve-foot and perfectly good lengths of lumber, she settled on the last board she'd cut, the most accurately measured though still not right and improperly angled. Cathy and Lynn were working between the tower's uppermost legs, the ones rearing up, so Cora had decided to stay out of their way by installing her brace on the side, which put her at a disadvantage for nailing, since the lower legs that she meant to join were ungrippably flat on the ground. On top of that, the too-short board flopped over whenever Cora, steadying it against one knee, contorted herself to tap with her hammer, timid taps, her hand choking the handle at its neck.

She wasn't getting any better in the fresh air or doing my windmill any good either, so I called her over to prop up the shaft while Gigi and I made adjustments to the tiller. As Cora ambled plumply across the yard, Gigi lowered her head and muttered. We had the tiller laid across two makeshift sawhorses, and leaning it upright was going to make our work harder, but I wanted Cora to successfully perform a task. She pulled up the pole and, like a rope climber resting, held it against herself with her hands above her head. "Don't bother moving your watch," Gigi said. "I'm already blind." From her angle Cora couldn't see the sunspot reflecting off the crystal into Gigi's eyes, so she stared earnestly at the time, ten o'clock, until I said, "It's catching the sun. Shift your wrist." This alerted her to Gigi's sarcasm, and she lowered on Gigi a look that seemed to dismiss her inch by inch by traveling with slow indifference from her face to her feet, where it stayed until Lynn, roused roughly by Cathy from one of her impromptu naps, came to exclaiming, "What time is it?" as was her habit. It was, by then, eleven. Patience was Cora's skill. At Lynn's eruption, she started, checked her hands, and re-settled her gaze a few feet from the spot she'd studied for an hour. After staring glazedly for a minute or two she started to shift her eyes back and forth between the two spots which, except for the foot of the tiller and its shadow, were unremarkable patches of dirt. Then she asked me if I'd hold the pole for a minute, and I took over her post. Like a moving picture of women devolving to her prehistoric state, she hunched gradually as she closed in on a point at the edge of the tiller's triangular shadow. She stopped, crouched, and worked a twig into the dirt. I thought she was investigating some half-buried object, but as soon as the twig was stuck into the ground, she wiped her pink palms on the seat of her pants and relieved me at the shaft.

After that, whenever I glanced up from my work, I caught Cora resting one hand on the other, rolling her forehead on the pole to look from side to side, exhibiting quick and fidgety signs that something in the air had proved salutary. There was anticipation in her restless gestures. Gigi noticed it, too. She stopped making the snide remarks whose frequency, volume, and nastiness indicated how much pleasure she was taking in her work. Since the motive and meaning behind the twig placement weren't clear to her, she viewed it with suspicion and accidentally stepped on the twig as soon as she had the chance. At noon, when we went in for lunch, Cora hung back. From the doorway I watched her right the trampled stick and plant another one at a distance of three or four feet from the first.

An hour later, she preceded us out, picked up the pole and dropped it at once, then repeated her ritual, again leaving a pace between the new twig and the last. Once she'd resumed her pose, half lifting, half hanging from the pole, Gigi and I resumed our work. We were building a base for the tiller, which had to sit solidly on the ground, balanced against the tower and the wind, but also had to be liftable, wieldy enough for the shifting of the windmill's heavy top. Dopily forgetting that the thing couldn't be moved through the rungs, we'd started with a tiller like a right triangle with its perpendicular abutted against the central pole. Now we were working more along the lines of a lever attached to the top of the shaft and broadening to a wide platform when it reached the ground. This would fulfill the sitting requirement, but the lifting and shifting were problems we hadn't completely considered yet. One accomplishment at a time was almost too many. Luckily, Gigi was as ignorant and smart as I, so we'd generally spot our mistake at the same time, and I'd quickly account for the flaw in our logic as if it were a lesson. "You see," I'd say, and invariably she'd propose a solution, which I would accept with teacherly deference to the student's need to experiment, just in case, though her answers were often the ones I'd have given, if not better. That's how we learn.

While we were adapting our platform to the foot of the tiller, Cora had returned to her staring attitude. Her fidgets had disappeared. With her temple resting against the pole and one arm softly curving up to an apparently effortless hold, she looked like a statue of pensiveness. As the tiller's shadow crept toward the spot she was contemplating, she seemed to remember her agitation and, with her head still at rest, began to slant her glance sideways every so often, shiftily, quickly, as if in calculation. Suddenly she said, "What time is it?" in a challenging tone. She was, you'll remember, wearing a watch. Gigi rolled her eyes at me. As soon as I'd turned over my wrist and opened my mouth to answer, Cora announced: "Two o'clock!"

I said, "Two o'clock."

Gigi said, "Too bad she's too big to wear."

Cora asked again if I'd relieve her for a minute. Then she walked to the place where the edge of the shadow intersected the circumference of her semicircle of sticks and, squatting on her haunches with her forearms on her knees, moved her suspended hand in a small arc that took in her twigs, said, "It's a sundial." Her smile was accomplished.

Gigi said, "It's a windmill."

I said, "Where's three?" Cora pointed it out. She started to smile again, but quickly checked herself and adopted the pursed look of thoughtfulness appropriate to the scientist awaiting proof.

"Gee," Gigi said, "I can't wait till three." Cora patronized her with a long look; now she could even measure a phenomenon as curious as Gigi. We picked up our work and, interrupted hourly when Cora made her marks, kept at it till six. Meanwhile, Cathy and Lynn had fitted the tower with seven randomly spaced braces. So it grew.

While everyone washed at the pump and went in, I tramped back and forth across the yard, gathering tools and lumber and stowing them in the cow cube. The wind and clouds were conspiring to storm. As I retrieved the firewood Molly had been sunning, I noticed Cora, still in position, upholding the pole. I came up behind her, tapped her shoulder. "Nature's time clock says punch out."

Pivoting her head where her hairline touched the wood, she smiled at me sideways, then, as if she thought I was merely referring to her sundial, turned her face downward again and gazed pleasantly at her feet. "Cora?" I said.

"I was wondering," she said, "when does the mail come?"

"Mail?" I said. "It hasn't come yet, so it's hard to say. You're expecting mail?"

"I was thinking, maybe I'll write a letter."

As she said this, more to her feet than me, I took the pole out of her hands and laid it and the tiller on the ground. Cora sagged. The center of the circle now, she cast a long, lumpy shadow over her six o'clock twig.

"Why don't you go in?" I said on another crossing. "Write that letter." She asked me what I was doing. I told her, "It looks like rain." She cast a worried glance at her semicircle of twigs. "Cora, go in." When I came back out, she had.

In the morning it was raining, and she was gone.

Late at night I'd left her sitting at the kitchen table, bent over a blank sheet of paper, tapping her teeth with a pen. Later still, when the wind got fierce and woke me, Clara Bow and Barbie, huddled in conversation in the living room, were the only women abreast downstairs, and I assumed Cora had gone to bed.

Making my rounds in the leaky dawn to tell the women not to wake up, I found Cora's bed empty. She wasn't in any of the other rooms, either. I fished her paper out of the trash, un-crumpled it, and read, "Dear Joe, How are you?"

"Wake up," I said, and shook Clara. "Cora's gone." I showed her the letter.

"I know." She swatted the paper away from her face. "I took her to the bus station in Eau Claire." At my look, Clara said, "What?" She blinked. "I didn't want to wake you."

"Do you know who this is?" I jabbed the letter with my finger. "This *Joe*? The *husband?*"

"It wasn't that bad."

"How do you know?"

Clara Bow had on her plain look, the protective impassive, but I could see through it. She was afraid—whether of my getting madder or being right, I couldn't tell. "She wanted to go home," she said.

"They always do," I said. "It's a sickness. They have to be stopped."

"Cora's an adult," she said. "Older than you. Older than me."

This altered my tack. I said, "She can't do that. She can't just give up and go home."

"She didn't give up. She got better. She wants to be where she belongs. Isn't that the point?" Without a single change of detail, Clara's expression was different, as if it were modeled of soft clay and, in the space of a second, had set. Now the watchfulness behind her eyes was confident, knew where to look. I unbent and creased the letter, mumbling that no one belonged where she might get hurt and wondering if I'd convinced myself with my protesting over Cora's departure—or was it just too early, with nothing finished, for Women Abreast to start to ravel?

▼▼▼

The women were stirring, Gigi and Cathy having their morning bicker, starting a series of muttered objections from Molly and groans from Lynn, Mary Belinda saying hello to the day with her usual grunts, loud and phlegmy, like a roll on snare drums, which made Joan whimper, then cover her head with her pillow and keen. Normally Clara Bow and I would dress in silence while this noise went on and, just as the cacophony reached its peak, we'd hear Cora climb heavily out of bed and thump across her room. When she stopped, so would Mary Belinda, and then, shortly, Joan. At the sudden silence in that bedroom, the women in the other would shut up. There would follow the rustling quiet of everyone dressing in compatible dislike, during which Barbie would come and get her clothes out of the bureau in our room, her arrival always minutes after Cathy had hissed her summary insult and Gigi had got the last word, which usually took the form of a physical threat. Now, without Cora to initiate peace, the noise kept building till the grunts reached machine gun pitch and the moans outdid the wind and the spat became a fight and the whole rusty motor of the house sputtering to life threatened to shake apart instead of starting to run. Clara had curled up on her side in bed with the sheet pulled up to her cheek and was shivering. I said, "Are you afraid of thunder?"

She looked up at me. "It isn't thundering."

"So why are you cowering?"

"I'm not cowering."

"What do you call it?"

Whatever else, it was a maddening counterpoint to the racket coming from the other bedrooms. "Nothing," she said and rolled her head so she was looking at my knees. "I'm not feeling well."

"What's wrong? You've been to the doctor three times this week."

She said, "Cystitis."

That was familiar, something I'd had once too, though I couldn't remember when or in what organ—that grave. "Sorry," I said. "Did he give you something for it?" Then a change in the tenor of the ruckus next door distracted me.

It was time to do something authoritative, which meant being myself, that is, huge. Going to the door of the worst offenders, Gigi et al., I filled the frame with my own. Molly stopped muttering, Lynn stopped groaning, but Gigi, who, like a vicious child bringing adult skills to a slumber party, was trying to strangle Cathy with a pillow, took a minute to attend to the new tone in the room. At the moment of noticing, she let up a little, and Cathy socked the pillow away, splitting a seam, which emitted a puff of foam pellets. Then she came up with a mouthful of foul words. Gigi faced me, dropped the pillow disdainfully, and said, "She provoked me."

"*You* provoke *me*," I said. "And I could easily snap your neck with one hand, but I haven't yet, but don't push me. Have you bothered to wonder what *I'm* doing here? Just another good Samaritan, you think?" This was effective. Cathy, whose only crime was a tendency to love too many people too often to love anyone, man or child, at length, looked at me dumbfounded, with her back to the wall and the collapsed pillow clasped in her lap. Gigi, who'd probably been a tad more aggressive then her résumé let on, stood, elbows back, bony shoulders thrust forward, giving me a narrow-eyed look of animal suspicion. I was growing enormously in their estimation. "Both of you," I pointed forked fin-

gers at Gigi and Cathy, "are on the verge of being booted out."
While they thought about that, reflected on what they'd abandoned for this Edenic existence, I leaned backwards into the hallway and shouted for Mary Belinda and Barbie.

When they were all assembled, I said, "As you can see, it's raining. In honor of the weather, I'm declaring a holiday. You can do what you like." I gave them a minute to consider how little there was to do, then said, "There are a few things that need doing if you're so inclined or find you have some spare time. Clara Bow's arranged to buy a pair of cows. Two of you could take the pickup and collect them, though I'm not saying how tractable they'll be, since I've never met a cow. If someone does this, someone else'll have to clear up the stuff in the shed. This'll mean milk, but it'll mean milking, too, so weigh the advantages and disadvantages. Also, fish are rumored to bite better when it rains. I'll be tending to some business that'll take me through the woods, so if anyone wants to chance meeting our outlaw member, who has a rifle, I'll be happy to escort you to the river. We don't have umbrellas. One more thing: Cora's gone. Mary Belinda's going to need help with the housework. We can take turns, or anyone who prefers can give up the outdoors for in. Today'd be a good day to catch up on the stink that's taking over the house—these sheets, for instance. Other than that—Clara Bow might be making a grocery run. If you go along, don't go hungry. We're broke."

Gigi said under her breath, "What else."

Molly narrowed her eyes a notch. "Where'd Cora go?"

"Home," I said. *"Comments?* Questions?" They shuffled and looked around, not exactly at me. Molly came up and, glancing impatiently past me, paused at the door with a nervous forward thrust to her stance. "Where are you going?" I said. I hadn't expected to sound hysterical.

Molly hadn't expected it either. She stepped back and said warily, "To shit."

Wisconsin had been such a simple idea: birch paper, a cabin, caves made of trees, pockets of dark where a person could hide. The means to this simplicity were settling deep into the underbrush, gnawing at the trees, making too much of a clearing. I remembered walking back to Mother after my night on the rock in Lake Superior, the winking dimness under the ceiling of fir, the silence, and now it seemed that on that morning, as on those long-ago shadowy summer days, I was supremely safe. And now that day also seemed as far away as being small in a world of indifferent enormity.

In my speech, I had mentioned some business. I thought I would regain my bearings by finding the cabin where I'd stayed as a kid. It was a rustic little wooden house sitting at a slant on a hill above a hollow in the beach called Bark Bay: curling linoleum, mouse-eaten convertible sofa and bunk beds, cold water only, aluminum cupboards, mosquitoes, and wild blueberry bushes nearby. I knew it would be different, smaller no doubt and maybe even boarded up and abandoned in favor of another cabin down the hill and down the overgrown beach less than a wilderness block away, where hot water ran and the waves in rough weather slapped a picture window above a bed with a neck-stretcher hanging from one post and where the owner of both cabins lived and let us shower during our week of renting the one above. As I waited for Barbie and Molly and Lynn to dress—Barbie for the doctor, Molly and Lynn to fish—it occurred to me that Mr. O'Hearn, the owner, with gray hair, a deep chuckle, and stinking cigars, fixed in my memory as simply old when I was beneath distinctions in any age over thirty and didn't know old wasn't static, might be boarded up, too, by now.

Molly interrupted this morbid thought. She was looking for fishing gear. We didn't have fishing gear. I unhemmed one of our quilts and rolled up the nylon thread for line while Molly hammered finishing nails into hooks and Lynn, instructed to look for bait, opened our last can of spaghetti. Seeing Molly's and my expressions, Lynn lifted a noodle and explained, "It looks just like worms."

"Maybe to you," Molly said. "Fish are smart. They have higher intelligence than anyone ever dreamed of."

"If they're so smart, why do they get caught?"

That, Molly explained, we couldn't hope to understand because we were only human.

Despite her respect for the mysteries of fish logic, Molly wasn't a bit intimidated by superior intelligence. The fish she and

Lynn brought back that night had been brutally murdered. She'd got impatient with her clumsy equipment and the fishes' predicted distaste for pasta, and had traded her branch and thread for a club, the surprising aspect of this new approach being its success. That day, she and Lynn clobbered five fish, and after that, whenever Molly went out with her club, we could expect an adequate, if ugly, dinner; once she'd thrashed a fish out of the water, Molly bashed its head to spare it protracted agony.

Walking through the woods that day, we were silent, Lynn pouting, Molly laying a heavy hand on branches here and there, testing them for fish resistance. Barbie was tripping along beside me with a sweet and faraway look on her face, not like her usual plain, evasive expression, but daydreamy, as if something remembered or imagined had called her mind away instead of the immediate or real pushing it off. For the first time, her youth struck me as more than a physical fact.

We stumbled on the river—truly, a stream—first and left Molly and Lynn on the bank. Molly's directions for tying a knot followed us; in tone, she commanded a troop. "Barbie," I said, "do you want to go to the doctor? You don't have to if you don't want to."

She tilted her head slightly and said, "I don't mind."

"It's not a matter of minding."

"What?"

"It's a matter of principle. It's your time."

Her soft laugh surprised me. Then, as suddenly, she was serious. She said, "I don't know how to pick up a cow."

"That was just a suggestion. In a long list. You don't have to do anything."

"I don't have anything to do."

At hearing this, the response I'd counted on from the rest of the women, I was prompted to tell her she could come with me. She said, "Where?"

"To look for a house where I stayed as a kid. On vacation."

"Here?"

"Yes. Close, anyway."

For a moment she walked along looking pensive, her hands in her pockets, her head slightly lowered. Her hair didn't swing when she tilted her head. It clung in strands to her cheeks and neck and shoulders. "No," she said finally, "that's all right." Pausing, she prodded a fallen branch, slimy with moss, and a mass of shiny black insects on its exposed underside dove for the dark.

" 'I don't mind.' 'That's all right.' Why do you do that?"

She seemed deeply absorbed in the bug migration. Her "what" was that of a student who defers answering by asking for the question again.

"What what?" I said.

"Do what?"

"Act as if your decisions are concessions."

"I do?"

"Yes, you do." I could see Abbot's chimney up ahead, and his smoke. "Don't go to the doctor."

"Why not?"

"Why? You're not sick, are you?"

"I don't know. Maybe."

"Maybe?" I said. "Do you feel sick?"

"No. But that doesn't mean I'm not, does it?"

Clara Bow Cole, I could overhear your conversations without eavesdropping. "Clara was fine till she went to the doctor," I said.

Not wanting to go any closer, I'd stopped. Barbie took a few steps past me, hesitated, and turned, her stance familiar—the hand on the hip, the thoughtful sidelong tilt of the head, not quite looking at me. "You know," she said. "I haven't gone to a doctor since I was born."

Stepping back into a screen of sopping ferns, I watched her go up to the door and knock. The door, painted a crimson as glossy as nail polish, was an odd spot of color, a bit of show business against the rough, weathered wood of the rest of the house and the unsunny forest. It swung in, and from my angle I couldn't see the man or anything inside or, in a second, Barbie.

The storm on the treetops was abating, but the raindrops detained for a time in the leaves continued to fall, gathering and plopping here and there like drips in the leaky low ceiling of foliage. The sound was round and musical and many times over-precise. The drumming on the treetops had drowned this out, the rain's second fall, but now that there was silence overhead and fat raindrops were splashing loud and low all around, I seemed

120

to be under a shell, like one of those paperweights that, shaken, contain a flurry of weather. The leaves were also letting in a little cloudy light, which gave the pooled rain here and there a glow and, when a raindrop fell just so, a twinkle. One of the winking wet spots on the ground turned out to be the eye of a frog, who sprang up from the slimy earth just as my foot came down. That was a false start. He landed back at my feet, where he squatted, shuddering. Then he belched and leapt past me. I followed his flight, but lost him as soon as he came down in the froggy muck. Just then a gun fired, and my shell was cracked. Unable to gauge the distance from the reverberant shot, I looked around, but didn't see Kathy, or any movement, or the red door, or the smoke.

No matter how lost I might be, I knew I'd come to a road if I walked, as long as I didn't go in a circle. What I finally came to was a house, which I recognized at once as our neighbor's on W. As I crossed the swampy yard, the official W.A. pickup truck went roaring by, headed for the road I'd been heading for when I set out that morning. Sodden and foolish, I followed the acrid smell of our truck's exhaust, squeezing brown water out of my arable hair and overalls as I walked and watching the sun break through the clouds. It was a cool autumn light, and I was looking for a summer cabin.

Running is too graceful a word for the thing I do when I hurry. Despite my month of intensive instruction in carriage and poise, I'm afraid I'm like Frankenstein's creation coming to life with borrowed limbs and a confused sense of urgency. This way, a reproach to my charm teachers, I got to 13, which I took, jogging and resting and jogging and resting and achieving my own kind of runner's high, that is, a blank brought on by too many jolts to the spine traveling upward and scrambling the brain, a bliss of sorts.

Finally, over a bridge that our river and doomed fishes went under, past clusters of trees with veiny, vined feet and the occasional sunspots of clearings, I came to a rusty mud road labeled, remarkably, "Bark Bay." I sank to my ankles in the clay, ungummed myself, and walked redfooted through the lush weeds until I came to a fork in the road. The right branch lifted and curved; the left descended into a dark tangle of bushes and trees

121

over whose lowering heads I could see the lake, and this was the one I took. Here the road was harder, eroded, rocks and old ridges of clay standing out in sharp relief. Gradually the trees parted, revealing the bay below, rough grass, smooth stones, ribbon of sand, breaking waves, and as if my senses all had their own memories I felt the cold water bruising my thighs, the pebbles between my toes, the tightening sunburn, the mosquito bites crusty with calamine lotion, saw the beach curving away in the shape of a horseshoe, bright light on the point, and, above it, the forest that, from my damp seat on its floor, seemed to end in midair where the land fell away; dizzy, I caught the smell, the low must with lake air breezing cleanly through, heard a branch snap—and jumped. The sound didn't stop. Somewhere nearby, the cracking limb creaked, then fell, a brief rustle.

Down by the road's end, blocked by trees, Mr. O'Hearn's cabin would be. Up a choked drive to the right I'd find ours. The drive had gone wild. I had to step over fallen birches and shoulder aside branches to get by. I ducked under a dripping low limb and, straightening, spotted the cabin.

I'd been prepared for overgrown disrepair. But besides being beaten and broken and askew, the cabin was morose in a way that had nothing to do with disuse. It was tiny and brutish, built of gapped boards, flat-faced, tar-roofed, unfinished. The porch I'd thought I remembered was nothing but a block of cement, now crumbled at the edges, propping a screen door that hung from its bottom hinge. I saw something move behind the dark window and guessed some family of animals had mistaken the place for a work of nature, which it was becoming, and moved in. The window, in my day, looked over a sprung sofa-bed that took up the corner of an L-shaped room, with a kitchen ahead and two pairs of bunk beds to the right; cornered in the L were two tiny rooms, one containing a toilet, the other a broken refrigerator. Pressing my face against the window, I could see the shadowy sink and stove, and sunlight, coming in a thin shaft from the facing window, glancing off a spring sticking out of the sofa's flattened seat. By angling my eyes, I could just make out the edge of a table with some bunchy thing—a cloth, the head of a mop, a wig—hanging off it. As I watched, the thing finished inching off the table and fell, its landing oddly audible and, odder still, sounding like a wince.

The door seemed to be stuck, not locked—the handle turned and the door gave a little but no more. So I threw my considerable weight against it, and in it went, its abrupt unsticking accompanied by a thump and a trill of ghostly gasps and squeaks. Huddled together, hugging the wall between window and door, was a group of staring children, and sitting at their feet, where my thrust had thrown her, a little girl who took one look at me and screamed.

I was as surprised as she, my first impulse to step back and close the door (I could tell because I was suddenly outside again). Then, with that shriek still in my ears, I kicked the clay off my feet and combed my fingers through my hair and reopened the door. This time the little one didn't scream. She'd scooted back against the others and had her arm wrapped around the nearest leg, which trembled. Her own limbs were like twigs. "Who are you?" I said. She looked up to her protector for help. He put his hand on her head—hard, it seemed—and stared at me. The others were giving me the same obstinate look. There were five of them, all with flat-cheeked faces, narrow eyes, long hair. The tallest, a girl, would've easily fit under my arm with room to grow. "What're you doing here?" I said.

I'd asked very nicely, but the kids were unmoved, like a tough little squad being questioned by the enemy. I stood there for a minute, smiling and trying to look harmless. Finally the big girl said, not so nicely, "What're you?"

"What do I look like?"

She clarified curtly, "Doing here."

"I asked first." Imitating children is not a very effective way of gaining their confidence. When it became clear that these could stare longer than I could endure being stared at, I told them exactly what I was doing there, but if I'd hoped my having been a kid once, too, right here, would soften them, I was mistaken. Childhood was apparently nothing to get nostalgic about. As I mentioned site-specific moments of mine, I noticed the kids' clothes, Levi's worked white at the thighs and nearly detached at the knees, polo shirts and button-downs worn almost transparent, on the edge of each fold in their rolled sleeves a hole, dangling threads. Once I got started on this childhood haunt of mine, however, I couldn't stop, even when I saw how inappropriate it was, even when I found myself getting desperately sad. "Do you mind if I look around?" I said.

The sitting little girl bellowed, "No!" and her brother ground down her head under his hand. Restraining her, he shifted, revealing more of the boy at his back, who was holding onto a jar half full of what looked like jelly, pink and sugary around the rim. When he noticed my glance, he tightened his grip and hid the jar behind him. It was too much, this fear for the poor valuable, so with a last strained smile, I turned and left. I couldn't stand being the monster.

But that's what I was, walking away, so big, my shadow immense, floundering before me over the uneven ground. Then I heard elfin steps running after me, and a childish voice called, "Miss?" The older sister—fourteen at most—caught up and, when I turned to her, hesitated. "If you want to," she said and shifted and shrugged. "Look around?"

"Yes?" I said, and she shuffled again, pushed back her hair, touched her lips with her hand, as if about to bite her thumb, the tough little adult who'd faced me a moment ago now imitating a child.

"If you want to—" she said. "My parents, you know, my mom and dad, they don't approve of us letting strangers in the house. I'm sorry about my sister. She didn't meant it. She's only four, you know—" she looked for a word and said, "shy."

I said, "I saw plenty."

Like a wading bird stuck in the mud, wanting to fly away but needing help, the girl cast around, looking from me to the woods on one side then the other, her hands fluttering with each jerky shift of her head. "But if you want to—" she said and, watching my face, sucked on her upper lip.

"No, I don't," I said, "but thanks."

I turned to walk away and heard her take a step after me. "Miss?" she said softly. I waited. "It's private here."

"Yes."

"Very private."

"And you're afraid of an invasion."

"Not an invasion." Her childish inflection was convincing this time. "But—"

"But wouldn't it be a shame if the cabin stopped being a secret? Look at it." She did. "It's a secret because nobody wants to know about it. That's not much of a secret. It's obscure. And if it stays secret," I said, "it'll just disappear. Do you see? It's already started."

"No," she said, "really. We're waiting for repairs. It's okay."

"It's not okay. You don't understand—what's inside, not the house. But I have one, too, a few miles away, and it's very private. If this collapses," I waved at the cabin, "come to mine. It's the last house on W going inland off 13—have you got that?" She made no sign. I said, "Why don't you come now?"

"No," she said, "no," reflexively fast, and as clearly as if she'd backed away I could see her withdraw. "We don't," she said, "my parents, you know, they don't like to go out."

"They're out now."

"They don't like to."

"They're not invited."

"Oh." Then she did back away. "Maybe. But thanks." Halfway down the drive she hopped a fallen tree and, on landing, paused and turned back to hiss, "Remember."

"Private, right. You remember."

As she ran back to the house, a shadow crossed the window. Five children couldn't last long on a jar of jelly. I couldn't help thinking that Clara Bow, an old hand at benefacting, would've known what to do, and I found myself wishing not that I'd had her along but that, for a moment, I'd *been* her. Then, when I barged in the door, no one would've screamed. And I would have known what to do about that paranoia; I could have *related*. It occurred to me that my own childhood was no basis for anything, and I wanted to know what I'd missed when I'd fallen asleep in the middle of Clara's story, about that fear of powerlessness she'd felt in the air and hunted down in dives and dark alleys and on the desolate nighttime shore of Lake Michigan, the answer she'd found, and I hurried, wanting very badly to get back to Mother and hear.

★   ★   ★

Unlike Cora, I was still on wristwatch time and, seeing 2:30, assumed I'd be home before dark if I took a diagonal shortcut; unfortunately, my wristwatch was not on time (except, perhaps, somewhere between California and Hawaii), and I got lost again— or, more precisely, when the sun started precipitously sinking, I panicked and assumed I was lost, which was just as good as not being where I was supposed to be. The forest was still wet and now cold, unpleasant to touch, as I went groping from tree to damp tree in the conviction that they'd lead me somewhere. They were at least substantial, while the shadowy spaces between them seemed treacherous.

Then something moved. A lot of things moved, but this was something sizable coming, I could tell by the meter and crash of the steps. Between trees, I froze. The steps stopped. I lunged for the closest fir, and the forest exploded, and I fell. The sound and the shock and the pain came at once, all over, as if I'd been bombed. Then the pain shrank to an ache in my leg and throbbed, and I knew I'd been shot. I bellowed in terror and rage. Finally I recovered enough of my wits to scream into the dark, "Don't shoot!" Kathy, as it must have been, ran away.

Better to be shot than to be mauled by a bear, I thought, but only briefly. I couldn't see my leg very well and was afraid to feel it for damage, but the blood running steadily into my shoe gave me a sense of the size of my wound: big. Certain I was crippled, I lay on the ground, making no effort to shake off the insects that climbed me en masse. The more I thought about the pain, the worse it became, until I knew I was not only crippled but dying, slowly, of the starvation and exposure that were sure to follow.

I was startled out of this pitiful reverie by the sound of a searching "Hello?" The voice was a man's. It seems I'd decided to call myself lost in the most found place in the forest. The man shouted again. While his first hello had been a question—where?— his second was a command—speak! So I did. Hello? Steps approached steadily, not hesitating once for an unexpected tree, and the man's white hair appeared like a beacon above me. Besides his hair, smooth as a skull, and the glint of his eyes, buttons, and hands, he was a shadow, featureless and tall; but he seemed to see me quite clearly. At any rate, he stared down at me for a long minute before saying, curtly, "Can you walk?"

This was his way, I've discovered, a brusqueness suggesting that his help sprang from an instinct so deep and doubtless that he couldn't do anything but follow its orders; little as he cared to, he was compelled. And that tone compelled me to answer, "Yes, thank you, I'm just resting."

"Then maybe you could direct me to the woman who was screaming a minute ago." He brandished a flashlight and lit up my leg. For an instant I was struck by the light and his showy timing, but I forgot them as soon as I got a good look at my wound. All that blood, I was mesmerized. Also, I thought I'd be sick. But then I remembered the doctor and said, "I had an accident." He didn't say anything—or, I should point out, hurry to help me. "Hunting," I said. "I dropped my gun."

"Where is it?"

"I dropped it."

"So you said. Hunting what?"

"Squirrel. Here I am, *bleeding.*"

"I repeat—can you walk?"

"How do I know?"

"You seem to've gotten away from your gun." He hunkered over my leg, pulled back the torn denim, palpated the neighboring shin and calf. "Lever yourself on your good leg," he said, getting a hold under my armpits and, remarkably, he hoisted me. Someday my windmill would go up like this. As soon as he had me unsteadily upright, the doctor stooped and, butting my middle with his shoulder, lifted me, shifted, grabbed my intact leg, and staggered in the direction he'd come from.

I said, "What are you doing?" He didn't answer. He probably couldn't. I weigh 185 pounds.

This wasn't chivalry. It was demeaning. Never have I been made more clunkily aware of my bulk: rump in the air, arms hanging down and no place to put them, leg pinned in Dr. Abbot's grip, which clamped and relaxed with each laborious step he took, head full of what was left of my blood, world upside down. Folded close, I could smell my own odor, the sweat and the clay and the rain and the panic, and this I might've called Feroc.

We were approaching his house. The door was lit up, shiny red, and the windows were bright, incredibly so, since I hadn't seen them, though it was a comfort to know that I hadn't been lost after all, but had found just the spot where I'd started that morning. From the front, the house looked small. Once inside, though, bumping upended down the hall that ran through the middle, I got the sense that I'd entered a trick building, house of mirrors, which contained an illusion of unfolding into infinity. I caught jumpy glimpses of neatly kept rooms on either side—an uncluttered desktop before walls of books, a real fireplace stacked with logs, dishes in a drainer (whiff of clove here), steam and a quivering clothes dryer, bedside table with spectacles and lamp. Then we swung left into a dark room where the doctor bowed and unloaded me. The light he turned on, like a huge articulated desk lamp rising from the floor, flooded my feet and gave the rest of the room a dim glow. I was on one of those tables where patients are put to be looked at by doctors. Instead of the crackling strip of paper, this table was covered with a soft sheet. The rest of the room was outfitted with standard medical decor, the cool counter and sink and jars of paraphernalia, but where the pastel walls with certificates or innocuous prints usually were there was dark paneling, unadorned.

With my head in shadow and my feet spotlit, I felt like a specimen awaiting vivisection. When the doctor closed a drawer and came forward holding scissors, I asked him again what he was doing. Scissors in hand, he held my ankle, pried off my shoe. Then I felt the cold edge of the blade snaking up my leg as he snipped through the hem of my pants and kept clipping along the inseam. "I'm going to cut off your pantleg at the knee. Any objections?" He tossed the trimmed piece on the floor. "Now. Before I take care of this, should I call someone to come pick you up?"

His head was right above the light, so I couldn't see his face. "Why not wait?" I said. "Then you can call a hearse."

"Don't be dramatic. This isn't serious."

"Not *serious?*" I said.

"It isn't serious," he said again, slowly, as if I were retarded. "A superficial wound. You were grazed."

"Then why couldn't I walk?"

"You tell me."

"You wouldn't let me."

"You were falling when I picked you up, but let's not worry the point. The effects of shock embarrass some people. Do you want me to call?"

"We don't have a phone."

"Wonderful." He left me for a minute, washed his hands at the sink, went through a cupboard, and came back with a bottle and a hank of gauze. I watched his face while he wetted the gauze. His eyes, lowered, but not on my leg, were shifting almost imperceptibly, as if he were watching a slow tennis match played by gnats. Suddenly, then, he was looking at me. "What exactly do you think you're doing?" he said.

"Bleeding," I said.

He lowered the stinging cold cloth onto my leg, which leapt. "What are you doing in my neck of the woods?"

"I got lost," I said, "and I'm truly sorry."

"In general."

"In general I'm not in your neck of the woods."

"I think you are."

"I think you're territorial and presumptuous," I said. He clamped his fingers tighter around my calf and pressed the gauze on my wound. "And your bedside manner's rotten. You're hurting my leg."

"And you're an unpleasant patient, but as you can see, I'm still treating you, which says something for one of us. I'm sure you know I've had quite a few visits lately—from women whose problems aren't a physician's business. I don't charge a fee for the privilege of my company, but I do expect some sort of satisfaction for my trouble. Call it the price of invasion of privacy. I repeat: What do you think you're doing?"

"You can read the constitution. It's a matter of public record."

"I've read the Constitution. It doesn't mention women."

"Our constitution."

After the stare that preceded his first question, he hadn't looked at me once. Now, as if he'd been performing a medical exercise on a mannequin and amusing himself by talking aloud, he dropped my leg and with a mild frown turned to the cupboard. He came back absently unspooling a bandage. I said, "We're a charitable organization for the rehabilitation of troubled women."

His hands stopped abruptly and he walked to the head of the table and looked down at my face. "One of whom is out there with a very real rifle," he said. "You didn't do this—though you might as well have, for all your rehabilitation." He turned the word into a curse. "But let's forget the trigger-happy troubled woman. What sort of charity do you dole out—what advice do you give to the girl I saw today? How do you rehabilitate her?"

I said, "We saved her life," but he wasn't listening. He was saying, "And what business do you have telling Mrs. Cole—"

I didn't find out what I'd been telling Mrs. Cole because, precisely then, Mrs. Cole appeared in the doorway and said in her sweetest way, "What business?"

The doctor didn't look up. Reassuming his preoccupied expression, moving down the table, he picked up my leg and started to wrap it. "What business?" Clara Bow stopped at my feet. "God, Beauty," she said, "I thought you were dead." She put a wadded piece of paper into my hand. Written on it in block letters was: BIG ONE SHOT AT DOCTORS. "I only found it twenty minutes ago, under the door, no way of knowing how long it'd been there—that gun's been going off every hour, I thought—" She laughed and dabbed at the toe of my shoe with her fingertips. Her speech was rapid, almost giddy, and the touch, however gingerly, was odd from someone who normally avoided physical contact, even the slight, innocuous sort most people can't help. Then, patting my foot as if she were afraid she'd provoked it, she smiled up at Dr. Abbot and said, "I know you wouldn't be lecturing her if she were in danger." Pat pat pat. "Would you?"

"I thought I was." This, from me, was soft and offhand as a pleasantry, but it fell like a brick on Clara's brittle mood. Her hand stopped its manic patting and lay flat on my toe for a second, then slid down to the edge of the table and held on. I raised Kathy's note so I could see Clara's face. She wasn't looking at me—or, really, even asking—when she said, "But you're all right?" She was watching the doctor's hands with that intensity that comes into a face when focus is a function of not-looking elsewhere.

"Only grazed," I said, but she didn't notice. The wrapping of the bandage around my leg seemed to have mesmerized both of them, their concentration so complete that I looked, too, but there was nothing remarkable about the bandaging, except that it might be excessive. Then I noticed Clara Bow's neck. Her head was downtilted in the doctor's direction at such an angle that I could see a vein pulsing in her throat, to the rhythm I could still feel in my toes. Quickly, without moving her head, she shifted her eyes to the doctor's face. The glance was so subtle, a secret, that he couldn't have seen it, but I felt his reaction. His hands, mechanically smooth up till then, passing the spool, missed a beat—just a beat—I wouldn't say fumbled. I remembered cystitis then.

Dr. Abbot, recovered, made one more revolution and, pulling the roll into the air, took up his scissors and cut. He plucked what looked like a tiny metal claw off the table, snagged the end of the cloth with it, slipped his palm under my calf and lifted my leg while he fastened the dressing. Dumbly, like everyone else, I was staring at this operation. Then I felt the doctor's fingers tighten on my calf, a tic, a pressure as brief as his pause in the unrolling a moment ago and just as little meant for me, but still it traveled, like heat, up my leg. Snatching it, my leg, out of his hand, I sat up and said, a squawk in so much quiet, "Let's get going." The pain was welcome. "Well?" I said. Clara was staring at me with a look surprised out of a daydream into doubt, as if I'd just leapt—and not politely—out of an idle thought of hers. "Well?" Now I was nearly shrieking. "Let's get going!"

"Can you?" she said, gently, concerned, Clara Bow Cole.

"Can I what?"

"Can you walk?"

"Can I walk?"

The doctor said, "Shock."

"Of course I can walk," I said. "I was only grazed."

"I knew you could do it," Dr. Abbot said in a tone that was, for all its ostensible gravity and good will, snide.

I said, "Go to hell."

Clara was coming around to support me. At this she stopped midstep and turned to the doctor. "Are you sure she's all right?"

"Sorry," he said. "You're out of my bailiwick." He carried his scissors and gauze to the cupboard. Replacing them, not looking back, he said, "If you can't make it, just flap your wings."

Clara Bow braced herself against the table and took my elbow. "Beauty," she said in a low voice, "I'm not going to ask you what's wrong."

"I bet you're not," I whispered back. "Are the doctor's days numbered?"

Her grip slipped for a second. "No." Using her shoulder to break my slide, I lowered myself off the table. Briefly she buckled. Then, seeming to stiffen from her feet up, she made herself into a dependable crutch and held me steady while I stepped. She said, "I ought to drop you for that."

So I let go of her and walked unsupported, though with great discomfort, to the door. "Well?" I said. "Why don't you?"

Worming her way under my arm again, she said in a motherly voice, "Now, don't be a martyr." With her arm around my back and her fingers dug in under my rib cage, she turned to the doctor. "Maybe we could borrow your car?"

"Why?" I said. "What's wrong with the truck?"

"I didn't bring it. I walked. I mean I ran."

"No wonder you thought I was dead."

"I had to. Molly and Gigi have the truck. They're getting the cows. Cathy and Lynn have the Cadillac—I don't know, don't ask me—and we couldn't find the keys to the Honda and Gigi wasn't home to hot-wire it."

I said, "We don't need a ride."

Abbot said, "Don't be absurd. I'll drive you."

"We'll walk."

I could feel Clara shift as she waved the doctor back with her free hand. At the door she left me propped against a wall while she stopped to light the lantern. To walk, I leaned on her again, with my hand on her shoulder and hers on my elbow, an arrangement that spared her the effort that first hold must have cost her, since it was overdone to the point of bruising my side, and the extent of Clara's overdoing, I'd discovered, reflected the force of the resistance she was overcoming. Limping into the glow the lantern cast, I remembered how unfriendly the woods were an hour earlier. Now they seemed homely, and the farther we got from the doctor's the homlier they became. Even Kathy seemed unlikely. "Clara," I said.

She said, "I meant to tell you. They took their vacation seriously."

"That night in Chicago, by the lake?"

"Gigi and Molly didn't come back with the cows."

"Clara Bow."

"I'm trying to tell you."

"I'm trying to ask you. That girl who got stabbed?"

"Don't you care about what's happening at home? All hell's broken loose."

She dropped her hand and the change in the balance between us made me feel like a bully, so I let go of her shoulder and limped unaided. As if lighting the way required all her concentration now, she was frowning at the lantern. I said, "Something happened today. I just want to know how you stopped feeling victimized."

"Not 'victimized.'"

"You know what I mean."

"I know. You didn't understand me."

"But I want to. What happened?"

"What happened today?'

I said, "You first."

"I told you," she said. "She died."

She hadn't told me that. "I know," I said, "but was it resolved?"

"She *died*. I call that resolved."

"How it happened, I mean."

"Beauty, I told you."

"She didn't say anything?"

Clara flinched. She blinked, and her features went smooth. "Help me," she said. I stopped, not knowing what to do, until she said again, "Help me," then, "That's what she said."

"There weren't any clues?"

"No."

"What about the knife?"

"The knife." She said this as if it were a new word, *knife.*

"There weren't any fingerprints?"

"There wasn't any knife."

"You said there was a knife."

"I know I said. There it was."

In a cold instant, a dark blink, I knew what I'd missed. "Where was yours?" I said.

"I didn't have one," she said. "All I had was lipstick."

Help me, the woman had said. So Clara had pulled out the knife—and put it back into her pocket, a lipstick.

She whispered. "What happened today?"

"Today." The children were best left alone. "It rained."

There's nothing like murder for putting an end to conversation. As we walked I wondered about that hand she'd started to doubt, whether she thought she could someday set foot in it again or thought it would crush her, and her charity looked like an attempt to coax chance, in the shape of that hand, into taking her back. Now, in the heart of Women Abreast, she was her own beneficiary.

The woods were unnaturally quiet and dark, no moon. We'd been walking so long to no sound but our steps that a bellow nearby made me leap. Jarred, my gimpy leg gave out, and I fell, realizing as I landed that I'd been unbalanced by a moo. I was much more comfortable sitting, so I stayed there, soaking up a puddle, for a minute. Clara Bow lowered the lantern and squatted in front of it. "What are you going to do?" she said. When I didn't respond, she said, "Do. You know."

"I thought you made it up," I said.

She said, "You didn't believe me."

"You said you made it up."

Her face was set in one of those frowns people make when they're weighing a price, with doubt and longing, of resistance and means. She stared at the flame and, after a minute, said, "I thought you made it up. My history," she said. She looked over the lantern at me, then slowly rose, lifting it.

This was more than I'd bargained for, in terms of rehabilitation, and for the first time since dropping my tiny Will, I felt responsibility weigh in as more than mass and momentary, more, that is, than myself going through the motions when something had to be done, and I didn't know if I was up to it.

Hanging on to a tree trunk, I got to my foot. Less than three yards from us, there was a wooden wall; we'd been walking blind. I limped and knocked and got in response a rustle and a moo. Clara Bow said softly: "Cows."

▼▼▼

Shades of all hell greeted us as we approached the door: bulb light, the strains of tinny jazz, a clink of glass on glass and a clunk, laughter, the hum of the generator, the drumming of water running in the tub upstairs. I smelled pizza, and my stomach rumbled. In the wake of a voluminous flush overhead, we made our way to the living room, where Gigi and Molly and Mary Belinda and Joan were ranged around a middling fire in various versions of prostration, from Gigi, propped on one elbow, to Joan, flat on her back. Twinkling Budweiser bottles, neatly aligned, circled the base of the fireplace. Gigi was trying to pour one-handed from a quart bottle of Jack Daniel's, apparently with some confusion as to where the bottle and glass met, so that neck and rim kept bumping till the tumbler overflowed. "Hey!" I said.

I seemed to be a hallucination of hers. Then she noticed the others looking and went from dumbstruck to suspicious. "I thought you were shot," she said.

"I was." She looked at my leg. "Shot. Grazed, actually." This absorbed, Gigi flickered a look at the marshaled brown bottles, then, with an expression approaching profundity, studied the puddle she'd made. "What is this?" I said. "My wake?"

"We thought we get kicked out anyway, you shot and all. When we just got the cows." Except for Joan, who was out cold, they were all deathly serious, like children trying to soften anticipated punishment by preempting its import. I only hoped they were so drunk that they'd forget the recovered amenities by morning, when they'd have to return to their stripped-down existence. Gigi came out of her study with, "We fixed the generator." Molly waved her wilting hand as if to show how little effort this had taken.

"The fire," Clara Bow said, and we all looked at it. "It's not smoking."

Gigi waved her hand its way. "It was," she said. "We fixed it. That's leftover boards."

There weren't any leftover boards. After a moment of mournful silence from Clara and me, Gigi started shifting glances sideways at us, each with its nervous measure of muddled calculation. She announced abruptly, "I won't tell you what those sluts been up to."

The radio, that new piece of furniture, started crooning "Embraceable You." I said, "Where did this stuff come from?"

"Basin."

"Bayfield, that is," Molly said.

"Bought with what?"

"Money."

"What money?"

Clara Bow was withholding comment, and I had no idea what our finances were but thought I could safely assume that the women had less. Looking past me at Clara, Gigi was saying, "That guy? Mr. Cows. He put 'em on sale." Not knowing much about the cattle transaction, I was hoping for Clara's intervention here, but: nothing.

Molly said, "We didn't have to buy the cows. We found some strays. It was free enterprise. You earn what you save. And then you spend it."

"There's no such thing as a stray cow."

"Tell it to Bessie and Betty."

These, it seemed, were the very beasts. I was not prepared for *names*. Touched by the gesture (and because there wasn't much else I could do), I said, well, clearly, there'd been a mistake. Two cows had been taken for free agents, and in the morning everything could be put right. And where, I asked, was Barbie? As usual, no one could say. After another round of deep concentration, Gigi looked up from her glass and squinted keenly at a spot in the air, as if her memory were visibly suspended there. "Last time I saw her," she said in an oracular fashion, "was when we put the cows away."

"That's right," Molly said, flourishing a weighty hand. "She was definitely there. A definite thing for animals."

Barbie did indeed have a thing for animals, and it took me a while of whispering to coax her out of the shed, where I found her sitting next to Bessie's or Betty's rump with her hand flat on the cow's udder, the two of them, animal and girl, perfectly still. She was teaching the cow to trust her. When I talked her out into the cool night, I stopped her, struck. There was something I wanted her to do tomorrow, I said, an errand of mercy for which I thought she might be well suited. The lantern lit her brows from below, giving her a fan of shadow lashes, a theatrical look of delight.

Considering what I told her about the cabin of children, she said slowly, "I don't know."

"Don't know?"

"They'll think it's a trap. You know," she said, "charity. That's how kids are."

No kids I knew. They would trust her, I said, I was certain. She was looking without comment at the house. We watched a light go on. She glanced at me. "It's too easy to flip a switch," I said. "We'll finish the windmill."

It was my way of warning her, but she said, "I like it dark. Like the pioneers." And I had my first glimmer of what might have prompted her cryptic submission to Women Abreast. Casually as I could, I asked her whether she wanted to go back. Her answer was slow and suspicious. Go back where?

Home? I said.

She deliberated again. "What if I don't get better?"

"What's wrong," I said.

She looked around distractedly. "Nothing, I guess, it depends." She tucked her hair behind her ear and said, as if it were a suggestion, "I have cystitis."

"Don't we all."

"We do?"

"No. I'm sorry."

"It's nothing big."

"Not that kind of sorry," I said. "How old did you tell the doctor you were?"

"My age."

"Which is what, these days?"

"Twenty-one." Her soft rasp of a voice was so unsure that I was sorry I'd made her say. The pain in my leg flared up, and I squatted on it to extinguish the lantern, then, limping, led Barbie into the house.

Inside, the women had sunk into an even deeper state of mellow, the fire purred, and Bunny Berrigan sang "I Can't Get Started." A flush above convulsed the pipes and Cathy, as if borne on the water, descended the stairs, pink-cheeked, dewy, trailing perfumed steam. Her perm had grown out a bit, giving her curls a sudden appearance, like a sculpted poodle's. Gigi rose up on her elbows and tried to twist to see the bather, but the effort was too much, and she collapsed, Cathy settled, and the room was still again. To no one in particular I said, "Did you buy groceries?" and no one in particular answered. I said, "What are we going to eat tomorrow?"

Molly said, "Fish."

Gigi groaned—and the lights went out. Quick as instinct, Barbie clamped onto my arm. The others shifted and muttered, then lapsed back into silence, bated this time, as if they were waiting. "The propane," I said. "That's all." Barbie loosened her grip on my arm, but kept her hand lightly there. A piece of wood in the fire fell with a hiss and sparks and a start of flame that lighted the faces around me, a brightening abrupt, upward, and brief as inspiration. In the hush that followed, the smell of pepperoni and beer mingled with Cathy's damp jasmine and Berrigan, still singing, lulled time for a minute and I wondered why I'd worried about what Barbie would do, since now it seemed so clear that she could stay, with us, and the others too, right here. Oddly the moment had for me the coloring, the scent, the timbre of nostalgia, though I'd never been through any moment like it, to remember. Then Gigi belched. That prompted a snicker from Cathy.

Clara Bow's voice startled me. "That was frivolous use of our fuel," she said. "Beauty's right." Except that I'd never said that. "Vacation's over," she said. "I don't know how you expect to become responsible if this is how you spend your free time. Beauty?" She paused, as if for assent, but not long enough to let me say a word. "Go to bed," she said. "If you tried to clean up now, you're so drunk it'd seem like a dream, so you can do it in the morning, when it won't be pretty." Now they were all looking at her, the minister of comfort become mistress of discipline, beery half-smiles slowly giving way to their customary expressions, the wary, the sardonic, the smug. "Look at Beauty," she said, and they did. "While you were wasting your time, she got shot trying—"

"It's nothing like that," I interrupted, baffled by her. "But it's late. We probably should go to bed."

The women came grudgingly to life and, with shifty glances at each other, lumbered to their feet. Then trudging like a family of sleepy, nudged bears, they made slow progress up the stairs. Barbie, the last, turned back on the bottom step to give me a quick look, a peculiar little quirk of concern, as if we had a secret and she were afraid I'd tell, but before I could study it, she was climbing again.

That left Clara and me. "Well!" she sighed, toeing a kleenex into Gigi's whiskey puddle and surveying the damage with abrupt little birdlike turns of her head.

"What was that?" I said.

"What?" Still looking around, she said, "I know it's your job. But you've been through a lot today."

"My job?"

Now she said, "What?"

I didn't know. "They were just having fun," I said, a little lamely. "It's not San Quentin."

"What?" she said again. "Are you upset? You're upset. I didn't know we allowed for a certain amount of backsliding."

"I'm not upset."

"Is it your leg? It hurts? You'd better go to bed."

Already she had her foot on the step, started up, and when I said, "In a minute," she paused for just an instant, long enough to turn and say, moving again, "Don't be foolish."

With everyone in bed, I thought I might recapture that peculiar sense of well-being in the household's—the keeper's—last moment awake, but Clara Bow's tone lingered, and as soon as I sat down the fire collapsed into charcoal and glow and the radio station ended its broadcasting day in static. Still I didn't want to go up yet, so it was with something like relief that I remembered Molly's fish, probably rotting somewhere: It should be seen to. A foray through the dark house in search of tomorrow's endangered dinner struck me as an act of repossession. Immediately I tripped over a bottle, which skittered and cracked into another then another and another until half the standing circle had gone down.

The least likely place for fish should have been the refrigerator, since until tonight, when the women "fixed" the generator, it hadn't been functional, but refrigeration is a deep faith, hard to shake, and when I unsealed the door a foul, oily odor overwhelmed me. Lifting the lantern, I found myself staring into a lineup of stunned fish faces—five, all bludgeoned into contortions previously unknown to fish, the first broken-mouthed, one-eyed, and bent in a right angle at the middle. Stowing the fish in an airtight space had been someone's sole post-operative gesture. They retained their scales and shattered bones and dying postures, and a look at these, along with the whiff of fleshy decay, relieved me of whatever vague notion I might have harbored about cleaning them. Then stepping back, about to close the door, I spotted the packet of mail that had been neatly stacked on the shelf above the day's catch. This was something I could handle.

The mail stunk. There were plenty of letters for Clara Bow Cole—from Sal, her stepsons, even Bill, if his last name was Dugan, and from most of the feminine charities in the free world, it seemed; also one return-addressless envelope stamped in red: PERSONAL AND CONFIDENTIAL. All of these were addressed c/o Women Abreast, Cornucopia, WI, and had, postal miracle, made it to our refrigerator. As an organization, we had prodigious junk mail and a handful of letters from the IRS requesting quarterly reports. And at the bottom of the pile was our bank statement.

I opened the envelope greedily, finally about to see exactly what "our" finances were, but what I found there put my puny greed to shame. It took me more than a minute to believe that figure, the balance, because I was not used to thinking of much more money than I could hold in my hand. It took me much longer—sorting through the checks to see that, yes, this did compute—to consider the implications. The checks, I mean, accounted for, along with the needs of Women Abreast, Clara Bow Cole's living expenses. My signature was nicely forged on payments to Sal and Bill, Penney's and Saks, Illinois Bell and Standard Oil and numerous unfamiliar names. When Clara Bow had told me, that day at the lake, that she'd put all her money into Women Abreast, I'd thought it was part of her test of my loyalty: with nothing to lose but Clara Bow Cole in the flesh, would I swim out and save her? But the woman had truly beggared herself. I was her benefactor now.

The next thing I knew, it was late. I'd made a fan of the IRS printouts and was reading each one. They were, apparently, identical. The idea of safeguarding this fortune by figuring out the taxes occupied me until I had to admit that the forms weren't going to teach me how to answer in a way that would satisfy everyone, or anyone, and this wasn't really my concern at all. It was a ruse.

I'd got more than I'd wanted, and so I wasn't satisfied. My height always made me an easy object for someone else's idea, a hypostatic human form, and if I'd resisted this, it was never wholeheartedly, since I was not so sure of a self that merited attention beyond what my stature received. But here again I *stood* for something (and what?), and suddenly it was not enough to merely stand, to be the figure on the other side of that enormous balance.

This was the night I decided to become the Beauty I'd impersonated, with authority. Solitude in a house in the woods was not enough. I wanted to be recognized.

However, my first act was secretive. I returned the mail to the refrigerator, but not the bank statement, which I took upstairs and, while Clara slept nearby, hid under my mattress, deep, where a change of sheets wouldn't disturb it.

▼▼▼

Arousing rendition of the national anthem woke the house at five A.M., provoking an unpatriotic outcry. From my bed I could hear the women encountering one by one the affronts of renewed consciousness: First they protested the noise; then, as their minds let in meaning, the flag; when they remembered its source, the radio; and, finally, Gigi, who'd bought it. A chorus of voices demanded that she go down and turn off— some said dismantle—the importunate thing. When she wouldn't, they condemned her. Out of the fracas came Cathy's voice saying, "... can't live without her ghetto blaster," and rather than let the situation turn ugly, I got up to disarm the radio. Clara, who'd been feigning sleep, sprang up as soon as I rose: "Where are you going?"

"To turn off the radio," I said.

"Don't," she told me. "Gigi should."

"Why should she?"

"It's hers."

The sound of mounting hostilities on all sides gave this soft talk the tone of battlefront espionage. "It's ours," I said. "And I left it on."

As I went she said, "Beauty—" but without much conviction, and when I looked back she didn't say anything else.

Now a gritty voice was announcing the news of the north with abrasively bright bonhomie for the hour—it presumed wakefulness. This was the other Wisconsin. Mine, upstairs, bemoaned the dawn. The newscaster was easily silenced, but the women went on. Going to them, I passed my room, and there stood Clara, poised in alert listening. "Getting them up?" she said.

I said, "It's five o'clock." Meaning: no.

"You shouldn't be up. Your leg."

"I'm fine," I said. "Go back to sleep."

"With all this noise?"

"Momentary. I was on my way—"

"I'm not tired."

"Then get up."

Clara Bow started to speak, stopped herself, lips parted, seemed to hark. This was how she got around vocal logic—cleared a small space for forgetting. Sharp again, she said, "We're all awake. We should get to work."

"What work?"

"What work?"

"Won't it wait?" I said.

She said, "Winter's coming."

"In September?"

"Okay," she said. 'It's only a few hours anyway." And she went stiff-backed to her bed and sat upright as if to say that while the loafers slept she at least would be at work, accounting for the passing minutes. Minutes, I remembered, were her only remaining commodity, and her appearance struck me all at once as pathetic—her scrub-brush hair, wan, pointed face, bony knees, sharp where her nightgown, washed thin in pump water and the Lava soap that had been one of her husky provisions, hung over them and sagged—as if she'd only become poor when I found out she was; and I decided to humor her, once the wenches were settled, by making out a work schedule with her, extended, to forestall winter. Then, ducking out, I glimpsed myself in the mirror, a woman who looked at least as tangled in the hair, taut in the face, hollow around the neck as the poor Clara Bow.

The baiting and bickering in the raucous room had assumed

a different tone than usual. First of all, the noise didn't let up when I loomed. Whereas my mere presence generally was enough to turn the verbal battle into a guerilla war of glances, this time, Gigi, the target of everyone's remarks, simply tipped her head up, shot an arch little look of amusement across her toes at me, then fell back, arms folded under her pillow, a picture of nonchalance. "What do you think," she said, "I'm some cousin of *Whitney Houston,* and I'm gonna tell you it run in the family? You never heard me call on you to claim no *Madonna* for a relation."

Lynn was prepared to answer, but interrupted herself: "What's wrong with Madonna?"

Cathy said, "What's wrong with Whitney Houston?"

Gigi shifted her head and fixed Cathy with a mocking look. " 'What's wrong with Whitney Houston?' " she said, and then, as if in answer, "What's wrong with civilization?"

In their exchanges, Gigi and Cathy usually came to a draw. Gigi had the subtler wit and a talent for implying superior strength, but Cathy knew the limits of her sparring equipment and knew just when to say "Shut up," which has the sound of a surrender but can be difficult to answer. This time, however, Gigi had got her with a question so broad and odd that no variation of "shut up" would suffice: Cathy rolled her eyes. I wanted to know what was wrong with civilization, and was about to ask, but Molly's cool response coming from the corner preempted me. "She has too many cousins."

Gigi's incipient smile at this froze in a grimace of distaste when Cathy, a little slow to get it, snickered. From the other room, silent till now, Mary Belinda rumbled ominously, "I know what that means."

Gigi shouted back, "Mary B., you got to be the quickest nigger this side of the Mississippi."

Cathy said, "What does that make you?"

With extremely sweet consideration, Gigi turned to her. "Honey," she said, "I was makin' a joke."

Molly laughed. That was too much for Cathy. She shook her curly hair, which was as stiff as straw and only quivered, looked Gigi flat in the face, and said, "Big. Deal."

Gigi was still staring back, her expression a caricaturist's sketch of scrutiny and wonder. Her tone was a slow marvel: "Girl, you got to be the whitest girl I ever saw. Everything be just as plain as your face." She held her gaze for a summary moment, then rolled her head back into the center of her pillow and contemplated the ceiling. Cathy clipped a whinny and with painful contempt mouthed the word "plain," which, as she took it, hit right where she could be hurt; and this haphazard strike was underscored by Gigi, who interrupted her musings to casually ask, "If men's not allowed here, s'at mean they not allowed, period?"

Last night, deflecting attention, she wouldn't say what "those sluts" had been up to, but now she was ready, or just pretending to be by way of blackmail. "They're not allowed," I said, "but neither is drinking or cow theft or what you might call misappropriation of funds."

Lynn had been listening with obvious interest. Now, very serious, she said, "You know, girls get masculine if they go without men. You know the way old women grow mustaches?"

Molly rose slowly with lowering eyes. "What man told you that? There's such a thing as nuns, and do they have mustaches? Well, a few, but in general? Or cancer of the cervix? No, not one nun, but no man told you that. You made it through puberty without a man, didn't you?"

Lynn said, "Just barely."

The time seemed propitious for me to say something. I said that men, nothing against them in general, were simply impractical now. The women were here for one problem or another, call them ailments, and though men might address the ache, they couldn't cure the disease, and furthermore, rather than risk catching something and being revealed as charlatans, they were sure to disappear as soon as the symptom resurfaced, as it certainly would.

That was my speech, and it was beautiful most of the way through, until, that is, I saw how generous the women's interest was. They looked sincerely curious, as if I were speaking in tongues and should be allowed, and this was a disconcerting switch from their normal policy of *trying* to look rapt, as if their tenure depended on the impression they were making. Their new lack of concern over appearances threw me. Meanwhile, they'd forgiven me my eventual digression and returned by way of Lynn's remark to the subject of adolescence. They seemed to be on the verge of reminiscing about teen sex and I, with my pale history, was prepared to be fascinated, when Gigi raised her head, looked over her feet at me, and fell back on her pillow—and the room went quiet.

I lingered there long enough to remind them how late last night had been and to try to ingratiate my way back into their confidence by offering them a few extra hours of sleep. They responded by settling down and assuming attitudes of slumber, so I backed out, bumping into Barbie, who was on her way to milk her new friends, and as we walked down the hall, I could hear the women resume. Clara Bow was sound asleep. I went downstairs and started the schedule anyway.

When they finished their furtive chatting and tired of lounging in bed, the women plodded down, performed their morning rituals in the woods, returned with the empty roll and some ideas about what items should go on the proverbial grocery list, remembered—groceries!—the fish and, displaying them filled the room with oily reek, announced the mail, and became confused. Molly took command. Apparently the last of the Coleman fuel had been put to some mysterious use yesterday, so she instructed her assistant, Lynn, to build a fire and then proceeded to gut the fish. While she was at it, Barbie appeared carrying a bucket. Gigi took one look at it, reared her head back in her skeptical way, looked again, and said to Barbie, "Milk?" Barbie didn't say. "No joke," Gigi said, then, "Hey. I think we should keep these guys."

Perhaps having forgotten that the cows weren't ours, Barbie took a protective step closer to her bucket. Suddenly Molly said, "Don't anybody drink that," with such force that we all froze, though no one was in anything even approaching drinking formation.

"What?" Gigi said, when she recovered. "How long since we had milk? And from the horse's mouth."

Cathy, a veteran dieter, said, "Not long enough," while Lynn murmured in disapproval, "Horse's mouth."

"It's not what you get at the supermarket," Molly said.

"It's crawling with bacteria." And the women, predictably, stared at the pail, as if the lurking germs might scale its sides.

First her cows, and now their milk; Barbie said woefully, "What do we do?"

Citing vague memories of junior high science, Molly declared that we would have to boil the milk and then, because we had no way of keeping it cold, we would have to drink it. This procedure she oversaw too, and under her tutelage breakfast was shaping up to be a regular feast: hot, whole milk and gamy, mutilated fish. I asked the company where Clara Bow was. Gigi said, "TKO."

Lynn translated: "Sleeping in."

They were all quiet for a few seconds. Then Gigi said, with the gingerly delicacy of a gangster "explaining" a disappearance, "She had some—agitation last night."

"She accused me of hiding the car keys," Lynn said.

Molly said, "She did? She didn't ask *me.*" She pulled the keys out of her pocket.

"Better let her rest," Gigi said to me, then to Molly: "You were commuting with the fire, lightweight."

"At least I could *find* my glass." Molly turned to me. "How's the leg?"

"Fine," I said. "A little stiff."

"I'll take a look at it later."

"Not *really* stiff. Fine, really."

"I insist."

Gigi said, "I sure would let her rest."

Through the window I'd seen Barbie washing the beer bottles under the pump, and I'd assumed this was her timid contribution to the household's present hubbub and cleaning to come, but now she approached with two bottles in each hand and held them out to be filled. This from any of the others would have provoked derision or rough questioning, but Barbie's fragile manner and whispery moves seemed to disarm the women, and Molly merely looked from the bottles to me, nonplussed. "Barbie," I said, "we can't keep them cold."

She looked over her shoulder at me, her expression freighted with significance, which escaped me. Softly she said,

"The kids," like a password. In spite of her misgivings, she was going to nourish the family of youngsters.

"Go ahead, Molly," I said. "It's charity." Barbie, already turning, shot an alarmed look back at me, as if I were betraying a confidence; but Molly meanwhile had tasted the milk and gave up four bottlesful without question.

The fish, however, was a success. Most of it fell into the fire, and soot and singeing sufficiently disguised the flavor of the salvaged remainder to make it palatable. Its savor was enhanced further by the sizable difference between our portions and our appetites. In short, breakfast was ravishing.

With Barbie directed cabinward, and so, safely out of the way while we disposed of her animal friends, I instructed Gigi to load the cows and went upstairs to consult with the bursar. But Clara Bow was not in her bed, which was made, her nightgown neatly folded on the pillow. I yelled her name out the window. Getting no answer, I started hunting for the checkbook.

The women were tidying up, so I disguised my search as an inspection. Gigi followed me around, peering where I peered and looking where I pointed, until I finally whirled on her and demanded, *"Would* you *load* the *cows."*

"Oh sure," she said, but didn't move.

"Well?"

"Do I look like Saint Francis and cows are gonna come to me?"

"Deputize someone. Just do it."

As I went up the stairs, I heard her say, "Hey, Cathy."

The bedroom was where I'd started, the obvious drawers and corners for putting away, so now I looked for hiding places. Our sparse furniture afforded few. Giving up, the lot exhausted, I lifted my mattress to see where I'd stashed the statement in the dark last night—and there, a few inches from that envelope, were two others like it, two more personal and confidential letters to Clara Bow, and the checkbook. I took the book and "my" statement and lingered for a long and finally, unfortunately scrupulous moment over the secret letters, which, along with the other statements, were gone next time I looked.

149

Gigi and Cathy were at each other again, so I told Cathy to go inside and send out Mary Belinda. Mary Belinda was impervious to Gigi. She was impervious to everything. As Cathy went, I said to Gigi, "Why do you pick at her?"

"Hey," she said. "That girl is makin' progress." Then it occurred to her, I think, that I, too, could push a cow around. "Why you call for Mary B.?" she said. "One more cow to move. Why not get Joan, too?"

"Gigi."

"It's a fact. Try to move Mary B. You got to go around her, like a mountain. You know her man beat on her? Big woman like that, she don't have to take it. But I tell you, that's her way of wearin' a man down."

"She left," I said. "She came here."

As if she'd anticipated this, Gigi already had a thoughtful frown on her face. "That got to be her most radical act," she said, and shook her head. "She move the mountain."

Just then Mary Belinda, looking not much like a mountain in motion, ambled out. "You can go in," I said. "We've got it." Smiling mildly at us, the truck, the cows, she paused for almost a minute, as if waiting for some mechanism inside to switch into reverse. Then, her pleasant expression unchanged, she turned around and went back to the house.

Apparently considering her point so well confirmed that it required no comment, Gigi took ahold of one impassive cow by the rope around its neck. Without Cathy worrying its rump, the stalled scenario I'd interrupted, the beast calmly followed Gigi up the ramp into the truck. The other wasn't as willing, and I had to push her. She wasn't contrary, just inert, apparently waiting for an explanation. Finally, frustrated, I smacked her rear and she shambled right up to Gigi, who said, "Shit. Stampede 'em." Then she climbed down and hitched the gate.

"That's it?" I said. "They stand there?"

Going around to the side of the truck, Gigi reached for the cows' ropes and tossed the free ends through the window on the passenger side. "I get in here and hold 'em," she said, and did. "It's their own fault if they don't sit down."

They sat or fell soon enough and laid low while we rocked along the bumpy road as Gigi tried to recall where she'd rustled

150

them. Rather than pointing out the first likely spot, as I'd expected her to do, she waited till we reached a farm fairly swarming with people—people far enough away, that is, to look bee-sized—and announced that this was it, her sly smile assuming that even I would see the foolishness of reversing the cows' fate now. "Gigi," I said, "there's a fence." And so there was, upright slats of wood wired close together. Skeptical, Gigi scanned it, then directed me to drive up to a tree, which seemed familiar, and yes, she remembered it well now: excellent cover.

The section of fence beyond the tree had been dismantled. I said, "You did this?"

"How else we gonna get the cows?"

"Wouldn't it have been easier to pay for the ones you were supposed to get?"

She shrugged, tossed the ropes out the window, and climbed out. Then came the answer: "This way, we got the cows *and* the cash."

"Which we have to spend anyway."

"—*and* the beer." An irrevocable gain. I subsided.

The cows were such *cows,* resisting us all the way again, while I thought about what excellent cover the tree and its attendant bushes would be for an advancing farmer attracted by the racket those heavy, hooved beasts couldn't help making. When we finally coerced them down the ramp, they just stood there, and I was all for pronouncing them returned and running, until Gigi suggested exactly that, reminding me of the exemplary role I should be playing. Stooping in the brush to one side of the breach, we unroped the cows and watched as they made their unbelievably slow bovine way to the fence. *"Go on,"* I encouraged Bessie, who promptly stopped, her rump still on our side. With a mournful shaking of her head, she tore a hank of grass out of the field and started to jaw it, and that was resettlement enough for me.

We got out of there speeding—until the road veered away from the farm and Gigi informed me that we were going the wrong way. Inverting Clara Bow's instructions to correct for my detour, she directed me round and about to the front of a farm that looked suspiciously like the one whose distant backyard we'd just penetrated. I was squinting, trying to spy out the returned

151

beasts, when the approaching farmer, Hecker, copied my squint and swiveled his head to see what was so interesting. Gigi, who'd been standing by blandly, turned to me and grinned.

The cows we got were just like the other two. But these were named—by Hecker, on the spot, as he explained they were "Brown Swiss"—Gretchen and Hans. Inferring my ignorance from a question I put to him about the welfare of the soon-to-be-orphaned heifers, the farmer detailed the mothers' diet for me: about fifty pounds of "silage," fifteen to twenty pounds of hay, some forage—per *day*. "Right," I nodded. "Can cows live on grass?"

His answer was not encouraging. But then he let us know that, treated right, these "girls" could be expected to give us up to seven-thousand pounds of milk a year, and I quickly figured that we hardly needed that much and could get by on grass. It didn't occur to me at the moment to wonder how much grass it would take to satisfy two cows used to seventy pounds of food per day, or where, in the woods, it would come from. Also, I forgot about winter.

Gigi and I drove away in silence, disbelieving the ease with which Hecker had bedded the cows in the truck. At the turn I looked back at the humming farm: the grazing cows on the rich green fields, the house with its porch in a tree's shade, two men crossing the slick, dirt yard, a girl running after them from the barn, the long, bright building, framed by two towering silos. "Silage," I said, and Gigi said, "Don't look at me."

"I tell you," she said, after some considering. "A bag of dog food's fifty pounds. They supposed to get that much *a day*? We better off buyin' food."

Before I'd become a millionairess I'd hoped to make Mother self-supporting. I said, "We could make it back by selling the milk."

Gigi rolled her gaze from the landscape to me. "What sucker you think's gonna buy it?" We'd both tasted the milk. "And you notice? Everyone around here got a cow. Even us."

It was all milk, I told her, and it shouldn't be hard to learn how to bring ours up to carton par.

"You see that stuff back there?" she said. "I mean. Machines."

"Yeah, but people drank milk before that 'stuff' existed."

"Yeah, but they didn't have Coke."

"You don't have to do it."

She looked out the window and said lightly, "I'm just saying, everyone got a cow."

We stopped in Cornucopia and bought groceries, nine bags.

Mary Belinda was sitting at the kitchen table, reading our junk mail. Joan, she told us, was in bed, and everyone else out. Coming back across the yard after showing the cows home, Gigi stopped at the pump and stooped, a study, so I joined her. The platform was frothy with suds salted with white crystals and smelled, as I stooped, too, of jasmine. "Those sluts?" I said.

Just then Clara Bow and Barbie emerged from the woods. They were walking together, spaced and not speaking, like soldiers in a drill. Unless she'd taken my own circuitous route home from the cabin, Barbie shouldn't have come that way, so, "Where were you?" I asked, but apparently assuming "you" was Clara, she turned right, hut, and without a word or look in our direction went into the barn manqué.

"Nowhere," Clara said and marched past us to the house.

When the door slammed, Gigi gleamed, her antagonism sensor engaged. "Ooo," she said, wagging her hand shoulder high. Suddenly she turned to me. "What she do to get in here?"

"Clara?" Killed someone, I was about to say, but a shout from the house interrupted: *Where* did all this *stuff* come from?"

"Ehlers!" I shouted back. That was the store. Clara Bow opened the door, focusing so clearly on a jar of something in her hand that I knew she must be thinking of the checkbook. She glanced at me. I rinsed my hands. She retreated into the kitchen. "She financed the whole affair," I said to Gigi.

"No lie." A moment passed while Gigi did some figuring. "So what you do?"

"I conned Clara Bow."

Gigi regarded me sidelong, her head back and eyes narrowing to that slit of skepticism that cut everything outrageous down to size. Slowly she followed me in.

Clara Bow was on the stairs. "Mail," I called, "in the fridge," and we met at the table. I handed hers over, piece by piece, that letter last. She glanced at it and looked for more. "The rest," I said, "is on the table."

Idly Clara Bow thumbed through and then, as idly, wondered, "Nothing else?"

"Mary Belinda?"

"What?"

Clara stood there for a minute, apparently unwilling to believe that was the lot, but just as reluctant to seem unwilling, and so, looking dull. Then, murmuring something about Barbie needing light, she went out carrying the lantern.

The rest of us were stocking the shelves when Molly showed up, a fish in each hand. She took one look at the groceries and dropped her sorry contribution in the sink. "Clara and Barbie come back?" she said.

"You walked right by them."

Together we looked out the window. Barbie had the barn door—that is, wall—wide open to the sunset. Clara Bow was not inside.

"How were they?" Molly said.

She knew something, so I said, "Guess."

She said, "I never guess."

"Then tell me."

"Would I be asking if I knew?" Turning, she spread her fishy hands. "So. What's with the windfall?"

▼▼▼

T his was the golden period of Women Abreast, I think. Are the poor in spirit blessed? Or the poor blessed in spirit? Anyway, there were minutes—oh, many of them—when it looked like it would work. The women were well fed and busy and not just not attacking one another; we were even menstruating together, as Molly announced after a day of duty burying the midden. This was, she said, what happened with sisters, roommates, and, sometimes, intimate friends. And the crickets were with us.

Leaving the barn to Barbie, who, prodded by Gigi and flush with the wisdom of one of my overdue books, learned to skim and strain, Clara worked on the windmill with me. In her new disciplinary way, she dispersed my crew, commanding each member to undertake some other task, and then she took their place, her sweeter self again, the Clara Bow I knew, I'd like to say, except that it might be misleading; she had her secrets, sparked against Barbie, harangued the other women, went out walking at night, insomniac, and then again was help itself, a puzzle. Her carpentry had not improved, but she attacked a nail, held a board in place, ran for a tool with an exuberance that almost (never) compensated for her lack of skill and was far more entertaining, until the nail had to come out, the board fell, or the

155

tool was wrong and she had to go for another, which she did as eagerly, and who wouldn't have been touched?

This was when Clara Bow first asked me a few personal questions. For instance, "Normal childhood?" After listening earnestly to statistics and a few details of my upbringing, she put out delicate probes, and I told her about my name and school and got somehow to the professor, to the subject of love. "Was it hard for you?" she said. "Since you're so—"

"What?" I asked her. "Big?" She didn't say. I didn't know what she meant: difficult the desire, the fulfillment, the act? Hard? I said. No. Not that or easy. It just didn't happen.

"But you're stunning," she said. "I would think."

Stunning, I said, was a good word, and what good was a stunned man? Unless, of course, you're trapshooting.

"Sometime he'd have to come to," she said, then thought about it. "Frank Abbot's bigger than you."

I'd been on the verge of confidence, but here it occurred to me that Clara Bow had mentioned once talking to "a Minnie Silverman," and so in her questions, encouraging for a moment, I started to suspect a test. I experimented with the notion by telling her a few romantic fibs, which she pretended to accept, and fair was fair, the weather, too.

So the windmill went together, sails to hub and hub to tower. It wasn't as picturesque as the ones glossily featured in my book's appendix, but when we roped it and, heaving like a pack of yeomen, towed it up into the air, there was no denying its virtues, foremost the fact that it existed. The women were still holding the rope when Clara Bow fell back, pronouncing, "It's turning!" We low creatures couldn't feel more than the faintest breeze, a feather, but sure enough, there was wind up there trying to push the sails out of the way; and slowly, groaning, they ground into motion. "We'd better hold it up," Clara said and ran. One of the blades swept down, I yelled, she ducked and grabbed a wooden leg. Absurd as she looked, so small, she was right, since we'd detached the balancing ramp before hoisting the tower. The others held on while we hammered the piece back into place. Then we all stood back and watched as the blades picked up speed and sailed. Unwired yet, the windmill generated nothing but an intermittent gust, but like the monumental Tinkertoy it was, it worked.

Going by Wisconsin time, which dilates, the electrician took a couple of days to hook up our whirligig to a generator, then to run the wires and, at the end of them, rework our system so a battery inside could store the power the other put out. Clara Bow and I were in the kitchen, still in sketchy pursuit of my past, when the refrigerator clicked and whirred. "Hey!" I said and turned to see. It seemed the same. I turned back to find Clara Bow gazing at me with the puzzled look she wore as she worded her questions. "What?" I said. She blinked, and then, with a smile visibly dismissing whatever she had in mind, clapped the table and said, "Let's put something in it."

"Milk."

"It's all we've got."

By "all" I assumed she meant "the only perishable," so, to be correct, I added, "Eggs," since we now had chickens, too, also from Hecker. The eggs, however, we agreed, required refrigeration only in principle, coming two a day as they did and going just as fast.

With Clara and Barbie still at odds, I did the errand into Barbie's territory, the barn, where the beer bottles of milk were kept in a bucket of pump water. Outside, Gigi and Molly were hammering on a coop styled like a lean-to. Each time they struck a blow, the little building shook and the chickens erupted and the wary cows, shuffling their haunches, tried to back away, but there was nowhere to back to. Standing between them, Barbie murmured condolences and administered strokes. In the half-dark, the girl had her own soft light. For a while, I'd noticed a new ease about her, something sleek, which I'd attributed to budding self-esteem, but now, as she left off cooing and smiled up at me, I could see that her appearance had actually changed. Her cheeks were undeniably fuller, her arms rounder; even her dirty hair looked glossier. Coming into Barbie's bloom straight from Clara Bow's pallor, I imagined their antagonism sapping one, feeding the other, since Clara seemed to have grown more pointed and wan than usual as Barbie waxed, her only flourishing her hair,

157

which she wanted trimmed, though every time I offered she had something else to do. The flush one, jealous of her milk, was suddenly alert when I plucked up the bottles. "Just putting them in the fridge," I said.

"I think I'll put this milk in the fridge," I said in passing to Molly and Gigi.

Gathering these three, a train, I carried the milk into the house and delivered it into the electrified refrigerator—which wasn't cold yet and, after the first surge, was hardly even humming audibly; and, I must admit, the visual interest was low, too, as the bulb inside turned out to be defective. Then someone upstairs who'd also discovered electricity, or perhaps was only hoping, flushed the toilet. That was gratifying, but as the gurgling in the pipes died, so did the refrigerator's hum. We were still assembled, attending, when the wind caught up and the Frigidaire bucked and the sink discretely burped. "Just getting the bugs out," I crowed over the subtle racket.

That night we set the antiquated lantern aside and ate under a flickering bulb, macaroni and cheese and bread and oranges and very chocolate milk accompanied by the refrigerator's whirr and the drain's staccato hiccups, in concert with all that made society advanced, progressive, and good, or so it seemed, as by way of fickle windmill we tapped what was always rushing by.

That was the best day of a good time, passing, too. Clara and I sat up late, after the others went to bed, and discussed the women's progress. We were both optimistic, but when Clara Bow included Barbie in her summary of successes, I was somewhat surprised. As her enthusiasm escalated, I found myself offering more and more reservations, weighting my opinion, where there was always room for improvement, to try and keep hers soundly grounded. Then she said, "Joan looks fine," and this was so improbable that I stopped talking. In a minute, Clara Bow did, too.

We were sitting before the fireplace in silent reflection, when there was a creak on the stairs. Cathy, in her highly flammable finery and carrying gilded, high-heeled sandals, tiptoed down into the hall. We looked at her, she looked at us. On the pads of her feet, she made a dancer's exit, out the door. I started up, but noticed Clara settling. Her smile had seen life. "Human nature," she said, tipping one hand, then, "animal instincts," tipping the other, and I heard a car drive up, a flare of music, a door slam. Staring into the fireplace as if the fire that wasn't there had mesmerized her, Clara Bow, lately the righteous mistress of discipline, was so unmoved that I thought she must know something, so I said stupidly, "What's she up to?"

"Seeing someone?"

"It's against the rules."

"What can you do?" This, with a shrug of resignation.

Something, I said, we should. "Men are Cathy's problem," I reminded her. "She's *married* to *six* of them."

Clara said, "You can't expect it to work for everyone."

Not five minutes earlier, she'd been the one with the cheery prognoses. Now, as if that had all been desultory speculation and she'd tired of it, she burrowed into her blanket, burying a yawn. Then she flung the blanket back and, caped in it, staggering as if under its weight, she stood, announcing: "Bedtime."

In re the stagger, I said, "Are you all right?"

"Fine," she said. My surprise at her sharpness must have looked like doubt, because she repeated with force, "I'm fine."

Quickly I gathered in my glance. Clara Bow adjusted her wrap. I thought I'd stay up a while, I said, and she said, "Fine." There was something sly in her smile, a glimmer of satisfaction, as if she'd predicted—to whom?—that I'd wait up for Cathy, or maybe it was her idea. Watching her climb the stairs, a child queen dragging her weighty royal robe, I felt I'd been maneuvered into playing the disciplinarian again. This made no sense, unless Clara Bow wanted out of the onerous role, which hadn't seemed to trouble her much lately, or wanted to share it, or simply wanted to create dissension. That is, it made a sort of multiple choice of sense, with none of the options especially sensible either. I chose to think that Clara's recent overtures would lead to trust, and then every little thing like this would be clear. I waited and, waiting, I fell asleep.

Trudging upstairs in the predawn murk, I nearly tripped over her. She was sleeping in the hallway, belly down on her blanket, gripping the two wadded corners above her shoulders, like someone sledding. *(Fine.)* I picked her up and put her in her bed. As soon as her head touched the pillow, she popped up in a panic and looked at her watch. Then, noticing me (I was the one trying to wrench my arm out from under her knees), she lay back down and, as if she'd dreamed her hurry, stretched langourously and yawned and seemed to sleep. After sticking my neck out to note that Cathy hadn't come in, I dropped into bed in my grimy clothes and slept the apprehensive sleep of the shortsighted. When I woke up a few hours later, Clara's bed was empty, the sound of violent retching was coming through the window, and Cathy was standing over me announcing her plans to elope.

And so began the rapid decline of Women Abreast. But wasn't this the golden period? you're probably saying, and so was I. *"Elope?"* I said. "Who's throwing up?"

"Barbie." She added, meaning to be reassuring, I suppose, "Molly's with her." Meanwhile, it occurred to me that she'd approached me lying down for a reason, so I jumped out of bed, asserting my height and jolting my brain, which prompted me to call for support. Cathy said, "She isn't here."

"So what's this business about eloping?" I said, lightly, in case she might be inclined to forget it.

She said, "I didn't have to tell you."

"No, and I'm glad you did. That was very thoughtful of you. But what about the thing itself? Telling doesn't make it better."

What she made of this, I don't know, since her response was: "Joe's all right."

"Joe?" I said. "The fiancé? He's all right? Weren't the other ones all right? What about them? Let's forget that you're breaking the law. But what about all those other all-right types—and here you are. It's proof you don't want to make the same mistake."

Mention of the law made her sullen, and when I finished she said, "I didn't say I was getting married."

"Elope," I said. "That's what you said." She looked at me stubbornly, sensing, maybe, that she had a definition on her side. "So you're just going to drop everything," I said, "and move in with some guy you hardly know?"

"I *know* him."

"How? You've been here."

160

"That's the thing." Abruptly, flattening her tone, she said, "I didn't have to tell you. But I did. That's all," and turned to go.

"When?" I stopped her as she reached the door. "When are you planning to go?" Not answering or turning back, she stopped, the hesitant movement of her shoulders eloquent: she'd meant to say more. "Don't go away mad," I said, "and don't disappear. Why don't you bring your Joe to meet us?" At this, Cathy did turn around, her expression wary, as if I might want to discredit the man. "I mean it," I said. "Introduce him. We'll be your family. You might need one sometime. A family."

"I have one." That was an understatement. "I didn't have to come here either, you know." She paused again, not looking at me this time, then said that Joe would be by that night and if he wanted to come in for a minute, it was up to him, he was a free agent, and it was a free country. With that, she walked out.

Almost relieved at how plain Barbie's problem—still audible—was, I went down and out to her. When I cautiously touched her back, she bent in a fresh paroxysm. A few feet off, Molly was watching with an oddly irritated look which prompted me to ask her what was the matter. "She's a silly girl," she said and walked away.

"Silly?" I said to Barbie, who was quiet again. "Did she want you to go to the doctor?"

"No."

"Maybe you should."

Weak and red-faced and teary, she straightened and made a pathetic attempt at looking robust. "I'm OK now."

"At least come inside where there's a toilet," I said. "Look—you got your feet dirty." While she scuffed her toes in the dirt, I went and fetched some soggy toilet paper from the nearby birch dispenser, but when I bent to wipe her off, she shrank. I had to hold her ankle.

"I'm OK," she insisted, redder still.

"OK," I said, "but your feet are dirty and you can't go in with dirty feet." Tolerating my hand on her elbow and arguing all the way that she could've rinsed off at the pump, she let me lead her into the house and up to the bathroom, where we stood

161

together at the sink and waited for the rusty water to run. I asked her: "Flu?" She shrugged. "It's not food poisoning," I said. "No one else is sick."

"Clara Bow was." Splash.

"She was? Where is she?"

Bent to take a mouthful from the tap, Barbie tipped her head my way, "Maybe *she* went to the doctor," and drank.

Clara's voice came from behind me: "I did. I told you I had a condition."

"You said you were fine. Fine—that was the word."

"I am."

"So's Barbie. Just puking her guts out, that's all. And Joe, too. He's all right. He's the one eloping with a bigamist. But he's all right. And so is Cathy. Everyone's A-OK. We're in terrific, tip-top shape."

Barbie gargled through this, then patted her face and, eyes ahead, shouldered past Clara Bow, who was frowning at me in pinched perplexity as if I'd spoken in a foreign tongue. "Is something wrong?" she said. Then she swayed. I reached out to steady her, she flinched and held the doorjamb for support. "Can you trim my hair?" she said.

Waiting for my response, again as if she were afraid she wouldn't understand me, she put me off balance, too, so instead of critiquing her timing, I said I didn't know, I'd probably make a mess of it. "I guess I can cut it," she said, and, remembering how she'd looked last time she'd done the job, I said I would.

Sitting primly on the toilet while I made timid snips at her curls, the lush growth, she asked me to elaborate on my apparent panic. There wasn't much to tell. "So everything *is* fine," she said, when I finished. "Cathy's to be expected, Barbie has a bug, it's minor with me, and I'm being treated." She rose to look into the mirror. "Cut it shorter."

So far, I'd just polished, so I clipped a little closer. Still, Clara wasn't satisfied, and when I argued, she held her hand out for the scissors. This went on, the curls gradually disappearing and Clara Bow, with every glance at her reflection, looking brighter, less likely to totter, until she was almost as cropped as when I'd met her and, pocketing the shears, I refused to cut anymore. She wanted to be bald, it seemed, but when I said, "Lots of gray, look," she subsided and, even with some hair left on her head, seemed to feel better; and so, after the bartering over every quarter-inch and a few words about Cathy in between, did I. I sputtered some tap water on the comb and sprinkled the woman's shorn head, a blessing compliments of the windmill.

We would receive Cathy's beau in the living room. Clara Bow and I, as mom and dad, sat politely upright on the sofa, while Barbie occupied her fireside chair, back to the room, with Molly on the arm, bent with her head out of view to talk in low tones to her. In response to each of Barbie's murmurs, Molly leaned in further, until all that showed of her neck was one bony lump between her humped shoulder blades. Abruptly she uncoiled, rising, and crossed the room to stand by the sofa, just as Lynn wandered in with an unhappy face. She sat on the floor and built a little igloo of woe around herself. Instead of her customary name brand beer T-shirt, she was wearing a blouse of blue shot with tinsel.

Mary Belinda periodically interrupted whatever mysterious task kept her in the kitchen to look across the hall at us; Joan was indisposed; Cathy was dressing—or at least doing plenty of walking to and fro past the top of the stairs, each time sending a message of jasmine floating down; and that was how we were ranged and arranged when Joe came to the door.

I'd expected one of the logger types who frequented the bars where she must have met him, but Joe was the other type, the sort who sat off to one side and watched instead of played the game of pool and contributed the jukebox tunes that made the players roll their eyes. His shirt buttons were done up but for one and his hair, not long or short, was combed smooth and to the side (right) and his face wore the appealing look of someone who is always early no matter how hard he tries to be on time. "Let's see," he said and identified us, mixing up only Molly and Barbie, provoking a grimace from Molly, who fastened her attention on the library. Clara and I said at once, "Joe?" We laughed at the coincidence.

"Right," he said, and smiled, and we ran out of conversation.

When Cathy decided that our discomfort had lasted long enough and made her fragrant descent, Joe was nudging Lynn with his toe and asking her: Why so glum? She'd fallen asleep, but his prodding roused her, and she unblinkingly resumed her sulk with a reproachful glance in it for him, wasted, since by then Cathy had usurped Joe's attention. "We've all met!" he called up to her. She paused briefly, like a beauty contestant on a runway, so we could admire her dress, another flimsy pink number she'd been lucky enough to pack with her work clothes. The permed part of her hair was tied like a ball at the back of her head.

"Joe has been eager to meet you," she said, beaming around at us, a truly convincing performance until she got to Lynn and, like Joe but with more force, prodded her with her pointed shoe: "What's wrong with you?"

"Nothing."

"What? Do you want to come with?" This was Joe.

Lynn shot the rest of us a look that asked us to disappear. "Right," she said, low. "And be odd?"

"Odd? If you're going to be odd, I take back the offer," Joe smiled, pleased with his joke, but Lynn didn't.

"Oh, come on," Cathy said. "If she wants to be a baby."

But Joe persisted. "I think there's someone at George's who'd be happy to see you," he said to Lynn.

Amazed that in one week—or was it longer?—Cathy and Lynn had developed a social life elaborate enough to allow a third-party allusion like "someone," I sat bemused through the rest: Lynn's grudging acceptance of an invitation she'd been pining for all evening, her sudden fluster over how she looked and her flight upstairs, Clara's attempt at polite conversation during the long wait ("So you live around here?"). Then the lights went out. This gave conversation a boost. Out of the general exclamations came Cathy's voice, "Lynn probably tried to use the blow-dryer. She has no conception."

Joe said, I assume to me, "Your setup can't carry a blow-dryer? I happen to work at Bayfield Electric and—" but Cathy interrupted him, at Lynn's appearance, no doubt, since the next thing I heard was Joe's, "Nice to meet you," as he was hustled out the door.

"A nice man," Clara said.

Molly said dryly, "They're all nice."

An agreeable general hum followed that, then movement, the rustle, the shuffle, the creak, the sinking of the cushion beneath me as Clara got up. In the ensuing silence, a hollowing of the room, I thought I'd been left alone, but Barbie's voice, "Beauty?" didn't surprise me. A timid murmuring, it sounded like solitude speaking.

I said, "Yes?" but she hesitated, and when she finally asked, I was certain she'd switched questions on me. "Should I take some more food to the Cleavers?"

I said, "The Cleavers?"

"The kids."

"The *Cleavers?*" I said again; whose joke was that? "You never told me," I said. "How'd it go?"

"Okay, I guess . . . I took the milk."

"And?"

"I don't know. I guess they got it."

"You guess?"

"They were hiding, I guess. You know, like you said."

Clara disappeared for spells, Cathy eloped, Lynn saw "someone," and now Barbie kept a family secret. In a circle expanding and getting ever weaker at its center, where I was, this seemed like just one more ripple, so I didn't challenge Barbie. "Yes, go ahead," I said. "Take the *Cleavers* food." But already she'd stolen away and left me addressing that reflective ghost who'd murmured my name.

I sat there darkly for most of the night, doing an unscientific sort of analysis: if Joe disappointed Cathy; if I discouraged Lynn or,

we'd all been sitting on Cathy's bags—except Joan, who was sleeping—and as we stood and sidestepped and hefted and she fussed, Joe plunged into the fray with his hands out to help. Through the bustle, Clara Bow stood aside, attending. When Cathy bent near her to retrieve a cosmetic case, Clara put a hand on her shoulder. Cathy looked up, paused a second, bent again. Clara touched her shoulder. Cathy stood up with her case and said: *"What?"*

By then, this hitch in the general momentum had brought everyone's attention around. Now, at the center of it, Clara Bow unhooked her earrings, the diamond studs she always wore. In her extended palm, they twinkled. This time Cathy's *what?* was just a look, with a hint of *well?* "You wanted to borrow them," Clara said.

Cathy said, "So?"

"So, do."

"That was Thursday." Cathy shifted and said in a dubious voice, "I'm leaving now." She pointed her thumb at Joe's car, then, following the arc her arm described, swung around. Her cosmetic case bumped her thigh when she stopped abruptly and turned back to Clara, who was still standing with her open hand out. "WHAT?"

"Borrow them." Clara's hand inched closer to Cathy. "It's a custom. It means we'll stay in touch."

Cathy said, "We will?"

"It's symbolic." She tensed her arm and the diamonds jumped. "A parting custom. Would you take them?"

Molly and Gigi spoke at once. Molly: "Why don't you just give them to her?" Gigi: "I'll take 'em."

Joe, clearly a man who respected ritual leave-takings, had stayed politely out of this, lifting the luggage and bundles one by one from our arrested hands and carrying them to the car. When, at last, he relieved Cathy of the case, Clara Bow caught the hand he'd freed and folded the earrings into it. Joe's touch had reminded Cathy of her company manners. She opened her hand, admired the gems, and said, "They're real, aren't they?" Gratefully she backed away. "Thanks," she said. "Thanks, everybody."

"We didn't give you no diamond earrings," Gigi said. "Don't be an asshole."

I walked to the car and said take care as Cathy fluffed into the front seat, and off they went. When I got back to my bevy, Clara was holding the door open for all the insects that wanted in and giving Molly a rare look of disgust. "I had no idea you could be so obtuse," she said.

"Is it my fault it's a dumb custom?"

Lynn, still mistily watching the fading cloud from Joe's catalytic converter, said, "I think it's beautiful."

Gigi followed Clara in, saying as she passed me, "How you think some diamond earrings look on Lynn?" As the door closed on her, I heard her mutter, "beautiful," and snort.

"Obtuse," Molly said to me, pronouncing it as two words. Then, her gaze dwindling to Barbie, who was standing at my side, she said, "I'm the only human here who thinks with her head." Barbie shifted closer to me.

"Molly," I said, "why don't you go fishing? We're getting sick of pasta and beans," then, at a sharp look from Mary Belinda, "not that the pasta and beans aren't excellent."

Going in, Mary B. said flatly, as if to herself, "If it comes home like last time, someone else can cook it." She patted her helmet of hair.

"Someone else always cooks it," Molly said. "As I was saying." She pointed to her head, that lone wonder of cogitation. Since she'd lost Cathy, she adopted Lynn as her fishing apprentice, after first trying to draft Barbie, who, I argued, brought milk and eggs to the table and so shouldn't have to procure meat, too. Molly said ha ha.

As the fishers stalked single file into the woods, Barbie eased away from me. Then something caught her attention, and I looked: a few feet from Molly and Lynn's exit, a glint of buckle, a flash of hand, the red of a bandana. When my eye reached that, the red, it was ducking behind the fir the hand held, then dashing away. "Ex-member," I said. "Fully rehabilitated, as you can see." No doubt assumed dead, I must have been a surprise to the hunter. This imagined start went to my head, the notion of myself as risen, unkillable, and I laughed, feeling a brief affinity with the towering windmill, whose sails swept majestically through the choppy air. "Look at that," I said, and Barbie obediently did. Her pained, pink look was chastening. "Barbie, you're feverish," I said. "Will you go to the doctor? Or is he the problem?"

Still facing the windmill, she gave me only her oblique cheek to decipher; so I stepped around to see her better and noticed Clara Bow standing at the kitchen door. As soon as I saw her, she said, "Clockwork," nodding at the windmill.

"Some farewell," I said, "the epitome of PR," wasting time and wishing her away so I could get back to Barbie; but Clara Bow persisted. She sparkled. "Hey," I said. "Where'd you get those earrings?"

She touched a fingertip to an earlobe. "Standbys."

"How about that?" I said to Barbie, who smiled a perfunctory smile. "Had two pairs and wouldn't let Cathy borrow one."

"Maybe the ones she didn't want to loan her—oh nothing."

"Lend." I'd spoken low, and Barbie always did, and Clara, in her eagerness to hear but not appear eager, was tottering on the edge of the doorstep. After a few long seconds of silence, Barbie excused herself with a mention of Gretchen and Hans.

"Guess who I saw?" I said, going past Clara. A gunshot gave away the answer and brought brief silence to the kitchen, where Gigi had been jittering around, playing the cupboard doors and countertops and drying pots and pans like tympani.

"Like the Fourth of July," she said, and resumed her percussive tour, tempering her tune to a sadness that was like no July Fourth I'd ever had, then picking up tempo again, until I told her that behind the very cupboard door she was denting there were sacks of seeds which could be planted, remember? She'd been there when I'd bought them, at Ehlers, on our initial grocery binge. She took one of the little brown bags off the shelf and turned it over in her hand, remembered, yeah, but not the instructions. Back then when, between Frosted Flakes and Scot Tissue, seeds had struck us as something else our household should have, a woman had stopped in the aisle to explain the how-tos of late planting and hardy vegetables, though perhaps not this late or this hardy. (She was especially well versed on beets, so we had many sacks of beet seeds.) I repeated as much of her teachings as

I could recall, while Gigi examined the sacks one by one. When she proceeded out, frowning, I turned and found that Clara Bow had gone. Gigi yelled from across the yard, "I got to do this in the rain?"

Free of Clara, I went through the drizzle to the barn to hear what Barbie wasn't saying. She was sitting half in shadow, her legs stretched out in the milky light coming under the uptipped wall. As I ducked under the door into an ambience of rustle and cluck, Barbie said, "Is there hay here?"

I didn't know.

Could we get some?

I supposed.

"You have to," she said. "For winter." She laid a hand on Gretchen's flank, or was it Hans's, and in an uninflected voice said, "I didn't tell you everything. You know, in the park. When we applied. What I wrote—"

"We couldn't read much of it," I said, because she seemed embarrassed.

"You probably think I'm some dip who goes around—" Without looking up, she stopped, and I didn't have to look up either to know that Clara Bow was at the barn door.

I made a smooth pretense of continuity by saying apropos of hay, "Farmer Hecker mentioned grain." The only help I got in this attempt came from Clara Bow, who did a snap impression of someone who'd come to the barn expressly to discuss what our beasts and fowl would eat come winter; but Barbie didn't even pay attention, got up in the middle of this conversation meant for her and drifted to the door. As soon as she stepped out, Clara stopped talking. We sat there, not saying a word, while Barbie visited the hens.

Then she was at the door again, to say that she was going to find Molly and Lynn. Fishing was something she thought she should learn. We all should, I said. With a rod.

"What if I don't have one?"

Clara waited until Barbie walked away to say, "Why wouldn't she?" With that, she left me long enough to wonder what the girl, who less than an hour ago had cringed from Molly, was up to, then came back out, stopping to say as she went by that I was right, we should all learn to fish.

Remember that string of fish she'd trailed home a hundred years ago? I did, a minute later. I was being misled. And because everyone was out, and I was left alone, there seemed to be a plot afoot to make me paranoid. I ran inside and up the stairs and jacked my mattress up: no mail. There wasn't a hiding place in the room that someone smart or persistent couldn't be expected to find. The rest of the house, too, as I stood there reviewing it room by room on mental slides, seemed too bare, the furniture too sparse, the shelves and drawers too few and obvious to conceal anything. As I projected the kitchen, the real door down there opened and shut; I dropped the mattress, and was down the hall before it settled.

Barbie met me on the stairs. "Too rainy," she said. It wasn't any rainier than when she left. "Are you coming down?"

I said, "Did you meet Clara?"

No.

Unsurprised that Clara Bow was out in the too rainy woods to be met or missed, Barbie preceded me down. She took her fireside chair, tucked her feet up under her, letting one arm fall flat, palm up, on the cushion and holding it above the elbow with her other hand, a tense lock on the lax, as if she were gauging her own blood pressure. While she took her time, I leaned on the bookcase and inconspicuously turned each volume upside down, shaking loose only the introduction to animal husbandry.

"What I was saying," Barbie said, "I don't want attention—about the thing, the application—I knew right after I wrote it, that's what it looked like, I wanted attention, but that wasn't it. It was," she thought, and I had time to see that she'd started the conversation without me, back at the barn, "an answer. The reason we were applying—we had to say, you know. I didn't want sympathy." Her soft voice was flat, as proof. She squeezed her arm and curled the hand at the end of it, watching her fingers, then peered around at me, briefly. "The thing is, I was sticking to the facts, like what led up to it wasn't important." She looked me in the eye again and said, "I was an abortion," then returned to her flexing hand. I might not have impressed upon you how

173

infrequently Barbie spoke more than a sentence, if that. Then this. "I was. It was when my mom was mad at her boyfriend, so she banged against the wall and had me, I mean like a miscarriage, but on purpose. The lucky thing was, she knocked herself out and someone wondered what the banging was and found us. The landlord, she said." She freed her hand to flutter it. "That didn't bother me, because I was a baby. It didn't bother me later either, but I'm telling you because of the effect.

"You know how people say they feel like they don't belong. I was like that all the time. That was the effect. I lived in different places, sometimes with my mom because of welfare." She tilted her head and considered me over her shoulder, not sure I understood benefits. "Sometimes with her cousins or her boyfriends, and then with my own friends when they got places—that was after Mom stopped wanting me around her boyfriends—but I was always a pain." She looked again. "I was. When you're a kid people have to do things for you, and when you get older they still have to—give you food and stuff, you know. So I thought I had to make people like me enough to want me around. That was the boyfriend thing. That was how I made it till I was sixteen, when I got a job at the Sav-on and I could pay for things." Her hand fell flat. "There I was. I didn't have to make anybody want me. Except my boss, but that was different. That was the first time I thought about killing myself. It was like being an abortion all over again, if you know what I mean."

I admitted that I didn't.

"When I had to make people want me around, it was, like, something to do. Then I didn't have to. There was only me. I mean, being dead didn't seem like such a drag." She gave this sentence a cheerful little fillip.

When she peered over her shoulder again, her eyes slightly wider than usual, waiting, I said, "I want you around."

With a sweet smile of condescension, she said, "That was years ago."

"Still."

"I didn't want sympathy, I said. I'm telling you for a *reason*." Then the purposeful girl laid her exercised hand in her lap and looked at it and told me she'd found the secret of life.

Of course I asked her what it was.

174

She gave me another quizzical glance. "It's a secret."

I was still unprepared for what she'd already told me, let alone the news that life had a secret, one that might be found by Barbie, how to react?—so I only looked my most receptive, as I was, waiting for the denouement. She hesitated for a long time, then said with a sort of resolve, "I'm not really twenty-one."

Gigi came into the room and announced that the seeds were planted. When I turned to look at her, she said, "Duh."

"The seeds?" I said. "Already?" and she told me most of them had been "arranged," the rest making a random sampling, an experiment. Barbie used this distraction to get to the door where Gigi stood, her muddy hands spread, prophetlike. Barbie ducked under a raised arm, saying as she went that she was "just" going to give Hans and Gretch some water.

I wondered after her but most of me, the massive, was stuck with Gigi, who apologized broadly for interrupting and, after wiping her hands front and back on the seat of her jeans, sprawled in Barbie's armchair and, almost unassisted, conducted a conversation I remember only as interminable.

I was inching away from the bookcase, easing Gigi to a conclusion, when Clara Bow came to the door, took in the room with a quick look, and asked where Barbie was. Even standing still, waiting for an answer, she suggested movement. Her short wet hair was standing up in finger-raked furrows. I told her where, and she said, "No, she isn't."

"I don't think she came back in," I said. "I didn't hear her." Gigi hadn't either.

Mary Belinda hadn't seen her. Neither had Joan. Clara said, "She isn't fishing."

"I know."

"You do?"

"She came back. Too rainy."

It was coming down harder now, and sharp, and we were standing in it, side by side, looking into the woods where twilight already was. The rain's needlework covered me with gooseflesh.

"She didn't say she was going somewhere?"

"To the barn."

But she might have, that *rea*son. Knowing I wouldn't get an answer, I hollered her name into the woods. A jolly, mocking echo rolled back and Molly, lips still shaped in the grimace that ended Barbie's name, came strolling out of the shadow, attended by Lynn, who took quick, earnest steps to keep up.

As she approached, Molly raised her arms in a victory sign, dangling a beaten fish from each hand.

"Go upstairs," I said, "and pack your things. I'll give you a check for gas and whatever you need to get started. You're leaving tonight."

She didn't even ask why. She appraised me for a cool minute. Then she flung the fish into the mud. "I was right on the mark," she said. "That girl doesn't even know what to do with *herself.* You're the one who wants the kid, just the way you wanted us—getting out is fine with me, the sooner the better. I didn't need you to tell me to figure it out—you're just like everybody I thought I was getting away from. You're only bigger and worse."

Clara's hand caught my arm and held it at my side, and Molly, as if I'd meant to hit her, proving her point, smirked.

Clara said, "You'd better go."

"Hey." Molly raised her hands like someone at gunpoint. "I said I'm going. I was simply making a statement first. Independent people can do that." She looked deliberately at Lynn, at Gigi, at Clara, at me, then, making the same slow time she'd kept when coming out of the woods, she walked past us and into the house.

Gigi was uncharacteristically silent. Lynn still wore her earnest, lagging look. Clara's hold on my arm tightened for a second before she let me go, saying, with her toe tapping one of the fish, "We can't eat these. You two go in and promote some other dinner." Then she picked up the tapped fish and marched toward our landfill. I picked up the other and followed.

While Lynn and Gigi lingered in the yard, Clara waited. When they went in, she turned to me. "What happened?"

I'd expected something else, slightly more advanced, since Molly after all had said quite clearly, "the kid." However, I had to consider again the fact that the only man Barbie had seen since she'd been here, as far as I could see, was Dr. Abbot. Looking down at the trash heap, I said finally, "She scared Barbie away."

"What do you mean?"

"Just that. She scared her."

"How? And where's Barbie?"

"I don't know."

"Then how do you know?"

"Do you see Barbie anywhere? Did Molly deny it?"

"Deny it? You didn't accuse her."

"And I didn't have to, either."

Clara looked unsatisfied, so I told her what I'd seen lately of Molly and Barbie together. Her doubt shifted its focus. "Where would Barbie go?" she said, as if it were impossible for Barbie to go anywhere. "It doesn't make—" She glanced up. "I was thinking about what she wrote."

"She won't," I said. "She as good as told me so." As good as gave me a testimonial, as I saw things now.

Everything Clara Bow had said so far had a soft tone of speculation about it, a dullness that indicated how much of her mind was taken up with what she wasn't saying, but here our conversation and her concentration seemed to meet, and she said in brisk summary, "Then I'm sure she'll be fine."

The neat brusqueness of it made me stare. Clara sucked in her cheek and looked away. "What's that supposed to mean?" I said.

Waiting, I could see the corner of her eye, moving. Finally she said, "It means, she's managed before."

"Haven't we all?" This brought her face around. I raised my eyebrows: well?

"Managed," she said. "She's not the sensitive plant you think she is."

"How do you know what I think she is? Or if she's not?"

"I did some cursory checking in Chicago."

"You—when?"

"Before we left. A precaution. This is an investment."

"You what? Verified their stories?"

"Yes. If they were verifiable."

"Barbie's?"

"I filled in the blanks," she said. "Young girl, old story. It's not that I'm not sympathetic."

This chilled me, for myself, and for Barbie, what she'd presented to me, the unverifiable. For myself, I said, "Why didn't you tell me?"

"I didn't want to undermine your confidence."

In? At the sound of a sputter and chug in the drive—the Honda—Clara perked. "They'll be wondering," she said. After a token hesitation, in case I wasn't completely satisfied and might want to clear up a point or two, quickly, in view of our more immediate and pressing concerns, she started for the house, walking at such a clip that I, whose legs are legion, had to hurry to match her pace.

My explanation of Barbie's disappearance and Molly's dismissal didn't satisfy the others either, so I organized a search. I put, I mean, the women's curiosity into exhausting practice. Clara said she'd go "that way," pointing into the absolute dark, and would stop and ask the doctor if he'd seen Barbie. I suggested that Gigi go along, and Clara took a prolonged minute to acknowledge that this was wise. Mary Belinda, wiser still, refused to go out in the night, even when Clara offered her the lantern, earning a look of disgust from Gigi. Lynn had what she formally referred to as a "previous engagement."

With Clara and Gigi dispatched, I traveled north in the pickup toward the Cleavers' cabin. Driving, I was not so lucky as before and had to make a few passes before I found the turnoff, where I parked, and walked the rest of the way.

The cabin was as I'd found it before, apparently deserted, with one difference: the door was locked, not just blocked by a little girl. I stood at the corner for a long time, listening for a whisper, then went crashing away, advertising my departure. Silently, I snuck up again, but: nothing. "Barbie," I called out, "if you're in there—you can come back. Molly's gone. I know about—" I hesitated. "Everything!" I said. There was no echo in that forest where branches and underbrush crackled and hissed in the gusty rain. My words hung in the dense air. The only silence was in the cabin, and it was shut up tight.

The noise I made going this time wasn't for the children.

Clara and Gigi's report was negative, though it took a while to get to it, since Gigi had been so impressed with Dr. Abbot that, in view of his stature, she seemed to have forgotten Barbie. "We saw the monument," was what she said. "Hey," she squinted, turned her head to size me up sideways, her most acute angle, "he got to be as big as you are." Her long look gave this observation all the weight of a proposition.

Clara said, "He hasn't seen her since her last appointment. We took the path, and then we went along the river, but not a sign."

Mary Belinda, who'd been lumpishly silent through all of this, abruptly brushed the air with her thick hand and said, "I don't know why you went looking in the first place. That girl's not the kind to take off just so somebody'll look. And if she's not the kind, you won't find her."

"Yeah," Gigi said. "Particularly in the dark. *In* the rain." Then she shrugged and, as if answering herself, said, "Least it was something to do."

"So," Clara Bow said. "We were wasting our time."

"Maybe. Maybe not." Mary B. lifted her hand again but not so far and studied her palm with lowered eyes. "I didn't see anybody go looking for Cora."

I said, "We knew where she went."

Her eyes rose from her hand. "We did?"

"She went home."

This creased the woman's brow, as if the thought that had been coming at me, accusatory, had suddenly turned in. The reversal seemed to have tugged us along, since we sat watching, silent, as Mary Belinda thought, her concentration surfacing as a frown and then sinking again. Gigi jumped up. "Shit," she said. "Give me the creeps."

Mary B. smiled vaguely. "Barbie? The Lord takes care of that kind."

I snapped. "Oh, he's done a great job so far."

She lifted herself heavily, still wearing that mild smile, and said, "How do you know?"

I wasn't above retorting, "How do you?" but her lofty expression gave me the feeling she did. She took her knowing self upstairs and, after the creaking overhead had ceased, the rest of us went to bed, too, without supper.

An inventory:

An armed Kathy haunts the woods, *ours,* not any of the other miles of forest thereabout; we give her a sense of security.

Elizabeth might wallow in a sinkhole somewhere, but, more likely, flagged a Cornucopian and offered her flask and rode that rocky gin back to Chicago in a dream, from which she needn't wake, or extricate us.

Cora cooks stew for her husband, who, summoned by telephone to the bus station, studied her peaceful silence and has since come to suspect that he harbors the brainwashed victim of a cult more potent than his own.

Joe, a waning bachelor and never a very good one, pesters Cathy to marry him. For once she is reluctant, and this turns out to be a strange aphrodisiac.

The opposite of suicidal, Barbie quickens, playing meanwhile Wendy to the Cleavers' lost children. How do they live?

Molly stops at a house on Route 2 and tells its occupants that she has been held captive by witches, in the secular sense, which she defines. Over coffee she becomes disgusted with her audience's personal Middle Age—they don't need a doctor—and moves on, as far as her half-tank of gas will take her, a small town where she settles until she sees that she knows better than everyone there.

Lynn dates, weaning herself from Mother. For a few days, she will tend the cows and hens, imagining that in a rural community this might look good on her courting résumé, but she quickly learns that people in these parts count on their kin to tend their beasts, and so, throwing up husbandry, she scrabbles for a position as a waitress and considers the big tippers.

The garden won't grow to entertain Gigi.

Mary Belinda reflects on the case of Cora.

Joan—Joan is constant, the control if this were a test, the proof that nothing but displacement has been effected here.

I am, with tentative huge hands, milking the cow, as Lynn hasn't started her education yet, in fact isn't even up, out late last night. Clara peers in under the angled door and, seeing me, smiles. Her usual efficient way is softened as she approaches, dilatory, like a mother creeping up on a scene, I remember, and I bend my head and milk. A tremor in the beast tells me that Clara has put her hand on Gretchen's flank. I look up and her eyes flit from my hands to my face, and she smiles, meanwhile petting the cow's rump. The absent-minded gesture touches me, Gretchen the medium.

In my ungainly life, I'd missed friendship like everything else, through the tokens, the attributes of friendship that could be observed by an outsider. Now, however, I had the sense of missing and having at once, of seeing those outward signs as not the thing itself, but this. It was Gretchen's bad luck to be in my grasp the first time I recognized friendship and, in the grip of it, forgot my strength.

The cow tossed her head and did a frantic cha-cha backwards, upsetting the milk and butting Clara Bow, who sprang back laughing, her hands raised like a crossing guard's. "Whoa, Beauty."

I raised my hands, too: empty; and she laughed again, and so did I.

She'd come in to propose that I give her a swimming lesson. I reminded her that I was an unlikely teacher, but she'd thought it out, had considered the Y, and knew how peewees were handled:

held up by the instructor. She lifted an imaginary peewee, said, "I'll show you."

This would be a real end to the test—no more wading in over her head and calling out for help if she learned how to swim, and I made up my mind she would, if I had to hold her up for a week while she figured out the peewee's part.

Announcing a manager's retreat, we suited ourselves and instructed Lynn to graze the cows (How? *"How?"* I said. "Lead them to grass and encourage them to eat it. Nobody had to teach Barbie." She was a natural, Lynn said.) and, as if we'd discussed our route beforehand, walked in agreeable silence down the drive, up the road, the long way to the lake again. In the fall warmth, the road and woods were steaming out yesterday's rain. Clara turned to me suddenly. "What do you see up there?" she said. "You're smiling like an idiot."

"Air's thin," I said.

"Well, cut it out. You're making me nervous." I tried to be sober, but in a minute she looked up and said, "You're doing it again." Something besides my immense good humor was tweaking her, and seeing this made sobriety come easier. "Where did you look for Barbie?" she said.

I told her. Then I told her the rest: about my old haunt, finding the children, Barbie's errands to them. This was such a relief, I felt the obscure beginnings of Women Abreast burbling up, as if a confession of secrecy, of past dishonesty, made a sound foundation for trust. Encouraged by her close attention, I described the cabin in detail, feeling gifted, so many secrets in store. She interrupted: "There were five?"

"Five?" I'd been talking about the Skinner family vacations.

"Kids."

"The Cleavers? Yes, five—that I saw."

"And the oldest was a girl? How old? Would you say?"

"A girl, yes, fourteen or fifteen—I guess—why?"

"But you're not sure you saw them all?"

"Not *sure,* no, but—what?"

"How do you think they get by? Five of them, and the oldest fourteen. She can't work."

Her compulsion disconcerted me. I said, "I think they scavenge. And Barbie took them—" But I'd already told her that.

And she remembered, said, "But now she won't be. So we should." After a second of dumbness from me, she articulated deliberately: "Take them food. Especially if Barbie's there."

"I'm not *sure* she is."

"But you think so, don't you?"

"I *think* so, but—why, especially, if she's there?"

Slowing, she gave me a look painfully short of disappointment, bland, as though I could be counted on for density. "She's one of ours."

"You can't tell *who's* there," I said. "They hide. For all I know, they might not be—"

"But if they eat the food," she said, "we'll know." Then, reassuringly, "I'll go with you."

She went ahead so brightly, lightened, that when she stopped and turned to me, the dawdler, I said, "You don't want to go *now,* do you?"

She showed me her empty hands. "With what?"

At the lot that we'd cut through last time, she popped the sign with the flat of her hand and sang out, "Shangri-la!" When I caught up, she was standing on a wooden platform, cement-founded, that had appeared in the clearing since our visit. "Dance floor," she said.

"Altar," I said.

"You got gloomy in a flash. Come on," she danced off the floor, through the trees, toward the drop-off. "Drown your sorrows." And she jumped.

My heart took a leap, too, and didn't return to its cage until the splash cleared and Clara Bow yelled a healthy hurry up. Pressing that exercised organ with my hand, I leaned over the edge and asked for reassurance: "No wading?"

"God! Come on!" she yelped. "It's freezing!"

I wasn't going to make it any warmer. As the teacher, I had to set a good example, so I took the slow way down, toehold to toehold, hugging the wall until I felt the water with my foot, and then I cast off backwards.

When Clara crooked her arms and hiked her torso, like a child expecting a lift, the old dread came back, a shrinking, but with it this encouraging thought: If I dropped her in the water, she wouldn't be hurt, unless she breathed in the lake, which would be her fault. I braced myself and stuck my arms out like a forklift. Because, I guess, I grimaced, Clara splashed me and said, "Come on, I only weigh ninety pounds." Then, when I'd changed my expression to suit her, she waded around me, surveying, and said, "Get down, would you? This isn't the circus." So I bent my knees until my arms were water-level, waist-high to the little woman. She laid herself across them and squirmed into a comfortable position, grinding her bony hips on my forearms. To get her entirely into the water and weightless, I squatted lower. This provoked a paddling panic from my student. She spluttered and yelled up at me, "I'm not a submarine, either."

"All you have to do is turn your head," I said. "Lesson one: If your face is in the water, you won't be able to breathe."

She got down and stood a few feet off to say, "You can't throw me in the water and expect me to come up swimming. I'm too old for that." She was earnest, waiting to see if we'd reached an understanding.

"Clara," I said, "you're not going to drown in water that only comes up to your waist."

"I'm not worried about drowning."

"Well, what?"

Reluctantly she got back on board and went right into a clever imitation of someone doing the crawl, stalled. With Clara Bow absorbed in her stationary flutter kick and stroke and the cold water numbing my arms till they barely tingled at her throes, I observed her progress from a growing distance and, as a spectator, decided she wouldn't get anywhere unless she tried to float; so I lowered my arms a little.

She clawed the water and promptly sank. In her exasperation, as she righted herself, she implied that she'd been on the verge of mastering propulsion and now, thanks to my premature unpropping of her, would have to start all over. This she did, climbed grimly back onto my arms, which her thrashing paroxysm had returned to life. As long as they were awake, I held her up, but when the deadening set in, I tried to introduce her to floating again, with the same results. Again and again she got irritated, and back up.

The last time, it was unintentional. I'd got to thinking about what she'd said about that hand, the supporting one, how helpless she'd felt—a lesson—when it had tossed her up in the air pocket. I felt, not helpless, but a little shaken, in the shifting, no Beauty to be standing there without a Clara Bow to balance, and that was when I dropped her. She stood up slowly and, instead of spitting and glaring, wiped her dripping face with her wet hand and trudged into shallower water and sat down.

"Giving up?" I said.

The rocks rolled and wedged my feet as I waded and weren't any fewer or smoother where Clara was, so I stayed standing, lumpily poised. Under water from the neck down and heavily still, like a little old lady taking the cure, she sat slightly hunched, gazing at the wall of rock two feet in front of her. There was nothing interesting about it, a lot of rock. "Clara," I said; she jumped, and so did I, at my loud voice. I tempered it. "I didn't intend to be your friend," I told her. "I wasn't interested in charity, unless it started at home. Everything I told you was a lie. Except the part about independence, and I mean mine." She'd stared at me for a few seconds of this, then turned back to the cliff, in that old critical pose: the tilted head, the thoughtful frown, the undertow. "I wanted to live here," I said. "It was the only place I could think of."

"Why are you telling me this?"

"I changed my mind," I said. "And I want you to know, and it won't make much sense if you don't know the rest." She didn't move, didn't look, didn't say a thing. "I needed money," I said, "and I read about you in the paper, so I knew you were rich and I knew you were—vulnerable—and after I did some research I knew you were generous and I knew how—that's why I settled on this, with women. I tailored it to you.

"It wasn't malicious. It was just selfish. I always thought I was a freak, and I guess I am, but I didn't want to live like one, what I thought living like one meant, I mean, I wanted a 'normal' life.

"I have a husband. Max. Max Silverman. And I have children, two of them, twins, Timothy and William." I'd been going along breakneck, but here I hit the rough—how to proceed? "They're *babies*," I said, and Clara said,

"My *sister*," flat and peremptory, as if I'd interrupted *her*.

I said, "What?"

She looked at me now. "I mentioned my sister, but I meant sister-in-law. She introduced me to my first husband, her brother."

"Listen to me," I said. "They were tiny."

"She was dying. That was the introduction."

Clara hadn't suddenly gone deaf or crazy. I'd only opened my mouth again to ask her (what?) when she blurted, "Beauty," then softened. "You don't have to tell me."

"I—"

"Let's get out of the water." *(Want to.)* She sprang up and started for the rock islet. My *why?* was drowned in the splash she made falling face down on the water. She was trying to swim, but her feet quickly sank, and then the rest of her, and then she got up and waded, pushing the water ahead of her as if she were annoyed with it. Behind, I was bewildered, with a momentary stranded panic; I'd told her too much, and not enough. Then I saw it, the solution: She already knew. She'd known from the first. After all, she'd verified everyone else's story—so why not mine? *I* was *her* project, and a success, as I'd proved by telling her as much as I had, which, in that case, was enough.

She was trying to scale the rock, but her climbing wasn't any better than her swimming. When I reached her, she was humped, holding onto an outjutting and walking in place on the slime right above the water line. I grabbed her foot to give a boost, but she didn't let go of the rock, kept pumping her legs as if she hadn't noticed my hold on her ankle. "Let go," I said.

"You," she said. "I can get up."

"You might die of exposure first."

As soon as I loosened my grip, she scrambled up, without a single slip, like a little animal who'd shaken off a trap. By the time I hoisted myself up after her, she'd already resumed her calm, assumed her Buddha pose, looking out on the lake. "Why don't you want to hear?" I said, the wounded animal now.

186

"It's not that I don't want to hear. I don't want you to tell me."

"Same difference."

"No."

"Why not?"

"I'm happier—"

"You wouldn't be. You didn't let me—"

Her head jerked around like a marionette's. "You think I don't know what makes me happy?" I must have looked miserable, because she said, the snap out of her voice, "I believe whatever you were going to say."

We sat there in silence, my grand plan for sealing our friendship dwindling to a feeble wish to save whatever was left of the day. Feebly, I suggested a second installment in her swimming lessons, and when that earned a moue, tried, "Weren't you going to tell me something?"

She said, "If you're still interested."

I hadn't been interested then, but now I was dying to hear, anything.

"I already told you most of it," she said. She seemed to be waiting for a word from me, but I didn't know what to say. "I told you about Ray," she said, "how he visited me in the hospital. That second time, when he was sorry he'd 'upset' me? He asked me, was there something he could do? Someone he could contact? Family? Friends? Well then, was there anything I needed? He could get it, he said. Tell him what. Tell him where."

This was not the mournful man who'd sat by her bed in the first installment, but the desperation was still there, transformed into solicitousness. Clara Bow gave him her keys, and when he left she asked the nurse: What about his sister? The nurse could not give out that information.

The man came back concerned. Her power had been shut off, and what, he wanted to know, did she eat? Mayonnaise and frozen pie crust, no good now anyway? In short, he did find something he could do, to "repay" her; he picked up her hospital tab and took her home and didn't once mention his sister, but guess whose room she, Clara, had then.

"You married him," I said.

"You know that."

"And his sister died."

"That night."

"That night?" I said.

"The night it happened. And he adopted me. He'd supported Sarah. Then he supported me. She'd lived there. Then I did. There was never a word—I'm talking about the way he courted me."

"Appropriated you, you mean."

"I guess, but you make it sound—"

"What?"

"Like a plot, which it wasn't. It was more like a rescue—me with my outburst and mayonnaise and no electricity."

I said, "It *was* a rescue."

With an impatient movement of her hand and her lips pressed, a breath, she told me, "Don't forget whose insurance card got me into the hospital in the first place. I never needed rescuing."

"Isn't that a rescue? The insurance?"

"No, if it weren't that, it would've been something else, and I'd've been fine. There's always something." As if she'd heard this, instead of said it herself, Clara tilted her head and frowned. "I was rescuing him," she said. "That's the point, isn't it obvious? I was replacing his sister. We blurred in the hospital for him, or on the beach, because he couldn't be there. He couldn't know, but I could—I was his way of knowing, as long as he didn't admit it, and he didn't. I said he didn't mention it. And that was an admission.

"It was the same with every one."

Every?

She named her husbands. Not exactly the same, she said, but they'd needed her, and she'd loved them for it. Simply that; she raised her hands, palms up, as if to say: What else? "It's a kind of power," she said. "People have to give it to you. And it got me every time. Someone needed me, and I turned out to be the worst possible thing that could have happened to him. You know what happened, every time." It wasn't a jinx, she said. It was punishment.

Maybe she deserved it, I said, but come on, what could she do: with *cancer? accident? crime?*

Nothing, she said, that was her point, until she saw: she could stay away.

All along I'd wondered what she was getting at, and now to find it was a point that I was supposed to have got long since— this was vaguely irritating. I mentally deployed my arguments against her faulty logic, but when I opened my mouth to marshal them, a whispering fly bussed my lip, and the point I finally got was stay, not *away* but *stay,* and closed my mouth, flicking the fretting bug.

I wanted to return to Mother, then, go home, but hesitated to disturb Clara Bow, who was sunk in silence, mourning, I sup- posed. The fly lit on her hand, and she jerked her arm. She blinked, with me again, and smiled. "I was determined to stay away from anyone who needed me," she said. *"Determined."*

The tone, the tense.

She said, "Do you know why Barbie ran away?" She had an idea, it seemed, but wouldn't look at me.

"She's pregnant," I said. "No wonder she had to see the doctor so much, hunh? They like to get involved in the early stages, you know, doctors. And Molly, I'm sure, was pressuring her to have an abortion. You said you knew Barbie's past?"

Clara had stood up slowly. "Why did you bring that up?" she said, so soft I had to strain to hear.

"You mean the doctor? Weren't you worried? It seemed apropos."

"It is," she snapped, "I knew that." Sweeping the lake, her gaze only brushed me, flitted away. "You don't understand any- thing."

I thought I understood *everything.* "Wait," I said, as she started climbing over the edge of our island. "I was only thinking of," she dropped into the water, "you." A woman should know.

I looked down from the rock. Clara was swimming. She sank, stood up, shook off the water, and plunged in again. The third time she came up, I shouted down: "More lessons?"

She stared down at the water, as she'd done before each surface dive, and I wasn't sure she'd heard me. Then she said, "No. Let's go home." And, shoving the lake out of the way with the heel of her hand, she started in.

On our way up the cliff, I hoped she would fall so I could

catch her and she would know I meant her well; but Clara Bow was surefooted. So we walked, shivering dry in the late lukewarm breeze, taking turns lagging and leading, startling each other with warnings of "watch out" and "ouch" and "look," to which we each reacted with the broad abruptness of gentlemanly mimes.

This is the twilight picture of home that greeted us: windows bright, windmill cranking, Lynn posing with a cow in front of the barn, her hand on the animal's sullen head. She smiled all the while we walked up the drive.

At the sound of a stirring in the kitchen, I mentioned our grocery status, low again, to which Clara Bow responded flatly, "We have two cows." Matter-of-fact as a butcher, she was.

I said, "You're not mad at Barbie?"

"No," she said, "I'm grateful to her."

"Then don't get bloodthirsty. Those are sacred cows. Hey," I shouted at Lynn. "What're you doing?"

The cow raised her head and Lynn, arm still extended, took a dainty step back. "See?" she said. "She likes me."

"Did she give you some milk?"

"As a matter of fact . . ."

"As a matter of fact?"

"No."

"No? Milk that cow," I said. "She's probably in pain."

Clara Bow said quietly, "You milked her this morning."

"Not that one, I didn't," I said. "I milked *Hans.*" We looked at each other in mild surprise.

And I was right. Later, when we were sitting down to a

dinner of macaroni and cheese drab with the morning's unpurified milk, Lynn carried in a sloshing pail, Gretchen's contribution, which had cost the new milkmaid something, it seemed, since her cheekbones were webbed with weepy mascara. I asked her why she was wearing mascara.

"Beauty," Clara said, her tone a reprimand.

Lynn looked from Clara Bow to me. She said, "I like to look nice."

She looked like a fright, but I didn't say that. I said, "We like you fine without."

Dabbing her lips with the corner of her napkin, Clara got up, murmured, "Excuse me," the hostess of old, and led Lynn by the elbow into the living room, where the two of them conferred in low voices until their dinner was cold. My attempt to eavesdrop was baffled by Gigi, who wanted to know what we'd decided, and it took me a minute to figure out what she meant, the purported business meeting. She demanded results. Finally my makeshift answers aborted her somewhat peculiar eagerness for executive action, and I was left to listen undistracted, just as Clara and Lynn concluded and returned to their congealed macaroni.

We were all silent. Clara Bow lowered her fork and raised her eyebrows: what? Gigi was idly watching her own long fingers shredding a paper napkin. "What did we decide today?" I said.

"Decide?"

"Our meeting."

"Meeting?" She frowned. "Nothing," she said to everyone. "This is a democratic body." Gigi snorted and pushed back her chair, scattering confetti. "What?" Clara said. "What's to decide?"

With a roll of her eyes so stupendous it would've shaken a smaller brain, Gigi left the room, Clara Bow saying, "Now wait—" She turned to me. "What was that about?"

"She was like that all day." Lynn carried her plate to the sink. "Driving me crazy."

I thought of Cathy, and so did Clara Bow, apparently, since we said at once, "Was she picking on you?"

From the stairs, Gigi pronounced: "No."

Lynn lowered her voice. "I was grazing the cows." She paused for a smile of self-approval. "And she came and *watched* me. What was I *doing?* I told her. Watching the cows. What were *they* doing? I told her, nothing, they were grazing. And she went away acting disgusted."

Clara gathered the remaining bits of napkin into a little hill. "Something must be bothering her."

"What?" Lynn said, stopping at the door. "Nothing's bothering her. That's what's bothering her, nothing."

I was the first to recover from Lynn's unexpected insight. "It's probably the season for theft," I said.

Clara said, "Beauty," a caution again.

"What? What were you two talking about?"

With her eyes on Mary Belinda, who stood at the sink, her broad back to us, Clara Bow suggested we adjourn to the living room. "Why?" I said. "We're all family."

"A *small* family," she said. "About to get smaller, I think."

"She wants to leave?"

Clara nodded. "Not that she said so. But she might as well have."

"That guy?"

"I think so." She was terse and intense, as if we were two operatives in danger.

"So . . . ?" I said. "Isn't that good?"

"Good?"

"Clara," I said. She *knew* this. "Everyone's leaving. And if they're not better off, at least they're not worse off. That's pretty good. It's not *bad.*"

"What about—" The question came as fast as a reflex, but slowed. She said, "Women Abreast?"

"We'll start over. We'll do better." She glanced at the table. "You don't think so?"

She looked me straight in the face and said, "Sure."

"What is it?"

"Is what?"

"The matter?"

"Nothing." After giving me a minute to guess, wrong, she told me it wouldn't be fair, it wouldn't be right, to let the women wander away if they were only "no worse off." We should try to keep them around, *sustain* them, she said, and wasn't it late? Wasn't I tired? She was. Swimming did her in.

★   ★   ★

I went to sleep reviewing likely explanations for this, Clara Bow's new attitude, as I saw it: (a) after my partial confession, she was afraid to be stuck here alone with me; (b) after the other part of my confession, of sincerity, she wanted to make Women Abreast work; (c) since I'd tarnished the doctor, she had to regroup; (d) all of the above, so when I woke up and found her bed empty, my confusion promoted a stomachache that demanded immediate medical attention. I'd never believed a word of those midnight walks, except the insomniac part, which a doctor could address. I was up and halfway dressed before I stopped myself, stalled on the unfamiliar moral territory of friendship. If I begrudged the doctor his chance to answer Clara Bow's doubts, then her doubts meant less to me than her company—meant, I mean, that I didn't mind winning her company by default, preferred an unhappy Clara Bow to an absent one. Would a real friend feel like that? Want the man her friend wanted to be the shit I was convinced the doctor was? I asked myself and answered, I don't know, and went back to bed exhausted.

When I dragged myself downstairs, Gigi and Lynn were sitting at the kitchen table, and Gigi greeted me, "Well?"—with bite. I was moving too slowly for her. She said, "You on the rag, or what?"

Interpreting her "Well?" I admitted that I didn't know what there was to do. Lynn, who'd been listening absently, got up to go out and tend the cows. Gigi stood. Trailing her fingertips along the table's edge, she looked at me sidelong and said we could get a TV. I took too long trying to read the way she'd sidled up to the suggestion—"get" by legal means?—and she dropped her hand so hard it made my elbow jump, then snatched it away like an offer retracted and without a word went after Lynn.

Clara Bow was still not home, and the circumstantial nature of my case against the doctor, Barbie's alleged condition, was beginning to look like such a big mistake, self-incrimination if the man turned out to be above reproach, sure to win me, instead of a friend at home, a wary neighbor, one more wary neighbor than I already had, that is, that when I answered a knock and found the very doctor at my door, I thought this was it.

Then, stepping into the small kitchen, a tall man, he said,

"Where's Clara?" And, suddenly, nothing could have been more absurd than his commanding tone.

"Clara?" I said. "Did she have an appointment?"

The man treated me to one of his pauses, a margin for error, then said coolly, "Do you mind if I call her?"

"Go ahead," I said. I was cool, too, and he didn't call. Instead, he took another look around the kitchen, and, when his gaze came back to me, asked, "Where is she?"

"Out. Would you like to leave a message?"

"No. I'll wait."

"Fine."

He seated himself elegantly, a slow and unfussy arrangement, as if about to watch a play—which would be staged in the corner to the left of my shoulder. Just as I was wondering whether he could hold that pose until Clara Bow came home, then wondering where she was, the doctor's hand shot out and pinned my wrist to the table.

His abrupt move, the scuff of the chair, covered Clara Bow's approach. She stopped outside the screen door, looking like someone who might've gotten the wrong house. "Where is she?" Dr. Abbot said, his tone, like his grip, not sharp but stern.

"Right behind you."

He held my hand hostage while he swiveled to see for himself. Clara had had a minute to prepare, and when the doctor turned, then rose, she became a busy woman, who, as she breezed by, hardly had time to brush us with a smile and, "I can't talk to you now, Frank."

He said, "Wait." Hurried, she hovered at the foot of the stairs. The doctor held out his hand. "What's that?" At "that," I noticed the transistor radio she was holding. What interested Dr. Abbot was the tangle of wires, one coiled around a couple of pennies, that protruded from the open battery compartment. Lifting the weighted coil with one finger, he said, "Did you do this?"

"No." She gathered in the radio. "I have batteries." Before he could speak, as he was clearly about to, she got back to the stairs, under a patter of pleasantries, she'd talk to him later, would try to stop by, and sprinted up.

I was pleased to see the man nonplussed. My moment of silent gloating was cut short, however, when he swung around and said curtly, "I didn't hurt your hand." We both looked at my hand, caught indeed in the middle of an injured act, flexing. I flattened it on the table. "Did I?"

Walking overhead, Clara crossed my "No." I said, "No," again and then, when the doctor still seemed not to hear, "I'm sorry," and for an instant was, the man so dumbly attentive to the silence above.

But he came around sharply. "For what?"

I retreated into a polite nothing, sorry he hadn't had a chance to talk to Clara Bow, and he hmm'ed and headed for the door before I finished. We heard a step. He stopped, the door ajar. Sweetly I said, "Perhaps you'd like to stay?" And he was gone.

Clara's quick step on the stairs told me that the monitoring had been mutual. "What was that?"

"Which that?" I said.

"Every time I find you two together, it looks like extortion," she said. "That."

"So why didn't you do anything?"

"You're a big girl."

"I don't think extortion is the word you want," I said. "Inquisition. That's the mode. He thinks he knows something."

"What?"

"What? You tell me."

She was confused, but then, clearing, concerned. "It's nothing I've said. If that's what you mean." Carefully, balancing a thought, she sat down in the doctor's chair and for a minute pressed her folded hands against her frowning lips. Opening her hands as if to conduct her words, she said, "He underestimates me."

"You?"

"He thinks I'm weak." I wasn't arguing, but she said, "He does. Why else would he worry about—" and she closed her hands abruptly.

I suggested: "Me?" I read her bland expression as a yes. "He'll see," I said.

"You think so?" Her eyes wandered. "I found the cabin. No one's there." I'd just had time to catch up when she added, "The Cleavers. Deserted."

"Wasn't it locked?" I asked, then remembered the radio.

Not a sound in the house, but Clara Bow harked. "Where's Mary Belinda?"

Of course our breakfastlessness should have been a clue, but I'd been preoccupied. After a clattering tour of the bedrooms, Clara shouted for the shepherdesses, who, like me, needed only to hear the question to notice the answer: gone. "What?" Gigi said, with enthusiasm. "Something happen to her?"

Clara hesitated, hung her hand on the bib of her overalls, and with patently false nonchalance assured the women, "It's all right. Just go back to work."

Assessing Clara sideways, Gigi hovered. "What?" she said, meaning "elaborate," and Lynn stopped at the door.

"Really," Clara said. "It's nothing to worry about." She filled the kettle, lit the burner, then, glancing up from her match and discovering Gigi, said, "Well?"

Gigi looked at me. I shrugged. This was enough for Lynn, who left, but Gigi lingered for another minute, watching for a sign that things would become as interesting as Clara Bow seemed to be suggesting they might. When none came and she went out, too, I looked at Clara, the little woman attending the kettle. She turned around: "What?"

" 'What?' Why'd you do that?"

"What?"

"You know nothing happened to Mary Belinda."

"No I don't."

"Were her things upstairs?" Her silence this time meant no. "She made a deliberate exit," I said, "and you know it. She's been on the verge for days. And now you've got those two thinking something's wrong."

Clara Bow stamped her foot. This, I swear, the woman did, and snapped, "Something is." Then, "Now maybe they'll think twice before sneaking away."

"No they *won't*," I said. "They know Mary Belinda can take care of herself. It's sure to occur to them. It's why she came here. Why they all did, opportunists. They're opportunists. And when the opportunities look better somewhere else, they'll go."

"Oh, just like that."

"What else?" I said. "Who's left? Three out of ten, and one barely counts."

Then Clara Bow Cole said, "You're not counting me."

I was still absorbing the full impact of this as Clara started up the stairs, murmuring, "I'm not an opportunist."

"I wasn't talking about you," I called up after her.

"That's what I mean," she shouted back, "exactly what I mean," and the kettle began to whistle.

I went at once to our two representatives in the field. I praised Lynn's grazing. I gathered Gigi and took her to town, where we bought a television, fertilizer, three quarts of oil, five gallons of house paint (yellow, her choice), brushes, a sewing machine, and yards of the fabrics that she liked or thought Lynn would like or said looked like Clara Bow.

did my belated best, but my earlier efforts, my original plan, founded on the principle of failure, were well on their way now, independent of me, and Women Abreast, like an Andy Hardy movie where not getting the show staged would mean no sequel, the end of everything familiar, briefly became a place of desperately cheerful industry.

Clara Bow greeted every suggestion with what I might justifiably call acclaim, then settled down to each project with indiscriminate seriousness. Unfortunately, Gigi and Lynn, as the last salvageable remnants of Women Abreast—besides Joan, who was resting—had to bear the full burden of Clara's enthusiasm. For instance:

Gigi was painting the house. This was her new occupation, not urgent, not really even necessary, but legitimate and just demanding enough to keep her respectably busy and at the same time allow her to watch through the window Phil Donahue and "All My Children," two sources of great satisfaction for Gigi. But when Clara Bow set up a ladder alongside her, studied her technique, then began to paint, too, pausing after every few painstaking strokes to refer to the master's methods, Gigi couldn't help but look a little closer at this exceptionally interesting work she seemed to be doing. Grand attention belittled the homely ef-

199

fect, even Phil could not sustain this scrutiny, and Gigi soon enough dropped her brush into her bucket, saying, "You like it so much, you do it."

While Clara was still clinging to that job, I tried to interest Gigi in sewing. Now she was wary, however, an artist not about to be patronized, and at first looked on with folded arms and angled face as I instructed her. The intricacies of cutting a pattern and piecing it together and my expertise—one skill my size had forced upon me, after all—with interfacing and armholes and pleats gradually impressed her and, though she was also wary of revealing anything besides skepticism, I could see that competitive gleam starting to glow in her sly eyes.

When the windmill failed us, she erupted and slugged the powerless machine so hard I thought our sewing days were over. I went downstairs to wait out the blackout and give her time to simmer and, in a few minutes, heard the machine humming. Returning to the sewing room, I found Gigi examining her first buttonhole, testing it with her finger. When she noticed me, she gathered the cloth around her hooked finger and pulled, until she lined up the next x'ed spot.

Then it started to rain. The sound on the window was sharp, insistent, and I knew that Clara Bow, the painter, would have to come inside. I headed her off in the kitchen. She took a step back, put her hand on the door. "Do you know what that is?"

"What?" I said.

"Snow." She said it as if snowing were a crime against her. "It's snowing."

Mostly afraid she'd find a way to oversell sewing to Gigi, keyed up for action as she was after three days of excruciatingly neat painting, I took her word on this atrocity of the weather and began to outline steps we could take to meet winter, but, as if I hadn't said a word, she interrupted me, incredulous, "And the garden's just starting to sprout."

I had mentioned firewood for us, grain and hay for the cows, and Clara was suggesting that we go to Bayfield to buy Burpee packets so we could use the pictures on them to identify the few doomed shoots that had broken our soil. At first I thought this was one more misguided step in her courtship of Gigi, who was no more attached to her seedlings than she was to the wind-mill she'd helped erect or the cows she'd kidnapped, but when she stopped speaking—a low, compressed way she'd developed lately, as if improvising from necessity—and stared past me for a second, out the window, I realized with a funny pang that this indeed was Clara's way of confronting winter.

It was even clearer when, after our trip to Bayfield, she took those Burpee packets to the patch and, without involving Gigi in the identification, staked them to the plants she thought they pictured, markings carefully set out in the last light on a muddy island in the middle of the matted, shapeless yard, like little makeshift tombstones.

This was a blue night for Clara Bow, the first of a few. We were sitting fireside in what seemed to me companionable silence, when I looked up from a hem to find her stiffly upright, ankles crossed, fingers laced, eyes focused on nothing. "Clara?" I said and, as she made the slight shift of focus from nothing to me, asked her if anything was wrong. Her answer—no, nothing, why?—was sharp, so I subsided, but then my silence seemed to irritate her as much as the question. She snapped out of her trance again to accuse me of staring at her. Unobtrusive as I tried to make my presence, after a few still minutes she asked what was the matter with me.

When this happened again, and sensing the restless pause that preceded the stiffness, I tried to leave as the mood brewed, Clara asked where I was going—asked as she might a stirring child who'd been told to stay put. After a while, I was stiffening at the first hint of a shift from Clara's chair, and the moods seemed to be mine, not hers.

My concern about her and Gigi was unnecessary, not because she'd learned a thing from her painting lesson but because she'd already done in the sewing by providing us with the pattern. It was a piece of *Vogue* artistry she'd picked up in Duluth in her immediate enthusiasm over our acquisition of a sewing machine; her eye was uncanny.

Like all *Vogue* patterns, this one was a challenge, which Gigi and I met with the available wool instead of the suggested taffeta, an exercise, as I saw it and assumed anybody would, since nothing could have been more remote from clothed reality than the woman sketched in stark style on the packet that enveloped the pieces. And almost any dress without a body in it, particularly a severe dress, is not especially impressive, so when this one was put together, laid on the bed, awaiting hemming, it did look like a Home Ec project, flat and plain and earnest with accomplishment.

Prepared to pin the hem, I was growing impatient with Gigi, who, instead of putting on the dress, was going about meticulously folding the scraps of fabrics scattered around the room, and I had to watch her refold a few of these useless remnants before I finally saw that she wanted to be left alone. This was disconcerting. Gigi was not body-modest, could be seen most mornings in the hallway wearing nothing or almost, and the little vanity she had she guarded carefully, concealed her pride in nonchalance, so that a casual change and bored tolerance of my help would have seemed to suit her here. The clearer it became that she wasn't going to try on the dress until I left, the stranger this seemed, and I was reluctant to go. But when she gave me one of her disgusted looks and roughly picked up the sewing project, I got out of there.

While I was waiting, Clara Bow came to the foot of the stairs and asked what I was doing. Head cocked to consider, she said I looked as nervous as a bridegroom.

"That's ridiculous," I said. "Bridegrooms aren't nervous anymore."

Gigi froze when I opened the door. As if her arm were being twisted by an invisible imp, she had her hand awkwardly at her back, the dress already half-unbuttoned, and on her face an expression even more disgusted than the one I'd left. Since there was no mirror in the room, I don't know what she thought she looked like, but from my vantage point the dress was ridiculously right for her. The rich, winy red of the wool brought out a rose in her skin, and the cut, with neckline draped shoulder to shoulder, waist cinched, skirt shaped softly to her hips, made the fineness of her bones as obvious as the bones themselves had always been. Her pose enhanced the dress's effect, the tilt of her chin and the angle of her twisted arm giving her figure a look of gawky, instructive defiance that was real and nearly regal.

Then there was her hair, plaited and left so long that the braids were hardly discernible through the frizz. And her feet were bare.

"You look great," I said, "a beautiful job." She stared back for a second, pitying me my pointlessness, since this was an exercise after all, this sophisticated costume, nothing she would ever wear. At Clara's step behind me, Gigi dropped her eyes and sank into her usual sulky posture and jerked free the button in her hand.

As her parting gesture, she stole the truck. Clara Bow woke me with the news the next day. By the time I was sensible enough to understand what she'd said, she was pacing, coming blindly at the bed as if she'd bump into it, abruptly halting at the edge and, after a blank second, executing a neat about-face, while she waited for me to get up and go with her to the police.

On a turn she caught sight of me, awake but not roused, and burst out in wild exasperation, "She's in Kansas by now."

I said, "I don't want to go to the police."

She stared at me for a still moment, then said, "Do nothing?" This was a guess, and instantly she was reasoning. "What's that going to solve?" she said. "She's the same kleptomaniac she was to start with. *Except,* she's a felon. And she was a felon to start with, too, did you know that?"

"I gave her the truck."

"You didn't." She wheeled and resumed her pacing. "She knew we'd give her whatever she wanted. No one else would've. She wasn't used to—do you know what it was? What did it? That dress. That dress gave her ideas." She stopped midstep.

I said, "Did she take the dress?"

With her back to me, Clara snapped, "You know she didn't."

She turned haltingly and crouched down with her hands on the edge of the bed by my pillow, her head bent. "It's such a simple thing," she said, "just living here." Raising her head but not her eyes, she picked up a lock of my hair that was hanging over the edge of the bed and smoothed it across her palm, as lightly as if she were comforting it. "I'm sorry," she said. "It's too bad."

The mood was upon her, so, except for a lame "it'll be okay," I didn't know what to say. In a minute she said, "Joan won't leave."

"No," I said. "But I don't know whether I'd call her 'here.'"

"No . . ."

"Why don't we regroup and—"

"We." She let go of my hair as if it had burned her. "This was your idea," she said. "Why don't you do something?"

I got out of bed.

L ynn had a more malleable self than Gigi. Somewhat Silly-Puttyish, it was shaped by the people and things and free-floating ideas it bumped into, not through opposition or synthesis as some selves are, but through accommodation. This was clear in the way she took direction from Cathy, then Barbie, then Clara Bow, but clearer as she watched TV. She didn't choose shows or change channels or make a point of catching certain programs. She watched whatever appeared when she turned on the set or found it running, and, regardless of subject, actors, or plot, she watched with a simple and sincere belief, not in the events that were being portrayed, but in television, which existed to entertain her, so she was entertained. Commercials received as much sober attention from her as anything else, and I believed that, given a blank check and told to purchase one of every type of item in a supermarket, she would fill her shopping cart with whatever brands she'd most recently seen advertised.

Because her conviction was so complete and so momentary, I knew Clara's tactics would work better on her than they could've on Gigi and would eventually fail, since Lynn would still be malleable, Lynn would be Lynn. Clara Bow attended her so closely that there wasn't room for me to do much more than watch, and wait for something to go wrong. It did during Clara's last doctor appointment. The woman was still disappearing—oh, those moods—for hours at a time, and this, the doctor's, was where I guessed she went, at any rate.

She'd become Lynn's best friend, her counsel and confidante while they taxied off to shop, did housework, carried wood, tended the cows, and during her extended absences I tried to fill in for her, lumping along and looking agreeable while Lynn went from task to task as if they were devotions. Listening to a minute description of a cow's digestive process, cribbed verbatim from one of my grossly overdue library books and delivered as narration by Lynn as she milked the exemplary beast, I was amazed by Clara's artfulness, her studied appeal, the lengths of her patience when she was pressed. Lynn looked up and said with a smile of wonder, "That's where we get the word ruminate." I smiled my own wonder and knew that I was a poor substitute, but didn't mind, as long as Clara Bow would come home soon and relieve me.

Then Cathy visited. She was dressed as well as any of the lucky women Lynn admired in soap operas—but the pavonine dress, the long, painted nails, the high heels, the bracelets tinkling silver charms, all advertising leisure, were nothing compared with Cathy's carriage, how she smiled, sleek. With a sweep and flutter of skirt she appropriated the sofa while Lynn, an armload of wood hugged to her bibbed breast, looked on like someone whimsy-struck, and said, "Aren't you cold?"

Cathy laughed. "Hardly," she said.

Lynn's expression was not so different from the one with which she'd regarded the cow while she'd said her piece, mystified by and at the same time certain of the strange workings that resulted in milk. "Hardly?" I said. "Where are you going in that dress?"

"Nowhere." The word was a yawn and led to a stretch, long and feline. Over her hand as it fell, spent, on the back of the sofa, Cathy looked slyly at me. "Just here," she said. "To see Lynn—" She broke off the word with mock petulance. "Would you put that wood down? Come and sit." And she rearranged her skirt to clear a space.

Dropping her burden, Lynn scurried to comply, stopping

short to wipe the dirt off her overalls, then her hands. "So," I said. "It must get pretty boring while Joe's at work."

"Boring?" She smiled complicitly at Lynn, who'd curled into the corner, turned as openly to Cathy as she turned to any TV show. "Thank God he's gone *some*times."

"Oh. That bad."

Her wry look at that barely brushed me before it connected with Lynn. When Cathy bent her head and whispered, Lynn answered with a laugh, low and wiser than she was, and I had the urge to run over and yank her away, but the clumsy bulk of me, stuck in the doorway where I'd stood, slouched to fit, ever since Cathy'd commandeered the room, wouldn't move. Since I'd only danced dumb attention on Lynn, I hadn't made the necessary impression, and anything contrary from me now would only bring Cathy's prior imprint into sharper relief. I could stick there, as Clara's representative, a clear eye on Cathy's charlatanism and Lynn's fickle leanings; but even in this respect, I wasn't much good. When Cathy looked up with exaggerated surprise at finding me still within eavesdropping distance, I stared back with commensurate obtuseness, but then Lynn looked up, too, frankly and innocently annoyed, and I felt myself shrinking to a movable size. Cathy asked nonchalantly, "Where is everybody?"

"Out," I said. She smiled down at her nails. "Lynn," I said, "I'm going after Clara. If I take a while, remember the cows." I left her glancing down at her own grubby fingernails.

On the momentum of my word I did start out in the doctor's direction, but the chance that Clara might be there and I would have to tell her something kept deflecting me until I found myself headed for Bark Bay. Now that even this summer seemed a simpler time, the wrecked cabin offered a morbid sort of comfort, but when I finally got there night was on me and I could barely see it.

What I saw in the last light was someone carrying a bucket around the cabin to the door, which opened, revealing the flame— from where I stood, a spark—of a candle set down on the floor inside. I couldn't recognize anyone in that little light, but I thought I knew the sweet, pale voice that greeted the bucket. And the voice that answered belonged to a man—maybe not a man, he was slight enough and had hair long enough to confuse me as he crossed the yard; his voice, though, was an unmistakable bass, old enough to drink with impunity. This was the one, then, the missing Cleaver. The door closed, all dark.

My return to Mother was slower even than the crooked walk away, and the weather was with me, the prickly black sky raining sleet, first spit, then sheets of it. By the time I got home, I was crusted on one side and the front of the house was glazed. When the fire inside leapt, the window glittered. Then a shadow crossed the pane and Clara Bow looked out, her dim expression as dreary as it was where I stood. With the light behind her, she couldn't see me until I came closer, and then she disappeared from the window and, in a second, opened the door.

"Where's your coat?" she said. "You don't have one, do you? Lynn said you were looking for me." These came out as a series of accusations.

I picked the ice off my arm. "I couldn't find you."

"What was it?"

Listening, I couldn't locate Lynn, so I lowered my voice. "Is Cathy gone?"

"Cathy was here?" She frowned at this lapse in Lynn's confidence, then, struck by something, brightened. "She wants to come back?"

"Only to gloat."

"Oh." Absent-mindedly Clara pulled a comb out of her bib pocket and, handing it to me, turned back to the living room. Since the sleet had melted into my hair, which was braided anyway, I didn't know why she assumed I'd want a comb. The hair on her own turned head, I noticed, was beginning to fluff out again, though neatly now. "Was that why you were looking for me?" she said. "I never liked her."

"What about those earrings?" She'd got to the living room door and, at this, stopped and swiveled to show me her perplexed expression. "The diamond earrings you gave her," I said. "The ones she was wearing today."

"Oh." She shrugged. "A token."

When she left the hall, I stood for a minute in the puddle I was dripping, chilled, turning over the comb, which was as long as my palm's width—long for a palm, short for a comb—scalloped almost imperceptibly along the spine, with a nice, surprising heft, silver, I thought, pocketing it and walking into the room where there was a fire.

Our half-built house didn't hold heat well. The warmth from the fire, with the infinite cold of Wisconsin against it, was as hopeless as a drop of white paint in a vat of black and by the time it thinned out all the way to the living room walls it was well assimilated, so that, sitting on the sofa, I had hot toes, a warm face, and an icy, slowly numbing nape. The conversation went that way, too, Clara asking Lynn about Cathy, and Lynn making short, smiling replies, all pleasant and superficial, with the gap between each exchange growing longer and longer until it finally went on uninterrupted, silence like the cold. Then Lynn turned on the television, moved it closer to the fire, and lost herself in "Love Boat."

We sat like that—Lynn with her crew, myself flushed and stiff-necked, Clara neatly in the armchair, ankles crossed and face a polite blank, as if attending in form but not spirit a ladies' tea—for what seemed like hours but couldn't have been since the boat was still afloat when Clara Bow came sharply out of her deep thought to say to me: "You didn't have dinner."

"No," I said, surprised, "and I can't say I'm hungry."

"You have to eat. What's the last meal you had?"

"I'm really not hungry," I said. "Anybody feed Joan?"

"Yes, and don't change the subject." She said this in the no-nonsense tone of a nanny addressing a nonsensical child. To satisfy her, I went to the kitchen, where frostbite seemed more of a threat than starvation, and heated some soup, which I took into the living room. But Clara had got back to her study by then and paid not the slightest attention to this proof of my willingness to overcome stupidity. The soup went down like so many spoonsful of medicine. The Love Boat had docked at Fantasy Island, where Lynn was contented to be, the fire giving her face such a glow that the show might have been her own febrile fantasy.

Clara held her preoccupied pose for most of the evening, breaking it only twice, first to reprove me for not changing my wet clothes, then to suggest that I think about wiring the house to the power lines, after all. Both came as abruptly as the dinner break, the messages sharp and, once delivered, apparently forgotten, something programmatic about them and, then, about the way she got up and announced that it was time for bed. This was unlike the postdoctoral moods I'd become accustomed to, and I found out why a few minutes after we'd got into bed. Clara's voice came casually across the dark, "I had some interesting news today."

I waited, then when she didn't say, asked, "Yes?"

"Frank Abbot's decided to move back to Minneapolis and resume his practice."

Her tone, like gossip, crept up on me. I said, "Any reason?"

"He's a doctor."

"He's a doctor here."

Clara Bow was silent, and now I could faintly see her, only blinking, regular as time, like someone reduced by shock to automatic impulses—as she'd been all night, it seemed, and in that state without thinking she'd thought of my dinner, my wet clothes, my messy hair, just as a stunned mother in the aftermath of a wreck might tend to her child's untied shoelaces. A serene concern replaced the creeping sensation. "Why did he leave Minneapolis?" I said, prompting her as gently as if she really were in shock.

"It made him sick."

"Made him sick?"

"His wife was on a respirator. A doctor disconnected her." She turned her head to look at me. "She wanted to die. Frank wasn't her doctor."

"He couldn't—" What? I didn't know what "made him sick."

Patiently Clara Bow said, "They took him out of her room."

"If she wanted to die," I said.

"That was part of the sickness."

We lay there looking at each other like a pair of mute invalids listening together to news broadcast over a loudspeaker. Then Clara returned her gaze to the ceiling. It was minutes before she closed her eyes as if she were finally looking for sleep. When I said, "But he's all right now," I thought she smiled, but the clouds had shifted, and in the baffled moonlight it was hard to see.

▶▶▶

There was a job Cathy knew of, Lynn said in a sure and quiet tone to Clara Bow and me, as Cathy stood by waiting, wedging the door open, "She has connections." Cathy's expression, the glimpse I got of it in the second before the door swung shut, was fierce.

She was unhappy, I told Clara, and was trying to convince Lynn to the contrary in order to convince herself, and she'd succeed and that would make her more unhappy, a circumstance that she'd hold against Lynn. Then they'd both be unhappy and in time, with the proper finesse on our part . . .

Clara smiled amiably up at me, like a little diplomat who didn't know the native tongue. She'd been as blandly agreeable when I'd suggested that we go car shopping while Lynn was out interviewing, and that suggestion had been prompted by the same expression, Clara watching with a mild smile as the two women drove away in Joe's Dodge. Walking, I tried to talk her out of her peculiar complaisance, or at least talk my way under it, but I couldn't get past that smile. The harder I tried, the more remote she seemed behind it, until I heard in my own voice the same breaking pitch Clara's had reached when trying to raise the moribund Women Abreast.

With this in mind instead of the business at hand, it wasn't until "Cornucopia, unincorporated," that it occurred to me to wonder where we were going, since there was nowhere to buy a car within walking distance. In northern Wisconsin, you couldn't buy a car unless you already had one. That Clara hadn't thought of this indicated how deep down distracted she really was. Usually when she was evasive or abstracted she at least went through the motions of appearing practical, but now, as I took the turn into Cornucopia, where a person could, at most, rent a boat, she came along without question, as if she'd forgotten completely—or didn't care—what we were supposed to be doing.

Passing a church and a tiny yellow building billing itself as "Real Estate," we came to a bench and sat down under a flag and the legend, WISCONSIN'S NORTHERNMOST POST OFFICE. Across the street, in front of Ehlers, the town's one store, a few people were gathered around a man trying to unlock a car with a coat hanger. The group emitted an Ah, an Aww, and then the man passed the hanger to a boy next to him. While the boy worked at the lock, a lanky, gray-haired man separated from the others and hailed someone coming out of the building on our right. "Ed," he said, meeting the newcomer in the middle of the street, "you know about these things. Maybe you have an idea." The old man took the elbow of a girl who'd been standing slightly apart from the rest and introduced her as his niece who'd locked herself out of her car. Then Ed took his turn with the hanger. Then someone else, and another, and each person who happened along the street was called over by the uncle for expert consultation, until most of the town must have been assembled.

After we'd watched these proceedings for twenty minutes or so, I said, "Clara, we can't walk to a car dealer." She frowned, seeming to consider this, and I added, "I don't even know where one is." Then, because she was already placid again and our position on the bench seemed so incidental, I tried to reintroduce the notion of purpose by suggesting that we step around to the bar, George's, and revise our plans over a drink. I led, she followed.

Unlike the few bars I'd been in, George's was bright inside, with white sunlight from windows all around and the yellow glow of hanging lamps. A pool table, with ample standing space around it, took up one end of the room. The other was crowded with small wooden tables, and against the wall there was a pinball machine, which a tow-headed boy of nine or ten was operating while his little companion crowed and slapped the wall with each ping the machine emitted. Clara seemed contented to sip a beer and watch the boys try to launch their machine. While I restated our immediate predicament, her attention floated back from the game to me whenever a pause or inflection in my speech cued her to nod or raise her eyebrows, and she was slow about it. When I stopped talking, she smiled her tea-party smile at me and looked vaguely back at the game, then around at the Cornucopians who arrived all at once at the door, a boisterous crowd led by the uncle. One burly man, brown and wearing a red baseball cap, was at the center of the commotion, kept turning this way and that to smile at someone laying a hand on his shoulder.

"Must've unlocked her car," Clara murmured, her eyes already wandering from the bar to the pool table, where someone was racking up balls.

"Clara!" I said, and in the crush and breaking clatter, it came out a little wild.

She looked at me quickly, her attention so clear that for one startled second I felt I'd got into the still center of her thoughts. Then she blinked and as quickly frowned down at her beer and said, "You're right. We should find a car." Her hand closed on her glass and slid it a few inches closer to her.

"What if something happened?" I said. "We'd be stranded." Lifting her glass, she considered me with the concerned expression that had come to her face last night when she'd abruptly remembered my dinner, my wet clothes. "Not that something will," I said uncomfortably.

"No, you're right. Winter's coming."

"Well," I said. "We can't get one. That's the point."

With a flick of her hand toward the bar, she leaned in slightly and said, "We could rent a car from someone here. To get to a dealer. Or we could borrow one." She sat back and, as if reviewing a scene she'd staged, took a slow and careful look around. "They seem like nice people." At the bar the niece, sitting between two standing loggers who were talking at once, was splitting her attention between them with the small, strained smile of someone overwhelmed, the gold disks of her earrings dancing each time she turned her head. She'd locked her car. "Maybe we could even buy one," Clara said.

"Maybe they're home now," I said. She tilted her head. I said, "Cathy and Lynn."

With her head at that angle, she lowered her eyes to her hand and adjusted her glass again. "Lynn's leaving," she said, then uncertainly, "You know that."

I said, "She'll be back."

As she stared, her frown softened into the pleasant abstracted expression she'd worn most of the day, an act of self-hypnosis, it seemed. The woman was not distracted at all. She was focused right at the edge of her appearance. "Everyone's leaving," she murmured.

"Let's go." I stood up. "Let's go home."

My height impressed everyone but Clara. She said, "But the car."

"The car doesn't matter." I whispered, aware of the niece staring at me. "It's not winter yet."

She took a last thoughtful sip of her beer and got up and with one more bemused look around led me out into the cold afternoon where the sky, as if to spite me, was starting to sleet again and the white sun was frozen at the crown of the trees and the dark, silent town, ranged around the mellow light and noise of the bar, did seem winter-bound.

Lynn was heaped in blankets in front of the television with the sound turned up so loud that she hadn't heard us come in. She hadn't thought to start a fire; but crouched like a camper close to the set she seemed to be warming herself in its blare. When she saw us, she jumped up, looking so relieved that I think she would have leapt at us if the blankets hadn't swamped her feet and given her time in the untangling to turn her relief into the bland greeting we got when she finally came unwound: "Well." Clara went around her and, squatting with her back to us, started to stack logs in the fireplace. Bent to scoop up the blankets, Lynn said, "I found the cutest room."

Clara made a minute adjustment to the wood, as if it were a flower arrangement. "You already have a cute room," I said.

Lynn looked at me for a blank second, then said—and it seemed to make sense to her, "But now I have a job."

"Doing what?"

"Waitressing."

She shifted the blankets in her arms and yanked up one trailing corner. As she walked past me, I said, "Lynn," and heard her pause. "Why do you think Cathy took this sudden interest in you?"

This was rhetorical, but with Lynn standing there considering me I could see that she thought I was really asking, and my stupidity puzzled her. "She's my friend." She waited to see if there was a trick involved, a knock-knock sort of logic, then when none emerged, frowned to herself and went up the stairs.

Behind me the television was blasting a choral message from Kodak. The picture cast shadowy blue shapes on the walls and flickered like the ghost of a fire on Clara's bent back as she crumpled letters from our junk mail pile next to the fireplace and poked them into gaps in the kindling and logs. I turned down the television and switched on a light, and the room went dark. Clara struck a match. "Damn windmill," she said, and in her whisper the match died.

I went out to turn the damn windmill around. The wind had shifted and was sliding by the sails, barely sending a shiver through them as it passed. I dragged the lever around until they strained, then rocked, heavy with the sleet they'd collected, sodden—and we painted the *house,* I thought—so I reached up and hung on the one right above me and, with my own limbs stiff and slow-starting, fell back just in time to miss being mangled when the blades took that leap of inertia overcome. As I backed up again to get out of the new wind, the door opened behind me. Clara was standing there, the fire a glow deep in the house, the look of warmth, and I'd started in, a few steps, when something my eye had just glanced over registered, and I looked again.

A cow. She was lying humped up on her legs a few feet from the barn. With Clara catching up, I went over. "Hans," I said and bent and nudged her with my toe. Then I brushed off the sleet and jogged her shoulder.

"Beauty," Clara touched my back. When I looked up at her, she said, "Don't."

"I'm not," I said, because my nose was running and my eyes were watering in the cold. Then I stooped to brush off Hans's flanks and haunches, looking for a bullet wound, I said when Clara asked what I was doing, though with the cow's whole hide exposed and not a mark on it, I had to admit that we hadn't heard from our huntress in weeks. "A cow doesn't just die," I said.

"She probably froze."

"She's an animal."

"People freeze. They're animals. Maybe she was sick."

"She was fine—" Yesterday, I was about to say, but I hadn't seen her yesterday. In fact, I couldn't remember when, in the week of Lynn's husbandry, I'd last got a good look at Hans.

"Let's go in."

"We can't just leave her lying here."

"She's not going to get any deader—" She broke off, and just as she said, "Oh God," and started running for the house, I thought of it, too: we'd forgotten Joan, who'd been lying upstairs in that unheated house all day.

I ran up the stairs and stopped behind Clara at the door to Joan's bedroom. Her bed was empty. We made a quick check of the other bedrooms, then hurried back downstairs to find Lynn. She'd pulled one end of the sofa close to the fire and was sitting curled up in the corner with her suitcase near her knees, looking sidelong at us as we landed in the doorway, as if we'd gone crazy and that annoyed her. Then, quick as it touched us, her glance slid away and lighted on the real source of her irritation—the armchair, flush with the fireplace, crowding the heat.

"Joan?" I said, and the armchair responded with a rustle. Getting closer, I caught her tangy smell, unwashed woman. "How did you get down here?" Whenever she'd had to get somewhere, we'd had to help her.

Lynn said, "Don't look at me."

Joan's eyes were closed. "I wanted to get by the fire," she finally sighed.

Coming up on the other side of the armchair, Clara asked, "Are you all right?"

Joan rolled her head that way, so I could only see the corner of her eye as it fluttered open. "No," she said, a long breath, "I'm freezing and I'm starving."

Clara said, "That's a good sign." Then, with her hand laid on Joan's arm, she became abruptly efficient, telling Lynn to bring back those blankets and me to change my clothes while she heated up some soup. No, I was going back out, I said, to bury the cow, I said, looking at Lynn, who'd dropped her legs over her suitcase and was sitting with her elbows on her knees, her jaw cupped in her hands, unmoved. "When are you leaving?" I said.

"Tomorrow morning."

"Good. You can help bury the cow."

Clara took a step back, coming between me and Lynn, but I could see over her head. "The cow doesn't have to be buried tonight," she said.

Lynn said, "The cow died?"

"No," I said, "we're just going to bury her. It's an experiment. What do you think? The cow *died*. Hans is *dead*. And who knows how Gretchen is—do you?" I hadn't thought of Gretchen (let alone the chickens) until I mentioned her, mad as I was at Lynn for being the last and so poorly suited for that position, so before I started blaming the woman outright for epitomizing the essence of ending in the air, I went out, over Clara's protests, to check for survivors. By the time I got to the barn, necessarily cooled off a bit, I realized that, leaving like that, I'd given those two the impression that, damn them, I was going to bury the cow, which now seemed like an unbearable task being forced upon me, and I couldn't tell if that was Gretchen breathing or the wind.

There was a knock on the barn, "Beauty?" then Clara Bow ducked under the door with the lantern, lighting up Gretchen, hunkered down boulder-fashion and immobile as her dead friend. With a glance at me, Clara approached the cow and, holding the lantern straight up like a signal in one hand, bent to touch her, tentative as a test of the beast's solidity, between her knobby shoulder blades. Gretchen's tail swished and swatted her flank and Clara straightened sharply. She turned to me. "Warm," she said. Then, when we'd had an instant to absorb this, she returned to the door, pushed it up, took one step out into the night, and stopped, lantern extended, like an usher waiting. I ducked out after her, and as soon as I lowered the door and turned, she started for the house.

We didn't bury the cow that night. We dragged a mattress downstairs and stationed it in front of the fireplace, between the lantern and the Coleman stove, and sat on it, draped in blankets, like squaws.

By morning the fire was out, the wood gone, the fuel exhausted, and the weather, since we were still alive, somewhat warmer, if not warm. Lynn left early, jumping up, suitcase in hand, at the first faint tremble of a car on the drive, not even looking back to say " 'bye," and I could hardly blame her, but did nonetheless. Joan had only transported her immobility to the armchair, where she stayed all day, facing the fireplace as if staking out the best seat in the house for the next show of warmth, which was not to come.

We did what we could, Clara and I, took to the woods with ax and saw, but we were tired and the ax was unwieldy and the saw was worse and Clara's felled tree, which was rotten, turned to pulp instead of logs. It was also wet. So we proceeded to the task of cow interment, a mere attempt, since the earth, under its two inches of mush, was frozen or rocky—we were discouraged, our fingers numb, before we could determine which, and after that we didn't try. Even our one hale cow wouldn't be milked, when we thought of that. She shied, she showed us her butt, and, as if that weren't enough, she kicked. We tried to calm her with caresses, not even caring about the milk at that point, just wishing for one sign of compliance from any dark corner of nature, but she shifted and shuffled away from our hands and rolled her head like a slow old creature plagued by demons. As soon as we took a step away, she fell still.

Clara and I were like this: I said "Let's," and she said, "Yes, let's," or I just headed and she followed, and then I said it was hopeless and she agreed and dropped her spade or saw or hand. I kept catching her watching me, first by chance, when the momentum of the ax coming loose too fast jerked my head back, then deliberately, with looks snuck after a long pause of concentration feigned to put her off guard. The first few sneaked times I saw the turn of her head or the quick lowering of her eyes, but after that she was faster, and I could only feel the glance retracted before mine got to her. The way she was watching, I had to be someone about to do something, but I didn't know what. What I wanted to do, more than once, was say, "We're rich, the bank's an hour's walk, let's go," but this seemed, more than a gross breach of confidence, the wrong answer. Clara Bow wanted reassurance, I thought, a sign; she was waiting for something from me to convince her that we could survive not just the night and the coming winter but Wisconsin.

I'd already said enough times that everything would be all right that, with the women gone and things failing and breaking down willy-nilly, it wouldn't mean much anymore. And I couldn't very well bet my life, since there I was. Money, my word, myself—I had precious little else to offer by way of insurance—and then I thought of the children, the tiny ones. I wouldn't risk their lives on a bum chance, would I? I'd gone out of my way not to. Still, it took me a while to think it over—was it safe?—but then there we were, night coming again, side by side on the sofa, our hands and feet muffled in blankets, Clara Bow sitting up straight, silent, waiting, and, "My children," I finally said. "You remember. The twins." She didn't say, or look, and I said, "We could bring them up."

I waited for her reaction, but she didn't speak or turn her head or blink. Her only move was covert, under the blanket her hands slowly shifting to press the gathered wool against her abdomen, like an old woman afraid of her lap robe slipping. "We'll get things fixed up," I said, "and then maybe Sal—" I stopped—maybe not Sal—and saw Clara look at her lap. "The court always sides with the mother," I said.

220

Clara's hands flew up, spilling the blanket, and she cried out, "I told you, I know." She shot a look at the armchair, where Joan was sleeping or pretending to, then said again in a fierce whisper, "I *know.*"

Her vehemence, beside the point, disconcerted me. "I was frightened," I said. "They were too small. But *I* told *you,* I'm better now. And," I said, "they're bigger."

She jerked in her seat, held her belly again. She wouldn't look at me. "Clara?" I touched her elbow, and she sprang up. Dragging the blanket around her feet, she took the few steps to the fireplace and knelt and in the near-dark started raking her fingers through the pile of charred wood chunks and ashes, burnt bits of paper and envelopes. I got up and stooped next to her. "Clara?" I said again. "What are you doing?" She had her face close to the heap, trying to see, and when she sat back with a scrap in her hand, there was a smudge on her nose. I reached out, forefinger first, to wipe it off, and she flinched. The paper she'd plucked from the ashes was about the size of my hand, black and flaking at its uneven edges and singed in the middle—a cigar-shaped burn where it had been folded. She was holding it up in a delicate pinch, the way she'd held dead fish by their tails, and when she suddenly twitched it at me—take it—its one intact black corner broke off and the paper floated to the floor. I picked it up.

The thing was burned, and the room was dark, but this fragment stood out: "with a mother who would kill her own." Here is as much of the rest as I could read: "babies, too. Then it is not for me to" and "ause he is my son, I can only respect hi." I rooted through the ashes for those bits of envelope Clara had reburied, but I couldn't find what I was looking for, the corner without return address, as if now that I knew, I would recognize Minnie's mark in the blank, though this was really my way of using up the time and energy I would have liked to use to abuse the woman. When I stopped, Clara was watching my face, her own slightly turned. "I know I was wrong," I said, "and I can't change that." I spoke very clearly, giving each word a shape, to show her how far I'd come. "But if I *know,* then things are different. We'll go get Timmy and Will and you can see," and then I noticed that she was still staring, with her head at that angle somewhere between skepticism and aversion. I'd seen bystanders look at gory accidents that way, I looked again at the letter, which had fallen onto my lap, and I said, "Clara, what is it you think you know?" She stared. She didn't say. I said, "You think—"

"This is a *figure of speech,*" I said, holding out my hand with the letter on it. "I wouldn't *touch* my children. I *didn't* touch them." I crumpled the paper and it disintegrated. "A figure of speech," I said. "What did she tell you?" When she didn't answer, I asked her again. In the silence, in the dark, I had to look close to see her small, sickened face. "I saw them," I told her, "in the park, in a stroller, the day of the ad."

"Oh Beauty," she murmured, "oh God."

And I started to shake her, make her say, but caught myself, dropped my hands into my lap. "Tell me," I said.

"I only know what she told me."

"What?"

Her eyes had been fixed on me all this time, and now, when she lowered them, I felt it, a drop. "I'm so sorry," she said.

"They're *fine,*" I said, *"fine.* It's her word against mine, and you know me, you know what I told you. Whatever else she said, she lied."

"She paid for all this."

"What?"

"This." For a moment, her shadowy hands held an imaginary globe.

"You did," I said.

"She did."

"You. I saw the statement."

"Her money."

"I don't understand."

"Anything?" Clara's eyes flickered up. Bowed as she was, with her hands as they'd fallen, palm-up on her knees, she seemed to be begging. "You don't understand anything?"

"I left my babies with my mother-in-law. And then I came to you."

"And I went to her. I had your wallet, Beauty. She wanted to have you arrested. Not your husband, Max, he didn't, she said. Then you provided the solution. This. You got yourself out of the way, and she paid."

"But *you.*"

She hesitated. "I told you."

"No," I said, "you didn't."

"I love people who need me, and they die." This she had told me, and now she repeated it like a prayer out of habit, small and toneless, so that I had to lean in to hear her. "I wasn't afraid for you."

There was a rustle, a scratch, as her finger found a scrap of the letter, showing me in the dark. "I *am* weak," she said, "Frank knows. I've never gone anywhere alone, not even leaving, like this." She let out half a laugh, a huffed breath. "You provided a solution for everyone."

After my leg injury I was familiar with shock, so I knew I would be better shortly, if I sat still the sensible world would reclaim me, and it did; I remembered how hungry I was, and how cold, and how little I'd slept the last night. With a rustle and creak, Clara Bow was crouching close to me. She was patting my shoulder, flat-handed, lightly, like a child comforting somebody bigger, or like somebody big, someone clumsy, being careful, like me. Like my own, her tentative touch, while she murmured close that she was sorry. It was never my size that made me timid.

We sat, Clara Bow on her heels, I with my knees in a hug, in silence until Joan wheezed in her sleep, and Clara whispered, "You must be tired." We might as well sleep in our beds, she whispered, since it couldn't be any colder upstairs. Still we sat for another minute, as if mesmerized by the fire that should have been burning, before she tapped my shoulder; then we went up.

Those murmured "sorry"s were still in my ear, and I know how a lullabied baby must feel. Wakefulness, once the singer's smoothed away its rough edges, its confusion of forms, seems sweeter than sleep, safer and better known, but because this is another sort of sleep, a baby can't help slipping out of it into real slumber, the two are so close. This was, anyway, how I felt, lying there in the dark with Clara across from me—that everything else, the babies, the lying, Minnie, and the money, had been lulled, not me; but, of course, I fell asleep.

And must have dreamed everything back into place, since I woke in a fright, at a sound. It was still dark, deep night, and I could just make out Clara standing at the dresser, stiff, her hand

223

cocked, as if she'd been startled, too. Then she looked down, bent, and took a step back. Her heel slid. Something skittered across the floor, under the bed, struck the wall, and rolled back.

Clara'd frozen again; but when I reached down to feel on the floor for whatever she'd dropped, she came to, snatching something else off the dresser and, before she'd even retracted her hand, moving toward her bed. "Clara?" I said. I'd picked up a lipstick.

She'd bent over the bed, her back to me, her hands busy, elbows working, and all I got for an answer was the sound of a zipper, closure.

I sat up, pushing back blankets and blankets and sleep, and asked her what. What was she doing? She tugged and took a few unsteady steps backwards, balancing a weight that, when she rounded and leaned toward the door, turned out to be a suitcase. I heaved off my covers, saying, "Clara," swinging my legs down, "where are you going?" But she was already out the door, on the stairs, her stocking feet taking each step with a thud. They stopped, her heavy footsteps, halfway down, and I got to the door to see her saying to the black hall below:

"I'm going with Frank."

"Frank Abbot," I said. "He's gone."

She stood still only long enough, stiff-shouldered, while my voice died, to give me time to feel foolish, then started again. She reached the kitchen as I reached the stairs. I took a few, leapt, and the crash of my landing met silence; she'd stopped.

We looked at each other across the dark kitchen, Clara with her shoulder propping the door open a crack, letting in the wind in stabs, and I said, "I thought you believed me."

"I do."

"Clara." I took a step forward, she took a step back. "You said you weren't afraid—" She was silent. "But Clara, I don't believe any of that, I don't care about—" but she was backing out now, the wind rushing in, so I said: "But the *doctor.*"

She took her last backwards step and the door slammed and I jumped to open it. She was slogging through the yard, through the slush, in her socks, at a tilt, weighted down by her suitcase. "Barbie," I yelled from the step, and she stopped in front of the windmill. "There's a man." She turned as I told her, "not the doctor, a Cleaver, I saw him."

There were moonlight for a minute, showing me her face, white and tense, as if she were listening to a sound behind her, not me—but there was only the sweep of the sails. I told her about my last trip to the cabin, the candle, the bucket, the boy. Barbie's intimate voice. Clara said, "You're just telling me that."

No, I swore it, if she had to believe what she did about need, then the doctor was just as unsafe as I was.

"That's why," she said. "That's why you're telling me that."

No, I said, go ahead. Leave if you want. But not for *my* sake. "It's not fair," I said. "You're my *friend*."

"You don't know."

"You *are*."

"You reminded me of my sister," she wailed.

We'd been screaming across the yard at each other, but now there was only an echo, so pale: "You don't have a sister."

"I would have."

I opened my hand and that lipstick rolled into the curve of my fingers. I was nothing but huge. When I looked up, she was backing away, too close to the windmill, and I shouted, "Clara!" As if I'd swung at her, made a grab for her, threatened—but I hadn't, hadn't moved, I was shriveling right where I stood—she jumped back, and the blade caught her jaw. It lifted her into the air. Then I moved, I leapt with my arms out to catch her, but in the slush I slipped, and I fell on her. Timber. The last thing I heard before my own head hit the windmill was the cracking of Clara's small skull.

Some say our bodies know before we do the sensible disasters that await us, that they see the trauma coming and prepare us to bear it by sending us previews in nightmares that build up our tolerance to pain—or wear it down, perhaps, so we won't be inclined to resist what we can't. Maybe no one says so, but that's how the rest of that night was for me, like a dream that started while I slept a short sleep, sprawled over Clara, with my ear in the muck, and seemed to go on when I woke at a nudge and opened my eyes to the toes of two muddy work boots and twisted my sore head to see Kathy standing above me with the muzzle of her rifle a few inches from my raised shoulder.

"Don't shoot," I told her, but saw as soon as I said it that she wasn't about to, was holding the gun by the butt with one hand, like a hunter nudging a fallen animal for signs of life. She lowered her arm and took a step back. Her face was calculating and grim, like an image straight out of those bracing nightmares. It prepared me to look down at Clara. She was splayed in a backstroke, not moving. I raised up like a crab and laid my ear close to her lips, but the cold and the wet had dulled my senses so I couldn't tell if she was breathing. I put my hand on her heart—useless, too, since she was muffled with so many sweaters and sweatshirts, all soaking, we were soaked. I unbuttoned and lifted, undid her bib, and with my hand pressed on her fluttering heart, saw the swell of her breasts above her skinny ribs, then her belly, the way she'd laid her hand on it when I'd tried to bargain my children for faith.

I buttoned her back up and got to my feet with her draped on my arms, so wet and heavy I thought I was sinking. Kathy was gone. "Your van!" I yelled into the woods. *"Where's your van?"*

Her voice finally came, a faint, faraway shout, "No gas," and I dropped my head on Clara's stomach and cried for gas and cars and phones and main streets and hospital signs and electricity running from remote matrices through wires strapped high overhead.

This was a year ago.

It was a long walk, in the dark and the mud, twisting with Clara to keep from bumping her hanging head and feet into trees, and the first thing I saw clearly came at the end: the light by the doctor's front door. He had the door open before I got to it, was rushing to get the woman out of my arms, as if he'd been waiting a very long time, long enough maybe to feel relief first.

Like Kathy, I'd turned into one of those ghosts who could take shape in a second, then just as quickly fade, and floating in after the doctor, and hovering while he undid Clara's clothes, I was invisible—till his voice called me up, with a command: "What happened?"

"She ran into the windmill."

He said, "It's the back of her head," and looked up at me for the first time. Here was Bill again.

"No," I said, "she backed into the windmill." I started to describe it exactly, the sound the sails made, the way Clara took a step back and I shouted, and Dr. Abbot gently rolled Clara Bow's head off his palm and came around the table and slapped me.

I raised my hand to hit him back, but it was feeble; he was already bent over Clara again, saying, "Go get two blankets off my bed."

When I brought them, he had Clara undressed and was toweling off her body. He took the blankets, wrapped her in them, and lifted her off the table. I followed him out of the house to his car and stood by while he laid her on the back seat and buckled two seat belts around her.

The passenger door on my side was locked. As I rapped on the window, the car started up and slid back under my knuckles. One glimpse of the doctor's face before he turned on the headlights and disappeared: I believed Clara Bow's story, and I believed his, and I believed he was just the obstinate man to fool her into hedging her last chance at being outlived by someone she loved.

Even though I wasn't thinking too clearly, was in shock from my own bump, or so the doctor said sometime later, though we both know, we all suspect, that slapping wasn't indicated, I didn't chase the car. I went inside, where I waited nine days for news. I am still here.

I'd called every hospital in the upper half of Wisconsin, none of which had admitted Clara Bow Cole, I'd moved into the doctor's clothing, which fit, and his cupboards and sofa, and was starting on the operators in nearby Minnesota, three numbers apiece, when he brought her back, with a carful of paraphernalia and a subtler set version of that look.

At first because of that look and the way it coldly noted me, summed up my usefulness, and left me alone in a second, as he carried in an unconscious, pale Clara with two bags of liquid balanced on her stomach, I didn't ask how she was or would be.

227

Then, when she was the same, when her sleep and pallor outlasted his look, I didn't want to.

I did what the doctor said: changed Clara, her bed, her IV, and her bags, washed her and turned her to keep her from getting bedsores. This became more and more difficult as Clara's pregnancy progressed, a pillow for her neck, for her knees, for her belly—the only thing she seemed to know in her deep sleep was pain. When something hurt, her whole body winced, a tendon behind her knee twitched, a vein in her neck, her wrist. The first time she did this, I stopped midmotion, one hand under her, the other tilting her shoulder toward me. I stopped and stared at her face, waiting for the pain or bother or whatever made her shrink to go deeper and wake her up, but it didn't; it passed, and her face and flesh smoothed into stillness. The next time it happened, the doctor was standing across the bed from me. Clara'd got so big and unwieldy that it took two of us to turn her without pushing too hard or twisting her, and the doctor was lifting from one side while I caught and cushioned her head and belly on the other. As Clara's weight shifted from the doctor to me, her baby poked me in the palm, the right; in my left, Clara's mouth moved. I tilted up her cheek on my fingertips and stared. With all the effort it took not to shake her, to make her wake up and complain, my hand shook anyway until I couldn't tell who was trembling, Clara or me, so I looked to the doctor. He was watching my face.

In almost four months of orders and reports, questions and short answers, comings and goings and silent, staggered meals, his glances had checked me as they might a watch, and I'd got used to that, even liked it, the comfort of being useful, unremarkable, taken for granted. Now this look lasted a minute—or longer, I don't know, because I turned back to Clara, whose face was so smooth, and whose stillness spread into my fingers and through me and sat on whatever dumb nerve had lurched when she'd moved. The doctor had known all along that she wouldn't wake up.

I lowered Clara Bow onto her pillows, then slid my hands out and laid them on her belly, waiting for a flutter, while the doctor went silently out of the room, his tall, terse grace.

The baby was born three weeks later, early and still small enough to make it past Clara's miniature bones. The delivery took at least five times as long and five times as much work from me as mine had. Even though the doctor had given her a shot for the pain, Clara tried to contort her body around the contractions, like a fetus herself, so I had to hold her, do her pushing for her, and administer the oxygen mask when she strained, all the while trying to keep an eye on the doctor. He was not saying, so I had to—anyway, tried to—gauge the baby's progress and health from the way his eyes moved and he bent and his shoulders tensed. Terrified, I thought, and then I was, and then he looked up, and I felt Clara rest. "What?" I said, but no sound came from my dry throat. He just looked; so finally I walked around Clara Bow's raised knees.

There the baby was—hairless, red, scrawny, and slimy, trailing her cord into Clara—and he gave her to me. I breathed a hoarse protest, but he was already busy, bringing out the placenta, tying and clipping the cord, and there was nothing to do but stand deathly still and balance the baby, five pounds of blind life no bigger than my two palms put together. Then that baby, like an imp sent from hell to try me, started squirming, and I had to hold onto her.

229

The doctor was done. He was looking. He was brilliant. I said, "What do we call her?"

"Patricia?" I blinked. He said, "Maureen? Sioban? It's Saint Patrick's Day." I was so engrossed in maintaining the slithering infant that it took me a minute to even say, "Oh. March," I said. "Saint Patrick's Day." And we both looked at Clara.

I carried the orphan to the sink and, with her nestled in the crook of my arm, started sponging her clean with warm water. Then I felt the doctor behind me and turned. His arm went around me, I reached, curving over the baby, brushing his chest—he took a sharp step back, a wet spot on his shirt, and turned abruptly to the sink. He ran steaming water on a towel, wrung it till his fists were white, and carried it to the bed.

If we said a word in the hours between then and when he went to bed and I sat down on the sofa in the dark, I don't remember it. We met in the hall. Something, isn't it, the frantic coupling of monsters while the corpse of the woman they loved lies in the next room and her newborn infant sleeps nearby, maybe whimpers? We didn't notice, then.

In the morning, fighting roots and frozen earth, we buried Clara in the woods.

What of Women Abreast (you ask)? Late one night five months ago (when you, Maureen, were one month in the world, and the most contrary, sleepless baby ever born to woman), I opened the door to a boy whose long hair and low voice sent a small tremor of memory through me. He was Rick, he said, "Cleaver," and he wanted the doctor.

Frank drove, I held the baby, and Rick perched in the back, directing us to the house on W. It was the first time I'd been back. In the moonlit night, the place looked desolate, quite dead, until the light caught a blade of the windmill, which was turning. I asked Rick about Joan. He said, "Joan?" I looked in on the cow, but she wasn't there. The house was bare of all but the biggest pieces of furniture, the sofa, the armchair, the kitchen table—with, ranged around it, in the light of one fat candle, the Cleavers, small and gloomy, like children playing wake. "Why so glum, Munchkins?" I said, and they stared, and I remembered that I terrified them. I gave the baby to the oldest girl, who gripped her with such fierce relief that I had to stoop, murmuring reassurances against my own spookiness, and loosen her hard arms.

A sudden harsh cry came from upstairs, and the Cleavers shrank. Barbie, they thought, was dying.

Her labor lasted past dawn. I was an old hand at this, so deft and helpful that for one wild moment of Barbie's delirium the child, another girl, was to be named Beauty, a moment that mercifully passed into the fog out of which finally came Flora, a flower from the secret garden of Cleaver family history.

In the kitchen I collected one furious Maureen from a stiff and bleary Cleaver and, from (habit!) the refrigerator, a mound of mail that asked for money, warned me to fill out my many times over provided forms, threatened my incorporated self with action, confiscated (oh, a small pang) my bankroll, and told me I was looked for—though obviously not hard, since I am easily found.

I'm out in the dirt with leafy Maureen, who crawls like any baby bent on keeping her appointments, which, in being airlifted back to the very mud she started from, she can forget for a minute. She pats and dabbles, and when she scoops up a lump of red clay, I fold her miniature fist around it and tell her: Mother. Six months old, she's learned to laugh, not derisively yet, good little girl. She allows me; then she throws the dirt down, and she peals.

▼▼

Ellen Akins, a graduate of USC and Johns Hopkins, is the author of *Home Movie* and has published stories in *Georgia Review, Southern Review, Southwest Review,* and *New Stories from the South: The Year's Best, 1988.* She is also the recipient of grants from the National Endowment for the Arts and the Ingram Merrill Foundation and a Whiting Writer's Award.